The Ruins of Noe

For Jennifer

The Ruins of Noe

Book Two in the
Faerie Tales from the White Forest Series

Enjoy!

Danika Dinsmore

Hydra House ❖ Seattle, Washington

Library of Congress Cataloging-in-Publication Data

Dinsmore, Danika.
  The Ruins of Noe / Danika Dinsmore. -- 1st pbk. ed.
    p. cm. -- (Faerie Tales from the White Forest ; bk. 2)
  ISBN 978-0-9848301-2-1 (pbk.)
  I. Title.
  PZ7.D619Ru 2012
  [Fic]--dc23

                2012004172

ISBN: 978-0-9848301-2-1

Second printing.

Cover art:
Julie Fain
www.juliefain.com

Illustrations by:
Alison Woodward
alisonannwoodward.blogspot.com

Cover and interior design:
Tod McCoy
www.todmccoy.com

Copyeditor:
Jennifer D. Munro
www.jenniferdmunro.com

Published by:
Hydra House
1122 E Pike St. #1451
Seattle, WA 98122
www.hydrahousebooks.com

Printed through Lightning Source, Inc. in the United States of America.

For Satori

Do not go where the path may lead, go instead
where there is no path and leave a trail.

Ralph Waldo Emerson

Moonsrise Ridge
Ithcommon
Dmvyle
Gyllenhale
GREEN RIVER
SPRING RIVER
Green Lake
Dionsdale
Water Realm
Center Realm
Sun Dreaming Rocks
Tiragarrow
Precipice falls
Easyl
Rioscrea
Warm ponds
The White Forest
Village-nests
markets

nal Spring

arsh
farms
grobjahar

Singing Caves

Foradenn

Sea of
Tzajeck

The
White
forest
☆

REALM

Reed
forest

Lola
Spring

REALM

Thachreek

Air
Realm

Thorsa

Rivenbow

The
Elder
Hive

Erriondower

L
O
L
A

S
P
R
I
N
G

R
I
V
E
R

Bobbercurry

LOLA SPRING

LITTLE MOON CREEK

flying
fields

N

Grioth

Dottisdagh

Fire
Realm

No Moons Canyon

Foraglënn
Northern Echoes
Icecap Forest
Read Mountain
castle
Sage Peak
Sea of Izajeek
FOREVER BEACH
THE WHITE FOREST
E
W
The Dark forest
THE RIVER THAT RUNS BACKWARDS
Western Range
Eastern Range
Mystic forest
Ridge Sea Forest
Noe Valley
The Hollows
ONWIND CLIFFS
ILLUSIVE BEACH
INDAGO CRATER
Croilus
LAKE HILL
South Coast Forest
INDAGO BEACH
N

Acknowledgements

Thanks ~

Everyone in this business knows that it takes a village to build a book (and keep an author going). And building a book takes time, so these thank-yous span years. Writing is strange that way, as so much of it is this ethereal "work" to others. They just trust that at the end of some period of time we writers will produce something magical.

For that trust and support I'd like to thank: my husband Ken Ashdown for always being there when I return from my imaginary wanderings; publisher Tod McCoy and copy editor Jennifer Munro for kicking the story into shape; my honest critique partners Natalie Smith and Sara Nickerson; my brilliant beta readers (Darline Sanderson, Lilly Era, Heron and Liz Collins, Karyn and Kelly Hoskins, Angelica Taggart); my "Patrons of the Forest" (Dale Dinsmore, Kendal Dinsmore, Jeff Cecchettini, Laurie Burnett) for making the Brigitta book trailer happen; my magnificent book trailer crew (too many to list, check the credits on thewhiteforest.com—but special shouts to Mauri Bernstein and Kevin Barron); Gwendolyn Alley, Sequoia Hamilton, Francine Byrne, Dan Dinsmore, Trysh Lucas, and Jen Keller for much welcomed assistance on my first Imaginary Worlds Tour; Alison Woodward and Julie Fain for their fantastic artwork; Laurie Scheer for being the best cheerleader anyone could have; and Yvette Dudley-Neuman and Larry Ho for being my accountabilibuddies.

I couldn't have done it without you and I wouldn't have wanted to either.

Prologue

The female Nhord shuffled to wake her tired feet. It was the end of her shift and her male companion would be replacing her shortly. Their shift changes were the brief moments they had together to enjoy each other's company. It was not a life anyone, even the most steadfast Nhord, would wish for themselves. The two long-time friends had accepted their destinies, however, and took fierce pride in their lineage of Purview Sentries.

The male Nhord entered, a wild look in his double-lidded eyes. The female's first thought was that he looked quite handsome, standing in the entrance to the petrified sandcave with the sun setting behind his armored back.

It is time, he whispered.

What do you—you mean THE time?

He nodded and held up his right front flipperpaw. A little fuzzy light danced around inside the webbing between his claws.

The Knowing. She felt it too. It was crisp and clear and eternal. It called them.

This was what six generations of Nhords had been waiting for. She glanced back at the large, ancient ring behind her. She had imagined the great joy or relief that would flood her body at this moment, but she only nodded, tightened the straps of her supply pack, always at the ready, and stepped aside to make room for her friend.

The little light sailed from his flipperpaw, drawn to the

ring. Drawn home. It caught on the breeze wafting into the cave from the dry heat of the desert.

The male sentry approached the female and nuzzled her lip horn with his own. She blinked each of her four lids fully and slowly to indicate that she was ready.

Together they stood and watched the little light flutter and bump into the wall of the cave before spinning into the Purview and disappearing from sight. Together they stood and faced the Purview as the vine patterns around its frame began to move.

Chapter One

Brigitta concentrated on the black pebble in her hand. She turned it over and over in her palm, gathering its energy, and then tossed it over the embankment into Precipice Falls. She closed her eyes and visualized the rock falling downward, splashing into the water below, and spinning through the underground caverns of the Water Faerie Realm.

"Be the rock," she murmured to herself. "Follow the energy of the rock."

Brigitta couldn't focus her mind. She opened her eyes and sighed. How should she know what it felt like to be a rock or to travel through the forest's underground caverns? She wasn't even allowed to explore them, not until she was a First Elder Apprentice, which was silly considering she had already been outside the White Forest itself, something none of the other First Apprentices had ever done.

"I'd like to see First Apprentice Flanna fight off a carnivorous caterpillar." She picked up the rest of the pebbles sitting beside her and threw them over the embankment.

"Ow!" came a voice from below.

"Sorry, Minq!" called Brigitta, peeking over the edge as Minq's rodent-like face appeared.

He rubbed his eye with one of his long, droopy ears. "Why you throw rock?" he asked as he fluttered over the

3

embankment.

"Something Elder Dervia cooked up to keep me busy," Brigitta said, immediately wishing she could retract her comment. It was not a fair accusation since every Apprentice was required to learn empathing. What she really needed was to practice being more "Elderlike" and not saying spiteful things. "I'm supposed to learn how to be other things. Like that tree or the water or, someday, even you."

"If you me, who I?" Minq landed awkwardly on the grass and removed his translucent wings, the ones that had been gifted to him by High Priestess Ondelle herself. He had never completely gotten the hang of the wings, nor did he like to wear them in the water or when he slept. But he did enjoy flying to Precipice Falls with Brigitta every few moons to practice flying in the winds of the water's currents.

"You're my best friend," Brigitta said. My only friend, she thought to herself.

They both fell back into the grass and stared up at the clouds, huge and white like dreamy mountains. Clouds were the only things Brigitta was good at empathing. She had a particular affinity with clouds, having spent so many hours watching them while lying on her back in the lyllium fields northwest of Tiragarrow. It seemed natural to become a cloud, slow moving in flight, overlooking the forest.

As she relaxed and focused on cloud energy, letting go of all intrusive thoughts as she had been taught, she was suddenly looking down from a great height, passing over the Water Realm. Tiragarrow appeared below, alive with tiny faeries scurrying around preparing for a party. Watching them zip about, Brigitta grew dizzy and lost her concentration.

4

She shook her head clear and rolled over onto her stomach, turning her attention to her favorite section of the falls, where the streams of water were like hair billowing over a faerie woman's shoulder. Waterfalls were trickier to empath, even for a Water Faerie. They were more complex and changed too fast. It was easiest to empath things if they were still and most difficult if they had minds of their own. At least that's what she had been told. Empathing a thinking beast was advanced magic and dangerous for an untrained faerie.

Minq's mind might be harmless enough, she thought, glancing over at his pointy pale brown face before turning her attention back to the water. Elder Dervia's low voice echoed in her head. *Dismiss anything that isn't related to the energy of the object. Dismiss your thoughts.*

"Easier said then done," Brigitta murmured. She allowed that thought to drift away, like a flutterscarf on the wind, as she stared into the water, emptying her mind.

For a moment she felt herself rushing downward and a penetrating coolness overcame her. It was brief but exhilarating.

Brigitta shot up in surprise. "I did it!"

"What do?"

"I was the waterfall. Only for a moonsbreath. But I did it!"

Minq clapped his ears together like hands. Then he threw his wings back on and spun his ears around while he flapped, twirling straight up into the air.

Brigitta laughed and it felt good. She hadn't laughed much since moving to the Center Realm two seasons ago to apprentice with the Elders. She missed her momma and poppa and even her little sister Himalette, but whenever she visited them it didn't feel the same. Her momma was over-fussy, her poppa only wanted to know what the Elders were up to, and Himmy had a busy social life that centered around the latest faerie gossip.

Flying with Minq to Precipice Falls was one of Brigitta's few pleasures. That and visiting Gola the Drutan in her tree home just west of Grioth in the Fire Faerie Realm. Gola said she liked the faeries of Grioth best because they left her alone, although she always made time for Brigitta when she came by unannounced.

Something round and white dropped at Brigitta's feet and she picked it up. It was a broodnut. A message was carved into its shell, exposing the red inner meat: *Time to come home—Love, Momma.* Brigitta looked up to see Roucho, her poppa's new featherless delivery bird, flying back in the direction of Tiragarrow. She smiled sadly at the thought of her momma still referring to their cottage as Brigitta's home.

"Hey, Minq," Brigitta pointed to the departing bird. "It's time."

Minq stopped twirling and waved at the bird with one of his lengthy ears. He liked Roucho, the only other bald flying beast in the forest. He landed, closed his eyes, and opened his mouth.

Brigitta laughed again as she cracked the nut open and tossed the meaty center onto his pink tongue.

By the time Brigitta and Minq arrived in Tiragarrow, most of the local faeries, and some not so local ones, had already gathered outside of her family's cottage. Her Great Auntie Ferna, from the village-nest of Gyllenhale, sat on a stump chatting with Edl Featherkind. Himalette's numerous friends dangled from the tree branches in their brightest party-wear as the adult faeries exchanged stories of their own unveilings. Edl gave Brigitta and Minq a friendly wave as they landed on the new moss she and Pippet had planted in front of the cottage for the occasion. Brigitta waved back. Edl had lovely yellow wings with a thick V shape spreading out toward the ends like friendly green smiles, marking her as a Master Gardener. Her specialty was tingermint, but her moss was excellent as well, perfectly spongy and soft.

Edl and her companion Orl Featherkind, Tiragarrow's Caretaker, were among the small number of faeries who treated Brigitta no differently than they had before she had saved the White Forest, and her Elder destiny markings had been revealed. But it didn't really count, since Edl and Orl were friendly toward everyone.

Brigitta looked around for Orl, even though she felt a tinge of guilt whenever she saw him, feeling a bit responsible for his arm breaking after the stone curse hit the forest. He always told her the spell reversal had healed it, that it was better than ever, but she noticed how it had pained him through the Gray Months.

The Gray Months. The last season Brigitta had spent with her family in Tiragarrow before Water Elder Jorris had died, advancing Dervia of Dionsdale to Elder status, Flanna of Rioscrea to First Apprentice, and Brigitta to Second Apprentice. The cottage before her was no longer her home. She had been living in the Center Realm and performing her Second Apprentice duties for almost two seasons.

It was just as well because she was sure most of the faeries in Tiragarrow were suspicious of her. And why shouldn't they be? Hrathgar had become an Elder Apprentice when she returned from the Dark Forest, and she tried to steal the power of the Hourglass. Twice.

"What destiny mark Himalette have?" asked Minq.

"I don't know," replied Brigitta. "She's managed to keep it a secret from everyone. She's been wearing wingmitts for the past few moons."

The crowd hushed as Brigitta's parents, Mousha and Pippet, emerged from the cottage and stood on either side of the doorway. Mousha looked particularly pleased with himself, and Brigitta wondered with what invention he would kick off the unveiling. He nodded to the faeries gathered in front of the cottage and they began to hum and flap their wings in rhythm. Pippet started the traditional celebration song and everyone joined in.

Show your wings little faerie kin

Wings that carry on the wind

Show your wings and hold them high

Share with us your Task in life

Minq struggled to keep the rhythm and remember the words at the same time. Brigitta helped him along by reciting the words in his ear.

Show your wings little faerie kin

You have now grown into them

8

Show your wings and hold them high

Celebrate your Task in life

As the last notes of the song drifted away, Mousha gestured to the doorway. Sparkling pink and yellow bubbles shot out from the entrance of the cottage and everyone cheered. Children flew from the branches and caught them in their hands, squealing with delight. The bubbles were thick and didn't pop on impact. Instead, they settled in the tree branches, on the moss, and on everyone's heads. A neighbor boy stomped on one. It slipped out from underneath his foot and flew into Auntie Ferna's face. She tumbled backward from her tree stump, laughing and catching her balance with her strong wings. A mound of bubbles gathered at Brigitta's feet. Minq dislodged one from his right ear.

"Poppa!" called Himalette from inside the cottage. She appeared in a filmy lavender gown and held up a small box, out from which the crazed bubbles fired.

Mousha grabbed the box and reached inside. The bubbles stopped and he withdrew his goo-covered hand. The gathered faeries stifled their laughter.

"Go ahead, lola," Pippet urged Himalette forward.

Himalette regained her composure and glided to the edge of the porch, grinning from ear to ear. "Thank you all for coming to my unveiling. Afterwards we will have leaf races, a lantern dance, and Momma has made tingermint tea and pipberry pies."

Brigitta and Minq exchanged glances. Himalette's eyes shone with a child's innocence, but she had grown in the last season. Her hair was darker, her face had lost its roundness, and her wings extended farther from her back.

Minq placed his ear across Brigitta's shoulders and she rubbed her cheek against it. How happy her sister sounded. Had they really taken the same journey through the Dark Forest two season cycles ago? Had Himalette really managed to forget the dangers that lurked outside the White Forest, like a distant dream?

Brigitta grabbed Minq's ear and held it, suddenly overcome by sadness as she recalled Hrathgar Good's teary goodbye on the dungeon floor of the castle on Dead Mountain. His ear squeezed back, as if he were empathing her thoughts.

Himalette's smile danced with excitement as Mousha and Pippet took their places on either side of her. They both grasped a wingmitt and beamed at each other.

"Two moons, two wings, one heart, one destiny!" they called and lifted the wingmitts.

Underneath, Himalette's pink wings shone brightly. On the ends, in a deep rose to match her momma's markings, were two long bars with two filled circles sandwiched between them, like snuggling musical notes. The faeries cheered and fluttered their own wings as Himalette curtsied.

"What marking mean?" asked Minq, flapping his wings along with everyone else.

"She's been marked as a Song Master," said Brigitta. "She'll learn to write songs and arrange music for festivals."

"This important Life Task?"

"It's perfect for Himmy. She'll love it."

Her sister flew up and over everyone's heads, showering the crowd with multi-colored flower petals. She landed in front of her best friends and they hugged her and kissed her cheeks, admiring her markings and pointing to each other's empty wings, describing what signs they thought might appear there some day.

"Friends not have mark. She young for destiny?" asked Minq as Brigitta plucked a yellow petal from his snout.

"Yes, a bit, but if her heart knows what it wants . . ." Brigitta tried to push away her envy. Everyone knew Himmy's heart; she wore it on her sleeve. She'd always loved music. But how did Brigitta's markings reflect her own conflicted heart?

She watched her sister making goofy poses for her friends. How simple life would be to write songs all day and learn to play instruments. Sure, Brigitta would learn to play a durma as an Elder Apprentice, but it was a sacred instrument to be used when honoring the dead. It wasn't anything festive like a hoopflute or light and joyful like blossom bells. Durmas were about as serious as an instrument could get.

"Poppa must be happy. He loves musical inventions." Brigitta couldn't help smiling to herself when she thought about her poppa's thunderbug symphony. She peered into the cottage to see if he had one waiting inside.

Mousha and Pippet caught Brigitta's attention and motioned for her and Minq to join them. They were about to fly over when a short reddish Water Faerie girl with dark yellow wings dropped down in front of them.

"Brigitta! Minq!" The young faerie bounced up and down. She patted Minq on the head and he winced. "I thought maybe you were going to miss everything, Brigitta, because you had important Apprentice things to do."

"Hi Glennis, we were just—" started Brigitta.

"Not as exciting as your unveiling!" Glennis exclaimed, referring to Brigitta's surprise destiny revealing in front of the entire forest. "But how could any faerie beat that? It was the most amazing unveiling ever!"

"It's not like I planned it that way."

"I guess Himalette isn't like you. I thought since she had been to Faweh she would become an Elder Apprentice, too, or at least a Wising, but she didn't. That means another one will be unveiled. Maybe from my own village-nest!"

"Maybe, we haven't had one from Easyl in a—"

"What's it like living in the Hive?" Glennis leaned closer to Brigitta.

"We don't call it that, we—"

"Do you get to sit in on any Elder meetings?" Glennis's eyes grew wide and she lowered her voice. "What's High Priestess Ondelle really like?"

Brigitta took a slow breath to control her annoyance. She was about to tell Glennis it was none of her business when Pippet's strong arm landed on her shoulder.

"Hello, Glennis, nice to see you. I need to borrow Brigitta and Minq to help me with the refreshments." Pippet steered Brigitta toward the porch, laughing. Minq fluttered behind them.

"Thanks, Momma. Bog buggers, that Glennis is a real—" Brigitta stopped and sighed. "Elder-like, Elder-like," she mumbled to herself.

"Ah, lola, she means well. She looks up to you." Pippet hugged her daughter. "I'm glad you're here. You, too, Minq."

Once inside the kitchen, Pippet handed four trays of little pipberry pies to Minq, who balanced them on his hands and ears. After he had flown from the room, Pippet sat Brigitta down.

"I haven't seen you since Himalette had her change. Let me look at you."

"Aw, Momma, I'm not any different than I was the last time I saw you."

"You are, you've lost weight. And you're not sleeping, I can tell."

"I'm fine. I'm sleeping." Brigitta left out the part about not sleeping well, but that was nothing new. She hadn't slept well since returning from the Dark Forest.

Pippet wasn't listening. She was pulling ingredients off the shelves. "Nothing a little triple lyllium suclaide won't cure. That will fatten you up and bring sweet dreams."

"Momma, you don't have time to make suclaide."

Pippet reached into a jar and pulled out some leaves and white petals. "Hmmm, I'm out of lyllium root."

Brigitta placed her hand on Pippet's shoulder. "Mother, I'm fine. Please. It's Himalette's unveiling party. You have guests."

"So, I'm 'Mother' now?" Pippet touched Brigitta's cheek. Her eyes grew misty. "Guess you don't really need me anymore."

"Don't say that. Of course I need you."

"It was only a matter of time." Pippet dug into her pocket for a bit of cloth and dabbed her eyes with it. "My big lola."

"How can I be big and be a lola at the same time?" Brigitta joked and then hugged Pippet to keep the tears from her own eyes.

As she snuggled against her momma's warm body, Minq burst in through the door. "More pies! Faerie took all before get to table."

"That's because Momma makes the best pipberry pies in the entire forest."

Pippet gave Brigitta one final squeeze and then turned to pile more pies on the trays. Brigitta grabbed a ladle and started filling cups with the tea brewing in the vat over the fire. She glanced at Pippet's soft pink face and noticed new wrinkles around her eyes.

"And you should try her triple lyllium suclaide," Brigitta added. "It's a secret recipe. Maybe she'll have time to make a batch for us tomorrow."

Pippet beamed at her daughter. "Maybe."

Brigitta stared out over the party guests from the porch. Mousha and Orl Featherkind were stringing a thunderbug symphony, Minq was fluttering around delivering pies, Edl Featherkind and a skinny Air Faerie with silky sky blue wings were stretching candlewebs across tree holes, and Auntie Ferna sat on a sturdy branch shooting flutterscarves out of a long hollow branch.

The object of a leaf race was to be the first to collect one of each color of flutterscarf without touching them with your hands. Faerie children zipped around with giant leaves, trying to catch the elusive scarves that switched direction with the slightest breeze. Laughter filled the air as one boy used his wings to blow a scarf away from the faeries behind him.

Pippet floated past Brigitta with a tray of mugs. "You should join them. Have some fun."

Brigitta did want to join the fun. She wanted to forget about her worries and responsibilities and simply be a Tiragarrow faerie again. She lifted off from the porch, determined to have a good time, then stopped short as she felt an intense buzzing emanating from her chest. She dropped to the ground with a sharp cry, and several faeries turned to stare. Brigitta's hands went to her breast and found her hourglass necklace. It was warm and vibrating.

"Brigitta, what's wrong?" asked Glennis, hurtling herself toward Brigitta.

Fernatta stopped mid-scarf toss. The leaf racers turned to look as well. Pippet and Himalette flew to Brigitta's side.

Brigitta waved everyone off. "It's fine, it's just . . . my hourglass . . . Ondelle's never called me with it before."

"Ondelle's calling you?" Pippet looked astonished.

"Away from my unveiling party?" Himalette pouted and crossed her arms.

Several faeries began to whisper.

"I'm sorry, lola. Maybe she forgot?"

The partygoers slowly resumed their activities, buzzing quietly to each other. Pippet handed the tray of mugs to Glennis and shooed a disgruntled Himalette away. She stood arms akimbo and waited for an explanation.

"I have to go." Brigitta kissed her concerned mother's forehead. "Don't worry, Momma, I'm sure everything's just fine."

Chapter Two

Brigitta sped toward the Center Realm, taking a direct route rather than the roundabout one she usually took to avoid the popular sundreaming rocks along Spring River. The trees parted and she flew over the expanse of warm rocks lining the river, which created a shallow creek with little ponds of water that heated up in the sun.

Luckily, most of the local Water Faeries were gathered at Himalette's party, and the seasonal warmth of the Green Months, the best time for sundreaming, was waning as the Gray Months approached. Two older Earth Faeries floated on their backs in the ponds, an Air Faerie family picnicked on a table-shaped rock, and a Fire Faerie couple cuddled near the creek, so absorbed in each other they wouldn't have noticed if it were day or night. As she buzzed over them unnoticed, Brigitta relaxed.

Before she had been called to her Apprenticeship, Brigitta had spent most of the seasons after her return from the Dark Forest helping her momma around the cottage or in the quiet company of Minq and Gola. Himalette had been declared old enough to travel to her lessons on her own and the White Forest faeries had gone back to their simple pleasures. Even her poppa had returned to the numerous experiments that absorbed his time. Only her momma's concerned glances and the pesky questions from Glennis intruded on her attempt to forget about her troublesome destiny markings.

Then, in the middle of the Grow Months, Jorris had died and Brigitta had been called to the Center Realm. That was when the whispers and nervous teasing began. She was very young for an Elder Second Apprentice and it was easy to draw conclusions about the similarities between her and Hrathgar.

As she zipped through the trees, she reached down to the hourglass dangling from around her neck. It was still vibrating and warm.

Why would Ondelle call her with the hourglass? What could be so important? Brigitta hovered in the air, suddenly realizing it must have been a mistake. The High Priestess was calling the Elders together and had forgotten that Brigitta had her hourglass necklace. But how could Ondelle forget something like that? She let go and continued her journey.

She entered a final long stretch of slender silverwood trees and then burst into the Center Realm, pausing only for a moment to gaze upon the Hourglass of Protection. It was suspended in its usual manner by the many twisted branches of the two immense uul trees on either side of it. It was less than a full season since it had been turned and the protective field around the forest renewed, but checking up on it every day was a habit Brigitta couldn't break.

The sturdy branches cradled the crystal structure as the colorful sands silently tumbled. The only sounds were the chittering birds and a few grawping grovens.

Satisfied that things were in order, Brigitta headed for the Elder Chambers entrance, a tunnel carved into a stone mound surrounded by an unassuming copse of trees. The

Hive was the affectionate term many faeries used for the collection of caverns that made up the chambers, the living and training quarters, and the various dens for Elder magic practice and artistic pursuits. The caverns extended far below the ground, farther than Brigitta had ever imagined before her first official visit. And in the depths of the Hive were entrances to tunnels that diverged and spread beneath the entire forest.

When the Ancients created the White Forest to protect the elemental faeries from the outside world, they also created the Hive and its passages as further precaution, though against what Brigitta had no idea. The caverns seemed so counter to faerie nature that she often wondered if the Ancients could see in the dark. Or *hear in dark*, as Minq would put it. She pictured tall elegant Ancients with long ears trailing behind them and snickered at the irreverent thought.

Still smiling at the absurd image, she entered the tunnel and flew straight into First Water Apprentice Flanna of Rioscrea and First Fire Apprentice Thane of Tintlebar. Flanna startled and dropped the red fire flower she was carrying.

Flanna was a large Water Faerie, but well-proportioned and strong. She had bright yellow wings and hair so red it matched the flower. Thane was tall and thin with dark features and lovely cobalt wings that everyone admired, including Thane himself.

"Oh, sorry," Brigitta mumbled as she dropped down to pick up the flower.

Flanna brushed her aside and snatched up the flower. She wiped it off and scowled at Brigitta. "The tunnels are not a racetrack, Apprentice Brigitta."

"Ondelle called me," Brigitta held up her hourglass necklace, immediately regretting doing so.

Thane and Flanna exchanged looks.

"Well," was all Thane said.

"I hope you aren't in any trouble, dear," added Flanna, arranging the petals of her flower. "Your lack of discipline reflects directly on me, you realize."

"I'm sure it's nothing. Excuse me, Apprentice Flanna, Thane." Brigitta turned and flew off, feeling the heat of their stares as she continued through the passageway.

Flanna was nearly as old as her momma, but Brigitta thought she acted more like a spoiled child. And she was definitely never maternal toward Brigitta. One of Flanna's duties was taking all the Seconds to Green Lake north of Dionsdale for water studies, and Brigitta always got the feeling Flanna resented any progress she made.

She rounded a corner and stopped, hovering in the air. Was it just her imagination or did Flanna really think ill of her? She held the hourglass in her hand and closed her eyes, letting her thoughts go, and misting her mind out. Brigitta's mind-mist gravitated to Flanna's energy using the lingering feeling of Flanna's skin brushing against her.

A moonsbreath later Brigitta was looking into Thane's sparkling eyes.

I wonder what that's all about? said Flanna, her voice reverberating inside Brigitta's own head.

Do I detect a hint of jealousy? Thane replied.

Flanna playfully swatted him on the head with the flower. *Jealous of a Second Apprentice?* she replied. *Don't be silly. She's not that bright. Look, she doesn't even know not to pick up someone else's reddened fire flower.* She giggled like a young girl.

Thane laughed. *Is it damaged? I can pick another one.*

"Brigitta!"

Brigitta opened her eyes. Ondelle was traveling toward her through the passageway. Her expression was serious.

"Oh. I was just—"

"Practicing a little empathing?" asked Ondelle.

If Brigitta wasn't in trouble before, as Flanna had suggested, she was now. She let go of the necklace and landed on the ground.

"I just don't like others talking about me behind my back," she mumbled.

"Is that what they were doing?" asked Ondelle, her expression unreadable.

Brigitta only nodded.

Ondelle studied Brigitta with tired eyes. "We've been waiting for you," she finally said. "Come along."

"Waiting for me?" Brigitta asked as she trailed after Ondelle through the tunnel. "You meant to call me away from Himalette's unveiling party?"

Ondelle turned, puzzled for a moment. "Oh. I had forgotten." She glanced up the passageway and then back to Brigitta. "Do you need to return?"

"It's all right," said Brigitta, trying to read Ondelle's face. She was distracted, that was obvious, but when had Brigitta ever known the High Priestess to forget anything?

Ondelle continued and Brigitta trailed after her. As they drew closer to the Elder Chambers she thought about something else. It dawned on her that without much effort, she had empathed another faerie. Even though she was probably going to get a severe lecture from Water Elder Dervia about invasion of privacy and irresponsible behavior, she couldn't help feeling just a little bit smug.

Ondelle and Brigitta entered the first chamber, a high-ceilinged cavern lit by numerous webs of candles and slices of globelight strung along the walls. Nine wooden chairs and a long wooden table dominated the room. The furniture was as old as the Chambers, having been crafted by the Ancients themselves. The room served as the Elders' primary gathering space and was where they counseled the other White Forest faeries.

Earth Elder Adaire of the village-nest of Dmvyle, Air Elder Fozk of Fhorsa, Fire Elder Hammus of Bobbercurxy, and Water Elder Dervia of Dionsdale were clustered around a woven basket on the table. As Ondelle and Brigitta landed, the Elders turned away from the basket, blocking it from view. Fozk, whose white hair and beard looked as if they were made of clouds and his long blue wings from a piece of sky, nodded to Dervia.

"Really, Priestess," Dervia approached, flitting her forest green wings, their yellow destiny markings shimmering in the candlelight, "my Second Apprentice?" She sent a terse smile to Brigitta and then jerked her gaze back to Ondelle.

The Elders were known to be less cavalier than most other faeries, but the tone of the room was unusually grave. It didn't take any empathing at all to detect the dark mood. Not even Hammus, the smooth-faced socialite fond of playful jokes and festive parties, was smiling. He pulled his tawny wings together as he looked from one Elder to the next.

Ondelle simply gestured to Brigitta, who meekly followed her to the table.

The Elders stepped back. Adaire sat down in her chair, shaking her head. Her black and silver hair spilled out of her bun onto her stocky shoulders.

Ondelle reached into the basket and pulled back a blanket. Sleeping inside was a tiny newborn Earth Faerie with dark features and a square body.

"Brigitta, meet Duna of Dmvyle. Three moons old." Ondelle studied the baby.

"This has nothing to do with Dmvyle." Adaire pointed at the basket. "This has never happened in my village-nest before."

"This has never happened in any village-nest before, Elder Adaire," said Fozk.

"That we know of," added Hammus.

"I'm sure it would have been chronicled," said Dervia, "and Fernatta would have mentioned it. She has studied every journal as far back as they go."

The Elders gave exasperated sighs and paced about the room. Brigitta was very confused. She peered into the basket. The Earth Faerie baby had all her limbs and two honey-colored wings tucked beneath her.

"I don't understand," Brigitta said as the baby yawned and opened her eyes. They were crystal white. "Oh!" she exclaimed.

"She has no destiny." Ondelle reached in, picked the baby up, and cradled it in her arms. "The Ethereals have not visited her. If they had, her eyes would be colored. Green or

22

brown I would imagine by the look of her."

"Maybe they just haven't done it yet?" suggested Brigitta, who had never spent much time around newborn babies.

"Perhaps, though it would be quite unusual," answered Ondelle.

"Unusual?" blurted Fozk with a laugh.

"Unheard of," corrected Dervia.

The baby started to cry. Adaire grabbed a leaf from a bowl on the table and held it on Duna's tongue until she stopped crying.

"Yes, wean her on ceunias leaf." Dervia threw her hands in the air.

"She'll need a tremendous amount of it later to deal with the embarrassment of her village-nest," grunted Hammus.

"Embarrassment!" Adaire spun to face him.

"Enough!" Ondelle placed the baby back in the basket. "Elders, hold your tongues!"

Brigitta looked around the room at the agitated Elders. She had never heard the High Priestess raise her voice to anyone before. Not that she had ever been invited to their private gatherings before, but she was pretty sure this wasn't how they usually acted behind closed doors. Was one destiny-less child all that terrible? Surely the White Forest faeries would be kind to her and find something she liked to do.

Just then, the Center Realm sprite, Vivilia, flew into the room. "Ondelle, the baby's parents are getting worried. What shall I tell them?"

If there were such a thing, Brigitta would call Vivilia the Elder Sprite. She knew Vivilia as the sprite who had given her and Himalette the protection of Blue Spell when the forest had been threatened by Hrathgar's stone curse, something that had never made any sense to her according to what she knew about the laws of Blue Spell magic. Then again, there was a growing list of things she didn't understand and a growing list of things she'd learned that the Elders kept to themselves, like the fact that Ondelle had sent Vivilia up to Dead Mountain to check on Hrathgar, who in turn had used the sprite to sneak the stone spell into the White Forest in the first place.

Sometimes Brigitta saw Vivilia flying in or out of Ondelle's private den. She never spoke directly to Brigitta, but whenever their eyes met, the sprite would smile slightly, just enough to remind Brigitta of their shared history.

"Tell them . . . " Ondelle looked to the blank expressions of her Elders, "that they will all stay in the Center Realm tonight and we will have an answer in the morning. And give them anything they require."

Vivilia looked a bit put off by being requested to do the work of a Second Apprentice, but Brigitta figured none of the other Apprentices had been told about the baby. The sprite simply nodded and left the room.

"The parents, Vivilia, and the six of us are the only ones who know about this situation," said Ondelle, as if empathing Brigitta's thoughts.

"Not for long, I'm afraid," Fozk admitted.

Ondelle looked down at the baby and addressed Brigitta, "A child receives its destiny when the Ethereals visit it through its first dream. This usually happens—"

"Always happens," Dervia muttered.

"—within the first few hours of its birth," continued Ondelle. "So, what suppositions can you make from this?"

Brigitta wrinkled her brow in thought. "Well, maybe the baby hasn't had its first dream yet. Or maybe it can't dream at all?"

"Nothing we haven't covered already," said Dervia. "Simple empathing tells us the child dreams."

"Maybe it needs longer ones?" Brigitta suggested. "Or deeper ones? Have you tried giving it triple lyllium suclaide?"

"Ha!" called Hammus.

Brigitta's cheeks flushed and she clenched her teeth. What were they expecting she could do about any of this?

"We must find a spell for the parents," concluded Dervia. "Something that will make them forget this ever happened."

"I'm sure I can give some color to her eyes," said Adaire, contemplating the small bundle in the basket. "Perhaps a combination of hennabane and—"

"You mean lie to everyone in the forest?" blurted Brigitta in disbelief.

The Elders sank into silence.

"Ondelle, perhaps she isn't old enough to understand the implications," Dervia finally spoke up.

"Then why don't you explain them to her?" proposed Ondelle. Something in her tone stilled Brigitta's breath.

Dervia's jaw twitched. She lowered her voice. "I'd rather she be excused."

"Are you going to give me a forgetting spell, too?" chided Brigitta. She knew she was being insolent, but the words escaped before she could catch them in time.

Ondelle placed a hand on Brigitta's upper back between her wings, immediately calming the young faerie. She turned to look into Ondelle's black moon eyes. The High Priestess's fiery red wings fanned the air behind her.

"Why am I even here?" asked Brigitta. "What can I do that the Elders can't?"

Ondelle gestured with her hands and a kiss of wind flew out from them and into the tunnels. "Elder Adaire, take the child to its parents and make sure they are comfortable," she said.

Adaire picked up the basket and left the room. A moment later, the kiss of air returned, and with it a male Air Faerie with long graceful teal wings and a female Air Faerie with translucent purple ones, both sporting three bold bars of matching darker color on the tops of their wings, marking them as Perimeter Guards. The male carried a jar inside of which floated a fuzzy yellow light.

Brigitta gasped and ran to the jar. "A whisper light!"

"You know what this thing is?" the male guard asked as he landed. "We found it east of Rivenbow."

The three remaining Elders stiffened and their nervous glances returned. Ondelle observed Brigitta, expressionless.

Brigitta tapped on the glass and the whisper light tapped back. She thought about her first encounter with the floating lights, when Himalette almost followed one right into the River That Runs Backwards. She couldn't hear any whispers now. The glass must muffle the sounds.

"Did it say anything to you?" she asked innocently.

"Oh, uh, some nonsense about me deserving to be Lead Guard." The male cleared his throat. "Although Trease here seems to think it said something else." He indicated his guard partner, whose cheeks turned pink. "Tell them, Trease."

"It told me how elegant my wings are," she said quietly.

Brigitta burst out laughing. The Elders stared at her as she pointed to the jar.

"Whisper lights only tell you what you want to hear," she said, composing herself. "There's a whole field of them outside Gola's old tree in the Dark Forest."

A chill went down Brigitta's spine as she caught the worried looks on everyone's faces. The gravity of what she had just said dawned on her as she watched the fuzzy little light tapping against the inside of the jar.

For the first time in almost one thousand season cycles, something uninvited to the White Forest had gotten in.

Chapter Three

After Brigitta had relayed all of her experiences with whisper lights, Ondelle requested that she wait in her living quarters until further notice. Wait for what, she didn't know, but she was certain her name would come up in whatever heated discussion they had behind their heavy wooden doors. It seemed like everyone in the entire forest was talking about her behind her back.

But everything wasn't about her, she scolded herself. She was being self-absorbed, feeling sorry for herself, yet again.

She spiraled down the tunnel to the second level, where the six Apprentices and two Wisings lived. Brigitta was still not used to living underground. The air particles were treated with a glow, in much the same manner as a globelight, but on a larger scale, so that the tunnels were surprisingly light. It was being enclosed that Brigitta didn't like, especially in the narrow bits. It reminded her of the carnivorous caterpillar caverns in the Dark Forest.

As she rounded the bend, she nodded at Kiera and Lalam, the two Center Realm Wisings, who were headed in the other direction. The two Wisings were always more polite than the rest of the Apprentices, perhaps because they were destined to remain Apprentices their whole lives. Since there were only four Elder positions, there were always a few Wisings in the Center Realm who spent their time in service to the others.

The Elders were lucky that Air Faerie Perimeter Guards took their Life Task so seriously, Brigitta thought as she entered her room and closed the door. They were honored to keep a secret for the Elders and proud to have discovered something so unique. Perhaps that male guard would get his promotion after all.

They were so proud, though, that they hadn't completely grasped the significance of their find. What lurked in Faweh wasn't all pretty whisper lights. What if something more menacing had gotten in? What if something more menacing *could* get in?

"And what did that whisper light have to do with Duna of Dmvyle?" Brigitta asked out loud. She couldn't see how the two things were connected, but something in Ondelle's distracted gaze told her that they were.

She moved across her small space to the mirror over her desk and gazed at her reflection. Her dark auburn hair had come loose from its bands and she had a pipberry stain above her lips. No wonder none of the Elders had taken her seriously.

"Is it so bad for a faerie to choose her own destiny?" she asked her reflection as she licked her finger and rubbed the pink spot from her face.

"Would you have chosen yours?" her image replied.

Brigitta couldn't answer that. She didn't know.

"Auntie Ferna chose hers," Brigitta reminded herself. "She was an Elder when they had to banish the Hrathgars. Not many faeries know that, and the older ones have forgotten."

She stared into her image's olive eyes.

"I wonder what other secrets the Elders are keeping?" her image asked.

Brigitta had been thinking the same thing. Of course, that was what the Thought Mirror was for, to meditate on one's thoughts. It only spoke the thoughts of the faerie looking into it, and only if the faerie were alone. Brigitta liked being alone with her thoughts, although lying in the lyllium field was a much better place to do it.

She stretched out her wings. The eye glyph and element symbols had grown sharper since they had appeared, revealing her destiny as an Elder, and were a richer shade of green.

"Still there," her image pointed out the obvious, "and not going away."

There was a knock at the door. Her image froze.

"Come in," Brigitta called, moving to her bed and sitting down.

Brigitta startled as Ondelle opened the door and entered the room. She closed the door behind her. Her presence filled the space, as if the Great Moon itself had walked in the door.

"It has been a long time since I have been inside an Apprentice's room." She approached the mirror. Brigitta's frozen image faded away. "I still use my own Thought Mirror," she continued and smiled.

Brigitta sat silently on her bed while Ondelle surveyed the rest of the room. Her gaze landed on the necklace around Brigitta's neck, which was back to its original cool temperature. Brigitta's hand instinctively went to the hourglass.

Ondelle sat down on the bed next to Brigitta and

bounced up and down a little. "I believe these are the same beds from when I was an Apprentice."

She stopped bouncing and looked Brigitta straight on. Her deep black eyes conveyed knowledge and experience beyond the faerie realm and a heaviness that suggested she alone bore the weight of her kin.

"Do you like it here in the Hive?" Ondelle suddenly asked. The familiar term sounded strange coming from the High Priestess's lips.

"In the Hive? Oh, well . . ." Brigitta shrugged her wings.

"I had a difficult time making friends when I was your age," Ondelle said, then laughed. "I still do, as a matter of fact."

It had never dawned on Brigitta that Ondelle might need friends or that she cared about being lonely. At least, she assumed Ondelle was lonely. She was an only child, her mother had dispersed when she was quite young, and her father had dispersed just before Brigitta was born.

"About what happened earlier with First Apprentice Flanna." Ondelle stood up and began pacing the small room.

"It won't happen again," blurted Brigitta. "I promise."

"Not in that way," Ondelle agreed. "We will train you to empath others safely." She stopped pacing and looked down at Brigitta. "And wisely."

It was not the response Brigitta had expected to hear, but she waited for Ondelle to continue. She was certain Ondelle was not there to discuss her studies.

"Aside from your sister Himalette, who seems to have recovered from her experience, you, Vivilia, and I are the only living White Forest faeries who have been outside our forest. It sounds incredible, but it's true. The elemental

31

faeries have become, I'm afraid, isolated and . . . "

"Spoiled?" Brigitta suggested.

Ondelle laughed, "I was going to say 'comfortable' but I rather like your choice of words."

"Our faeries don't like the unknown," said Brigitta, "or anything out of the ordinary, do they?"

"No," Ondelle said through a sigh, "and things will get a lot less ordinary unless we do something about it." She drew closer to Brigitta and put her hand on the young faerie's cheek. Her palm felt soft and warm and Brigitta wanted to close her eyes and melt into it. "I just wish we didn't have to ask so much of you."

"Of me?" Brigitta sat up. "What can I do?"

"Come with me." Ondelle offered her hand. "There's something else I need to show you."

Ondelle led her farther into the Hive than Brigitta had ever traveled. As they descended, spiraling through the tunnels, the light grew dimmer and the passage narrower. The third level was where the four Elders and Ondelle lived, the fourth level where they practiced magic in various spell chambers, and the fifth level where they kept Center Realm herbs, potions, and important texts.

They landed in the fifth level in an odd cylindrical library. Between the shelves of books, dark tunnels radiated in four directions. The whisper light hovered in its jar on a wooden pedestal against the far wall. It glowed in the dim light with a kind of intelligence. Brigitta could swear that it was watching her.

"I wonder how it's still yellow," Brigitta wondered aloud, "and alive?"

"It shouldn't be?" asked Ondelle as she opened a

cupboard in the wall and removed a book. A hole appeared in the middle of the floor and she dropped down into it.

"Gola said they only last a few suns," said Brigitta as she followed.

They landed in a small antechamber with no tunnels. The light was reduced to an eerie green, thick vines stretched along the walls, and earthy roots met them coming up from the edges of the ceiling and floor.

Elder Dervia stood there looking especially nervous, and another faerie lay on a stone altar in the center of the room. At first Brigitta thought the faerie, a large male with grayish blue wings and matching grayish blue hair, was sleeping. But she couldn't detect an element bound to him. As she stepped closer, she realized it was Jorris of Rioscrea, the Water Faerie Elder Dervia had replaced.

"But . . ." Brigitta gasped, "Elder Jorris! Isn't he—I thought he had—"

"Died, yes," responded Ondelle, who nodded to Dervia.

"Ondelle, must we?" Dervia wrung her hands. "She's still a child."

"We have settled this matter," Ondelle said, alluding to their private meeting while Brigitta waited in her room. "The signs cannot be ignored."

Sighing in resignation, Dervia signaled to Brigitta, who crept closer and leaned over Jorris's body. He hadn't changed much, which Brigitta found astonishing. She remembered him as jovial and kind, and she knew it wasn't fair, but a part of her resented him for dying. His death had pulled her away from her days of shelling gundlebeans with her momma, daydreaming with Minq, and sorting seeds with Gola.

Dervia lifted Jorris's left eyelid with her finger. His glassy brown eye shone back. She let his eyelid drop again.

"When a faerie's destiny is fulfilled, he or she dies, and the Ethereals claim the spirit," said Ondelle. "You're familiar with dispersement, of course."

"His eyes!" Brigitta exclaimed. "I saw it happen to Hrathgar Good. Her eyes returned to crystal white when she died."

"Correct," said Ondelle. "His spirit has not been dispersed."

As soon as Ondelle spoke the words Brigitta felt it. Another presence was in the room like a soft, dark cloud hovering behind Dervia, as if listening in. Its water energy was a faint mist easily overlooked. She sensed it now.

"As with Duna, the Ancients should have visited him. A destiny at birth, a dispersement with death. Until Duna was born, we did not know if Jorris's condition was an isolated incident." Ondelle handed Brigitta the antiquated book she had taken from the library. "Read what it says on the inside cover, please."

Wary of the silent presence now making its way around the room, Brigitta took the book, which was so heavy she nearly dropped it. She opened the faded cover and was surprised to see a poem in bright blue ink, as if it had been written that morning. She cleared her throat and read:

When forest spirits cannot leave home

And babes keep eyes of crystal white

When tongues of Elders start to moan

So will come a guiding light

And she who calls it by its name

Who knows it from its forest kin

Will travel back to times of old

To make the balance right again.

Brigitta's heart dropped into her stomach. "Who wrote that?" she whispered, looking up from the book.

"We're not sure," replied Ondelle gently. "This is the very first White Forest book written by the very first Chronicler, so we suppose it was the Chronicler herself."

"It could be a nursery rhyme for all we know," added Dervia, although she sounded unconvinced of this.

"It's all true. The dead keeping their eyes, the child not getting her destiny . . . " The air in the antechamber suddenly felt very thin to Brigitta, and the walls too close, making her head spin. The book began to slip from her hand.

"And she who calls it by its name . . . I had suspected." Ondelle caught the book and tucked it under her arm. "Now you know why I summoned you."

"No, no I don't," stammered Brigitta. "Why me? Why not Himalette or Gola or . . . or . . . They've seen whisper lights, too!" She looked from Ondelle to Dervia and then dropped her head.

Ondelle took the young faerie by the shoulders. "I think you know the answer to that already." She lifted up Brigitta's chin to look into her eyes. "Brigitta, undispersed spirits do not relinquish their elements to the next generation. When a spirit is dispersed, a new child is born bound to that element. It is a cycle of balance."

Brigitta's eyes welled up with tears. "You mean no more Water Faeries will be born if Jorris isn't dispersed?"

"If this trend continues, no more faeries of any element will be born."

"Duna . . ." Brigitta's thought trailed off. The little destinyless Earth Faerie could be the last one of her kind.

"Also, we have no idea, without the Ancients, if the Hourglass spell will last through the season cycle. But we do know, without the Ancients, it cannot be turned."

Ondelle let go of Brigitta and straightened up, looking at Dervia with a combination of sadness and apology.

"You may be the one to explain everything to her mother and father." Dervia's thin lips trembled. "My Life Task includes protecting my Apprentices, not sending them headlong into situations for which they are unprepared!" With that Dervia flew up through the ceiling.

"I cannot insist you come with me," said Ondelle, ignoring Dervia's outburst. "I leave it completely up to you. There are dangers I know nothing about."

"Go with you where?" asked Brigitta, sensing Jorris's spirit slumping to the floor in despair.

"To the faerie ruins in the Valley of Noe. I will depart in four suns' time."

Chapter Four

Alone in the ancient library as the other Apprentices went about their duties, Brigitta wondered how her absence would be accounted for. What lies would be piled on top of the growing number of secrets? She glanced at the whisper light, still floating in its jar, still watching her. A choice had to be made about traveling to Noe, and Ondelle insisted Brigitta decide without her influence.

She turned her attention to the passageway on her left. Ondelle had informed her that it led to the Fire Faerie Realm and had granted her permission to use it. Being awarded this kind of privilege would have shocked her that morning, but so much can change between one sun's rising and setting.

The tunnel was dark and still. She didn't have to take this route, but it would mean avoiding any Elders and Apprentices. She rubbed her globelight until it shone brightly in all directions and entered the tunnel.

Sticking to the main passage wasn't easy. There were so many enticing smaller tunnels. She heard water rushing from a few and saw long roots dangling from the ceilings of others, roots so long they created tempting curtains to pass through. At one point there were markings on the walls in silvery-blue: three large circles with squares inside of them and another circle inside each square. Brigitta studied them a moment before moving on.

To her amazement, she wasn't frightened in the underground passageways. She felt rather comforted because no one except Ondelle knew where she was. There was something very delicious about that fact.

After several moonbeats, the main tunnel began to narrow and curve upward until Brigitta emerged from the stump of a large dead tree on the northeast border of the Fire Faerie Realm. Lola Spring River, the smaller of the two White Forest rivers, ran south here, then turned west toward Bobbercurxy, the largest village-nest of the realm. Hrathgar's childhood home.

She flew downriver to the bend, where she could just make out the colorful tents and flags of the Bobbercurxy marketplace, then crossed over the river and slipped into the silverwood trees on the other side. She kept south until she came to the fire flower farm. The flowers were pale pink, as they remained until a faerie's passion deepened the color.

Brigitta shook her head, recalling Flanna's red flower. What a frivolous plant, she thought. It wasn't good for eating and had no healing properties. She plucked a flower from the end of the last row and sniffed it. It was odorless. Who cared if it could stay fresh for many moons after it was picked if one couldn't even use it to scent a room?

The Master Gardener, Trovish of Grioth, was nowhere in sight. This didn't surprise Brigitta, as he was known to spend most of his time north at the Air Faerie marketplace in Rivenbow. For some reason, Air Faeries were especially fond of fire flowers. Perhaps they were the most frivolous faeries of all, she concluded. She stuffed the flower into her tunic pocket as she flew from the farm.

She followed a path southeast until she came to a

crooked tree with an enormous burl at the bottom, carved out to make room for Gola's home. It was smaller than her Dark Forest home, but Gola insisted she needed very little and preferred puttering around her expanding gardens to hiding in her tree.

As Brigitta approached, she could see Gola pushing a seed mixture into little holes in the burl. Brigitta and Minq had helped carve out the holes so that Gola could plant mosses and ivies on the outside of her home, something she could never do in the Dark Forest because the beasts insisted on eating or poisoning the mixture before it could sprout. It seemed to Brigitta that Gola, too, found more trivial things to do living in the White Forest. She had gotten *comfortable*.

As Brigitta approached, the little bat-winged Eyes perched on Gola's shoulder turned around and opened wide. If the Eyes could smile, she figured that's what they were doing, so she smiled back.

"Hello, dear child," Gola said without turning away from her task. Her barky fingers continued their work. "One moment and I'll fetch us some tingermint tea." Gola smoothed the seed mixture down with her thumb and then dropped the remainder of the mixture into a little silver bucket.

She slowly straightened herself to step away from her work, but her left foot was stuck. Brigitta watched in dismay as Gola bent down and ripped her foot away from the ground with her hands. She grunted as the roots of her foot broke free from the earth, and she lost her balance.

"Gola!" exclaimed Brigitta, steadying the old Drutan. "Are you all right?"

Gola gave a harsh chuckle, her empty eye sockets

squinting in the direction of Brigitta's voice. "A tree-woman of my age should know better than to stand in one place for so long!"

Her Eyes fluttered to the door and Brigitta followed, helping Gola into her tree-home. She led Gola to a chair and then went to the kitchen to dish out some tea. Gola raised her feet onto some old blankets piled under the table and let out a tremendous sigh.

"The earth calls to me and I find it harder and harder to resist." Her Eyes landed on her shoulder, closed themselves, and leaned into her barky neck.

Brigitta placed the mugs on the table and sat down. She glanced around the walls, at the small shelf holding Gola's moonstone pots, at another shelf of books, and at the fading map of Foraglenn.

"Gola, where are all your other Eyes?"

"Bah! Too much effort to hold all those images in my weary mind. I released them to the flying fields. The Air Faerie children are looking after them. Or vice versa, perhaps."

Her remaining pair of Eyes blinked open and gazed at Brigitta. Even they looked old and tired.

"Don't you need them?" Brigitta asked.

"You forget, dear, my destiny is complete. I could lie down right now in the fire flowers and root myself if I so desired."

"But you won't, will you?" Brigitta's voice caught in her throat.

"Not yet, child, not yet." Gola reached for her tea and took a sip. "First I must perfect this tea your mother makes so well."

"And there's Minq," Brigitta said quietly. "He would miss you."

"You didn't come here to talk about me rooting myself to the earth," said Gola, always one to get straight to the point. "Spill your thoughts."

Brigitta told Gola, whom Ondelle trusted completely, about the poem inside the ancient book that predicted the white-eyed baby, the non-dispersed Elder, and the naming of the whisper light. Then she relayed the heavy decision she had to make about traveling to Noe.

"Hmmm, I was aware of Elder Jorris's condition, but not the rest."

"You were?" asked Brigitta.

"I was asked to be advisor to your council, remember?" Gola gestured to her door with her tea mug. "Though none but Ondelle ever bothers to visit."

"Ondelle comes here? To your home?"

"You expect me to lug myself to the Center Realm?"

Brigitta didn't know how she felt about the fact that Gola kept things from her as well. As much as she loved Gola, there were seasons and seasons of her life that Brigitta knew nothing about.

Glancing up at the map of Foraglenn on the wall, she asked, "Were you ever in Noe? Is that how you got your map?"

Gola burst out laughing, "Good grovens, it would have taken half my life to get there and back!"

She placed her mug down on the table. The Eyes fixed their gaze on Brigitta. "After the Great World Cry left Faweh in complete chaos, and before the elemental faeries were moved to the White Forest, a young Noe faerie named

Narine gave me that map and asked me to tend to the whisper lights."

Brigitta choked on her drink. Gola waited patiently while she coughed and caught her breath. "She—who—what?" she managed. "How come you never told me?"

"I am telling you now."

"Who was she?"

"She was an Ancient, daughter to the High Sage of Noe. She saved my life and we became friends."

Brigitta stared at Gola in disbelief and annoyance. Why did Gola, and every other so-called wise being, always leave out the important details?

"Do not let your anger get the best of you," Gola pointed a barky finger in Brigitta's direction. "Listen. My destiny has always been entwined with that of the faeries, but it is not my place to interfere with yours. I answer my own calling, understand?"

"Yes," said Brigitta meekly. She gripped her mug in her lap and waited for Gola to continue.

"The elemental faeries could not hide in the White Forest forever and they were not meant to. It was far too dangerous after the Great World Cry, but the Ancients knew there would come a time when an attempt to heal Faweh was necessary. At that time, the whisper lights would be released and deliver their true messages to the old civilizations."

"What do you mean?" Brigitta could hold her tongue no longer. "What true messages?"

"That is as much as I know."

"But you said whisper lights only tell you what you want to hear," said Brigitta. "How would anyone know if the message they received was true?"

42

"You would know." Gola lifted a necklace from her tunic. Five black moonstones dangled on the chain and caught the light.

It was the kind of answer that always exasperated Brigitta. How do you know when you know something? She watched as Gola rubbed the glossy surface of the first stone with her thumb.

"I was new to the world when Narine saved my life; I had no destiny yet. My moonstones formed later that night." Gola emitted a soft snort. "It was no surprise when, over time, each one revealed a new service to the faeries. I was never bitter about my destiny, though, until young Hrathgar broke my heart."

Brigitta stared at the last moonstone on the chain. Ondelle had told her Gola's final destiny was to help save the White Forest from Hrathgar's curse. But Hrathgar had stolen the stone, so Gola didn't even know she was supposed to help the faeries until after she already had. Did that mean destiny was destiny no matter what?

As Brigitta pondered this question, invisible tendrils of energy wove out from the moonstone, criss-crossing toward her like twisting fingers reaching through the air. Without thinking, she leaned forward and touched it with her index finger. A cacophony of images swarmed through her mind—

A boy with starry eyes, dark footprints leading up a rocky path, a mossy field encased in vibrating glass, Elder Fozk with panic on his face and beard whipping in the wind, a winding circular metal structure inside a cave, Glennis leaning over the side of a boat with yellow sails—

The images vanished as quickly as they had appeared and she was back in Gola's den, her body tight with tension, her breath still. She gasped for a lungful of air as Gola felt her way around her kitchen, her pair of Eyes on the table, studying Brigitta face.

"I'm sorry," Brigitta said once she had caught her breath, "I didn't mean to touch it. I just . . . "

"Couldn't help it," said Gola as she opened a jar and scooped out some brown powder. Her Eyes fluttered to her shoulder and she dropped the powder into a beaker of clear liquid. She stirred the mixture with her thin wooden pinky. "You are one who always reaches for answers."

Brigitta didn't know if that was a good or bad thing, considering all the trouble Hrathgar had gotten into seeking too many answers for herself. But she was not like Hrathgar. Was she?

"What were all those images I saw?" asked Brigitta, trying to conjure them again.

"Possible choices you will have to make."

The images were unfamiliar. Even the ones of Fozk and Glennis were out of context, and the faeries looked seasons older. It felt as if Brigitta had, in a moment, seen her life spread before her, but that the events had happened many seasons in the past and she could barely recall them. It was discomforting. She made a mental note never to touch Gola's moonstones ever again.

Gola removed a spell seed from her shelf. She spun it around three times, dipped a finger into a jar of water, and added three drops to the top of the seed. It opened and she poured the mixture inside.

The images were not from the White Forest. Did that mean she had no choice but to leave her home again? Were any of the images of Noe or were they other journeys to come? When Gola's Eyes turned to her, she remembered the image of a boy, perhaps her own age. His eyes had been a deep crystal blue.

Gola handed her the spell seed. It weighed about the same as the one she had used on her trip to Dead Mountain.

"For strength?" asked Brigitta, thinking about the burst of energy Gola's potion had provided when she entered the cave of the River That Runs Backwards.

"For courage."

Chapter Five

Brigitta stared into the space just above the green zynthia sitting on the table in the Elder Chambers. Even though it was only one small crystal, the one she had brought back from Dead Mountain, just having it in the same room with her made her nervous. She knew how zynthias made one's mind weak and prone to suggestion. It was through green zynthia hypnosis that Hrathgar had managed to trick Vivilia into bringing the stone curse into the White Forest.

Brigitta took a deep breath and, as she released it, filled her mind with water energy, letting the cool presence settle there. She then imagined the water energy saturating her whole being, making her strong. At last she imagined this strength expanding, forming a protective shield around her, cocooning her inside.

She lowered her gaze. As it landed on the zynthia, she felt the crystal's power pushing through, and she pushed back. It was like pushing against a dark, thick cloud, elusive and unpredictable as it tried to slip past her. She pushed some more, struggling back and forth until the cloud finally enveloped her and her mind went blank.

Brigitta, a voice called from far away. A familiar voice. Where was it coming from? She couldn't see anything. She didn't know where she was.

"Brigitta?" Ondelle's face emerged from the haze.

Slowly, Brigitta grew conscious of her surroundings. She was sitting on the floor of the Elder Chambers as Ondelle held her by the shoulders.

"You did well." She smiled and helped Brigitta up.

A protective glass covered the green zynthia. Brigitta stared at it and nothing happened; she was safe.

"I didn't. The zynthia energy pushed through."

"The trick is never to push back." Ondelle looked into Brigitta's eyes. "It is about balance, always about balance."

"That's what Elder Dervia says."

"That's what all the Elders will tell you during your lessons, no matter which element is your focus."

"But the zynthia energy is different," Brigitta complained. "It doesn't react right with the elements. It's a mean energy. It wants something from me."

"When something is hungry, what do you do?"

"Feed it?"

"Exactly. I feed it my fire and air energy while reserving a balance for myself. There is no one way to do this. Practice will teach you your way."

Practicing with the zynthia had been Ondelle's idea. As promised, she hadn't pushed Brigitta to make a decision about going to Noe, but she wasn't going to delay any training. There were things she'd need to learn sooner or later, Ondelle had said.

"Why are you bringing it along?" asked Brigitta.

"It is a powerful tool. I'm sure it could be of use." Ondelle stared at the zynthia in the jar.

"Um, Ondelle," said Brigitta, "what exactly would you . . . would we be doing down in Noe?"

"We seek an item left behind by the Ancients."

47

"And this item will heal Faweh?" asked Brigitta.

"I am afraid it is not that simple," replied Ondelle, lost in thought as she contemplated the crystal. "But it is a step in the right direction."

She swept back around. "How did you enter Apprentice Flanna's mind?"

"She was just kind of open." Brigitta shrugged and then thought about it some more. At the time, she hadn't even hesitated. She had just done it. "I remember I held my hourglass and relaxed. I think Flanna was so open because she's in love with Thane."

Ondelle laughed. "I think you may be right." She touched the glass case. "Let us experiment. I will look into the zynthia and then open my mind to you. You will enter my mind and together we will be with the zynthia."

Brigitta's jaw dropped. Enter Ondelle's mind! That was completely absurd. But apparently Ondelle didn't think so, because she was lifting the glass again. Brigitta averted her eyes from the zynthia.

"Take hold of your necklace."

Brigitta's hand moved to her hourglass necklace and a moment later she felt a tickling energy around her, then a gentle prodding of cool air. She relaxed as much as possible and followed the energy back to Ondelle.

There, see? You are doing well.

Ondelle's mind was expansive. Brigitta suddenly felt larger than the entire forest, but completely focused at the same time. She could tell that all of the focus was Ondelle's doing, and that if not for the High Priestess' skill, she would have been scattered like sands in the wind. Through Ondelle's eyes, Brigitta gazed at the zynthia, no longer

48

afraid. She could see its sharp green facets shining like eyes.

The most important thing to remember, Ondelle's mind spoke through her, *is that when you empath a thinking beast, you must stay connected to your own center. Do not forget yourself or become lost in the maze of unfamiliar thought and feeling. Usually one uses a personal item or memory as an anchor. I believe, for you, holding your hourglass has this effect.*

I would have chosen it, Brigitta realized, *if you had asked me to pick something.* The sound of her own thoughts reverberated through her. They mingled with Ondelle's as they admired the zynthia in front of them. *It's beautiful*, Brigitta's voice echoed.

Abruptly, Ondelle's energy slipped, like someone had poked at the fabric of it. She quickly rebalanced her energy and then dropped the glass lid on the zynthia. Just as quickly, Brigitta was back in her own mind in the room. It wasn't like a zynthia hypnosis or moonstone vision, though, which left her dazed and confused. Her senses actually felt sharper, picking up the vibrations of every item in the room.

"Someone else is here," Ondelle said, looking around. "The zynthia reached out to them."

Brigitta sensed it, too, and both of their gazes landed on the wall on the other side of the chamber's entryway.

As Ondelle and Brigitta approached the hiding spot where Brigitta and her friends had spied on the Elders seasons before, they saw a young faerie collapsed on the ground.

She looked in their direction, eyes foggy.

"Glennis!" Brigitta exclaimed, rushing to her side. "She's a friend of Himalette's from Easyl," she told Ondelle.

"Brigitta." Glennis reached out to touch Brigitta's face,

as if she didn't quite believe it were real. Her eyes met Ondelle's and she straightened up. "Ondelle!"

"Are you all right?" asked Ondelle.

"Yes, I . . . I think so . . . " stammered Glennis as she shook her head clear of the zynthia hypnosis.

"You shouldn't have been spying!" snapped Brigitta. "That was wrong of you! How did you even know—" Brigitta stopped. Glennis was cousin to Dinnae, who had been in the tunnel with Brigitta when they had spied on the Elders. Dinnae had a big mouth.

"I should have sealed that crack," Ondelle stared through the tunnel, "although, we have not had very many young spies lately."

Ondelle turned her attention back to Glennis, and Brigitta knew what she was thinking. They couldn't allow Glennis to share what she had overheard. The last thing they needed was for the White Forest faeries to start panicking.

Brigitta grimaced. She was just as wrapped up in secrets as the Elders.

Glennis's eyes shone a fear with which Brigitta was familiar. She felt a pang of pity for the young Water Faerie. Once you start to know things that you didn't know before, Brigitta thought, there's no going back. Unless you were young enough to forget about it all, like her sister had.

But Glennis was not so young. She was, Brigitta realized, only slightly younger than Brigitta had been when she had left the forest seven seasons ago.

"Ondelle," she lowered her voice, "please don't put a spell on her, or hypnotize her to make her forget."

Ondelle looked shocked. "No, of course not."

"Let me talk with her. In private."

Glennis fluttered around Brigitta's living quarters. She flew over the bed, looked at the books on her shelves, the beautiful ceremony beads hanging from her cabinet, and then landed in front of the mirror.

"You can really talk to yourself?" Glennis waved at the mirror, and her image waved back.

"Yes, yes," Brigitta was starting to regret inviting Glennis back to her room. Perhaps a forgetting spell would have been easier after all. "Glennis, please, sit down, we need to talk."

Glennis made a face in the mirror and then sat down on a stool, the effects of the zynthia completely worn off. "I can't believe I'm in your room! You must love it here! Do you stay up all night talking with the other Apprentices?"

"I know it seems exciting to you, but it's not like that. There's a lot of responsibility." Brigitta tried to command some of Ondelle's authority in her voice. "We live in a realm where faeries are safe and happy. That's because the Elders keep it that way. Sometimes, the Elders know things that the other faeries don't. Things I don't even know about. But that's why we have Elders, so all the other faeries don't have to worry about anything. So that they can be Song Masters or Gardeners or Star Tellers—"

"I can keep a secret, Brigitta, if that's what you want to know." Glennis sat down next to Brigitta, who was surprised by her sudden directness. Her round face took on an unexpected seriousness. "You're leaving the White Forest again."

An image of the older Glennis flashed through Brigitta's

mind. The Glennis Brigitta had seen when she had touched Gola's moonstone. In the vision, Glennis had looked at her with the same solemn expression. Brigitta noticed there were little flecks of dark yellow in Glennis's eyes that matched her wings.

"Yes," she finally said, realizing it was true, "I am."

"I won't tell anyone our forest is in danger."

"I—we—appreciate it," said Brigitta, believing her. "Oh, and I need a favor."

"Another one?" laughed Glennis, fluttering her wings.

"If anything happens, and I don't return, I need you to be there for Himmy, like a sister. And to fly with Minq and to make sure Gola has help in her garden."

"You'll come back," Glennis insisted, "I know you will. And you'll tell me all about it." Then she was back in the air, zipping around the room.

"Sure, Glennis, I'll tell you everything."

"I don't see why you have to go. It's unreasonable. You're a child!" Pippet paced across the living room as Mousha sat in his favorite mushroom chair, which swallowed him up in its cushy folds.

"I told you, Momma, it's because I've been outside the forest before. It's because of what I've seen and what I know."

She looked to her father for support. His eyes were filled with concern as he tapped his little yellow wings together.

"I'll be with Ondelle, Poppa," she reasoned. "Ondelle is more wise than any other faerie. She won't let anything happen to me."

"But it's so far away, much farther than before . . . " Pippet's eyes teared up and her voice cracked. "And simply to get some old faerie artifact?"

Brigitta swallowed her guilt. If she told them about the rhyme, she'd have to tell them about everything else. If she told them about everything else, she would only frighten them. She did not want to frighten them, Himmy, or anyone else if she could help it. Hopefully, she and Ondelle could fix whatever needed fixing and nobody would know the difference.

"We'll get the artifact and come right back," Brigitta said quietly. "It's important, Momma, I told you. The artifact will help keep the forest safe in the future. It was made by the Ancient Ones. It's *sacred*."

"I suppose it doesn't matter what I think, does it?" Pippet cried. "Oh, you are just like your poppa!"

There was an uncomfortable silence in the room as Pippet continued to pace. Brigitta's heart went out to her mother. Mousha glanced at Pippet and cleared his throat.

"Might others have the opportunity to examine this artifact?" he asked, leaning forward in his chair.

"Mousha!" scolded Pippet.

Himalette burst into the room, carrying a little package. She twirled in the air, showing off her wing markings, and landed in front of Brigitta.

"I made you a going away present!" Himalette thrust the package in front of Brigitta's face.

"Oh!" Pippet exclaimed and rushed from the room, dabbing her teary eyes with her tunic. Mousha struggled out of his chair and followed Pippet into the kitchen.

"It's a song drop!" exclaimed Himalette, oblivious to

Pippet's outburst. "Song Master Helvine taught me to make it. I've been helping her since my Change. We released some unfinished songs on Green Lake today. It was amazing, all those notes bobbing on the water."

Brigitta took the package from her sister and opened the lid. Nestled in pink flower petals was a shiny silver teardrop the size of Brigitta's thumb.

"When you want to hear the song just drop it to the ground."

"It's lovely, Himmy. Thanks." She kissed her sister on the top of her head.

"It's my first one, but Helvine says I have a talent for it." Himalette's face lit up. "Tell Ondelle I made it. If she likes my song, maybe she'll let me make an official one for the Twilight Festival or even for the Festival of the Elements!"

"I'll be sure to tell her." Brigitta closed the package and tucked it into her pack. She doubted that Ondelle paid much attention to the choosing of festival songs, but she wasn't about to tell that to Himalette's eager face.

Mousha led Pippet back into the room. Pippet wore a strained smile, although Brigitta got the feeling it was only for Himalette's benefit. She held out a soft bag.

"Your suclaide."

"Thanks, Momma." Brigitta took the bag and squeezed Pippet's hand. "Well, I guess I should –"

"Wait!" exclaimed Mousha, "I've got something, too." He ran into his laboratory and retrieved a flat, green disc. He placed it in Brigitta's hand and crossed his arms.

"Uh . . . thanks . . . Poppa," Brigitta waved the floppy green thing in the air, releasing a faint boggy odor.

"No, not like that!" Mousha took the green disc back

from Brigitta and spoke directly into it, "Like this!"

He rolled it up into a ball and flung it through the air. It hit the far wall and stuck with a splat.

"Like this! Like this! Like this!" it called from the wall in Mousha's voice.

"I'm not sure what to call it yet," Mousha tapped his wings together. "Vocal traveler? Throwing voice? Vorple blat?"

"Vorple blat!" laughed Brigitta.

"How about talking stinkball?" suggested Himalette, holding her nose. Brigitta playfully swatted her on the head.

"Fabulous thing and not as difficult as it looks. I ground some of Gola's chatterbud seeds, mixed them with groven saliva . . ."

"Ewwww!" Brigitta and Himalette squealed, looking at each other in disgust.

Mousha fluttered to the wall and peeled the blob off, leaving a round green stain. "It was meant to stay spherical, so you could bounce it or roll it or play catch."

"Who would want to play catch with that?" asked Himalette.

Brigitta flew to her poppa and hugged him. "It's wonderful. I love it!" She retrieved a scarf from the wall of her old bedroom, took the slimy disc between two fingers, and wrapped the scarf around it.

"All you need now is to invent something to clean up after it," said Pippet, examining the stained wall.

Brigitta laughed and hugged Pippet, who let out a heavy sigh and hugged her daughter back. Brigitta was relieved that the tension in the room had finally dissipated, and that she could remember her family like this in the moons to come.

"No, no, Apprentice Brigitta," scolded Elder Dervia, "you're not concentrating!"

Brigitta was tired of concentrating. She had never concentrated so much in her life. She had spent the past few suns in the private company of each Elder, while the other Apprentices prepared the festival grounds for a full forest gathering. Everyone had been told Brigitta and Ondelle were traveling somewhere, but no other details had been revealed. If Brigitta had been bothered by suspicious glares before, the situation was now downright unbearable, so she kept to herself when not in training.

After a transformation lesson from Elder Adaire, a lesson on how to manipulate firepepper from Elder Hammus, and mind-misting practice with Elder Fozk, Elder Dervia had Brigitta working on cloud gathering, which seemed like a waste of time. How would changing the clouds have helped her fight off a giant toad or a rock dragon?

Dervia cleared her throat and stared down her long nose at Brigitta, who braced herself for another lecture on her lack of discipline. "I apologize. You are tired. We are all tired."

An apology from Elder Dervia, Brigitta thought, that's new. She looked into her mentor's eyes and was surprised to detect genuine fear and concern. Elder-like, she told herself and straightened up. "It's all right, Elder Dervia. I'll try again."

Dervia nodded and sat down on a rock. They were on the edge of Green Lake in the northern border of the

Water Realm. It was the best place in the forest to work with clouds, which gathered fluffy and white above them.

Taking a breath, Brigitta settled her mind and body, feeling only cloud energy. Slowly and carefully, she tested the weight of each one and found which held the most wetness. Guided by her gentle prodding, the cloud began to reform, graying as it grew denser.

"Yes," Dervia murmured. "Much better."

A subtle movement on the lake's surface drew Brigitta's attention and she lost her concentration. She groaned and was about to apologize when she noticed that the movement was due to raindrops pittering on the water as the cloud she had been working on released a gentle shower. She had done it! She turned to her mentor and smiled as the light rain continued to fall.

Dervia stood and took Brigitta's hands in her own. It was the first time the Elder had ever touched her. Her hands were cool and not unkind. "I am a harsh mentor, I realize. But much harsher tasks lie ahead for you."

Brigitta nodded.

The Elder gave Brigitta's hands a tight squeeze then turned her back around to face the lake. "Now, again."

Back in Brigitta's room, Minq watched as she placed her sister's song drop into a little pouch and placed the pouch, along with her mother's suclaide, into her pack. Saying goodbye to Minq was harder than she had expected, but she wasn't going to cry. Elders-in-training don't cry, she told herself.

"I wish you could come with us," she said as she picked up her father's new invention. The smell alone was enough to leave it behind. "Ondelle says there's limited energy for traveling to Noe and back, and she wouldn't want anyone to get left behind."

"Will not be same forest without you," said Minq.

Brigitta was about to place the "talking stinkball" in her cabinet, but Minq's comment reminded her how much she had missed her family when she was in the Dark Forest. She placed the disc, well wrapped, in her pack along with her other gifts, then added her globelight, two firestones, some herbs from Elder Adaire, and finally Gola's courage potion. Ondelle would carry the zynthia, thank the Dragon.

"If you ask me, I go," Minq told her, touching her arm with the tip of his ear. "You save life. I yours."

Brigitta looked down into his sad rodent face and gave in to her tears. She wrapped her arms around him. "I yours, too, Minq."

He patted her back with an ear. "Do not doubt self."

Brigitta smiled as she pulled away and wiped her face. For a simple ground creature, as Gola called him, he sometimes had surprising insight.

They said their final goodbyes and Minq left to fetch Gola for the forest-wide departure ceremony. Brigitta plopped herself in front of her Thought Mirror.

"*And she who calls it by its name, Who knows it from its forest kin, Will travel back to times of old, To make the balance right again,*" sang the image in the mirror. It had an annoying habit of reminding her of thoughts she'd rather ignore. She supposed that was the whole point.

"And how am I going to make the balance right again?"

asked Brigitta. "I can barely make rain."

"Who else would go with Ondelle?" her image asked. "Would you risk sending an Elder instead?"

"I'm sure we could do without one Elder for a few moons."

"The fate of the forest is at stake. What if no more elemental faeries are born? What if—"

"You're not helping!" Brigitta stomped away from her mirror and flopped onto her bed. She closed her eyes and counted her breaths.

Air Elder Fozk had encouraged mind-misting as a meditative practice. Brigitta lay very still and allowed her thoughts to drift away. They misted out of her room and reached through the halls, navigating around the forms of Apprentice faeries.

They spiraled down through the Hive, past doors and furnishings, mingling with the charged particles of air, and slipped through the cracks to the lowest secret chamber, where Elder Jorris lay.

As Brigitta's mind-mist gently explored, she sensed Jorris's undispersed spirit, restless and worried, pacing the room.

Chapter Six

Brigitta stood nervously by Ondelle's side while the crowd of faeries gathered below. She had stood twice before on the silver platform beneath the great Hourglass of Protection. The first time she had looked out over the frozen and broken bodies of hundreds of faeries the day of Hrathgar Evil's stone curse. The second time she had received Ondelle's hourglass necklace and her destiny markings in front of the entire forest. On this day, the White Forest faeries were mingled together rather than grouped by elemental realm. They had no idea what to expect. The gathering was unprecedented in the history of the White Forest, and the air was buzzing with curiosity.

Her momma, poppa, Himalette, and Auntie Ferna stood in the front row, as did Glennis, her shining eyes locked on Brigitta. Brigitta nodded in her direction and Glennis nodded back. With unconvincing smiles on their faces, unconvincing to Brigitta at least, the Elders sat at the base of the platform in their high-backed chairs.

No games or songs or dances had been arranged. It had been difficult enough just to invite them all on such short notice. Several faeries had brought food, and many had brought instruments. Brigitta was sure a spontaneous party would break out after she and Ondelle left, because that's what faeries did best. That's all they really know how to do, she thought sadly to herself.

She scanned the crowd and spied Gola and Minq at the back near the Fire Faerie grandstand. She was amazed Gola had managed the journey to the Center Realm, even with Minq's assistance. Brigitta's eyes filled with tears as she smiled at her loyal friends.

Gathered in the giant uul trees on either side of the Hourglass, Vivilia and several dozen other sprites observed the faeries pouring into the festival grounds. At the base of one of the trees, looking a bit disgruntled, stood the First and Second Apprentices, and sitting under the tree were Earth Wising Lalam and Fire Wising Kiera. Brigitta had a sudden longing to be sitting there with them.

Ondelle held up her hands to quiet the crowd.

"My White Forest kin," she began and the faeries settled themselves. "Many season cycles ago, my mentor, the wise and respected Oka Kan of Tintlebar, revealed to me that I would one day travel to the ruins of our ancestors in the Valley of Noe. As the moons passed and I became absorbed in the responsibilities of my Life Task as High Priestess, it did not seem likely that premonition would come to pass.

"Recently, however, we received a sign, a message that our ancestors left almost one-thousand season cycles ago. Our old kin sent it to remind us that there had been an important sacred item left behind."

An excited murmur rose from the crowd.

"An artifact," Ondelle continued, after the faeries had quieted down, "that was to be retrieved at a later time when we were stronger and wiser and the world outside less chaotic. This artifact was designed to make our forest safer in the generations to come."

Ondelle gestured to the two Air Faerie Perimeter Guards. They flitted to the platform and handed her the glass jar containing the bright whisper light. The crowd gasped and buzzed as Ondelle held it up over her head.

"It was written by Chevalde of Grobjahar, our first Chronicler, that we would receive a visitor one day," Ondelle gestured toward the whisper light. "A message would be delivered by this visitor when the time was right. But only one faerie would be able to hear the true message. That faerie would travel with a companion back to the ruins of Noe. That faerie has heard the true message."

Ondelle dropped the glass jar, and it broke neatly in two between them. Brigitta was briefly distracted by the skill it must have taken to create such a jar. The whisper light floated up, and Brigitta got the strange sensation, once again, that it was staring at her.

But it was silent. There were no whispers.

Ondelle pointed her scepter directly at Brigitta's chest. Her eyes narrowed and there was a brief flash that traveled from her face, down her body, and out her scepter, imperceptible to the gathering below, and quick enough to be dismissed by anyone else. Brigitta felt her hourglass necklace vibrate, and her body went numb. A warmth radiated from behind her, from the Great Hourglass itself. Blue waves of energy enveloped her and the scepter and then disappeared in a blink.

The whisper light shot forward, into her necklace, and vanished.

The crowd burst into excited calls. Pippet's jaw dropped open and Mousha fell back, too stunned to steady himself with his wings. The Apprentices' and Wisings' eyes grew

62

wide in astonishment. Even the Elders looked puzzled.

In shock, Brigitta stared up at Ondelle, who smiled and nodded at the crowd. Brigitta's tongue felt heavy in her mouth, and her head spun. What had the High Priestess done to her? She gazed out on the crowd as if in a dream.

Ondelle finished her going away speech, saying something about how precious Blue Spell was and how it was reserved for rare occasions. Brigitta was no longer listening. Her stomach was doing somersaults and her heart pounded in her chest.

Her mind snapped to attention again when the High Priestess pointed at her and bellowed, "Brigitta of Tiragarrow, by the authority granted to me as High Priestess, by the approval of the Council of Elders, and by the blessings of the Eternal Dragon, I grant you permission to leave the White Forest on our behalf and travel by faerie Blue Spell to the ruins in the Valley of Noe."

Securing her scepter into a holder in the front of the platform, so that it stood on its own, she continued, "This scepter, a gift from the Ancients, will stand here as a reminder of this momentous journey. Think of us when you gaze upon it. We look forward to a great celebration upon our return."

She placed her arm around Brigitta's shoulder and leaned close to her ear. "Say goodbye," she whispered.

Brigitta raised her hand without thinking and waved at the crowd. Mousha hugged Pippet as she wiped tears from her eyes.

"Farewell, my kin!" Ondelle called, gripping Brigitta tighter. "May joy fill your every task!"

A moment later, there was a blast from the scepter.

Brigitta's entire body was propelled backward, through the air. She panicked in anticipation of ramming straight into the Hourglass. Instead, she was propelled inside a tunnel of wind as images and colors collided around her. She could still feel Ondelle's strong grasp but couldn't turn her body to see her. Faster and faster they were sucked backward, as Brigitta's insides were squashed against her body. Her lungs felt like they would be crushed, and it was impossible to take a breath or swallow. The colors around her blurred by so fast that she could no longer isolate them. They appeared as one continuous stream of brownish-blue.

Expelled of all air, her chest began to ache and her heart pounded desperately. Just as she thought she would suffocate from lack of breath, everything stopped. She collapsed to the ground, too exhausted to open her eyes.

It felt as if she would never be able to move again.

Chapter Seven

When Brigitta did finally open her eyes, she had no concept of how much time had passed, but she knew she was no longer in the White Forest. She lay on the side of a hill in a patch of prickly brown grass. At the base of the lumpy hill, an unfriendly forest threatened to swallow any trespassers. The sky above was a grayish-red with a few grumbling clouds. A sickly haze obscured the sun.

With a dizzy head, Brigitta slowly got to her feet. Her insides ached as if she had been punched all over her body.

"Not the most comfortable way to travel, is it?" Ondelle's pained voice called from above her.

Up the hill, Ondelle sat on the steps of a dilapidated, weed-ridden platform, similar to the one they had just left behind. As Brigitta studied the hillside more carefully, she realized they were standing among the remains of what must have been grandstands, scattered about and camouflaged by the grasses, forming a U around the platform.

"This must have been where their own ceremonies took place," Ondelle said. "Although . . . " Ondelle's voice drifted away as she contemplated the arena. "Whatever used to sit on this platform is missing."

After scanning the entire hillside, Ondelle finally stood up. A little wobbly, she used the steps to steady herself and then stretched her arms, legs, and wings.

"You're sore, too?" asked Brigitta, fumbling her way to the platform.

"I'm bones and blood," laughed Ondelle, wincing. "I have never traveled by Blue Spell before, either."

Weak from the walk uphill, Brigitta was about to sit down when she remembered the ceremony. She grabbed her hourglass. It didn't feel any different.

"You lied to everyone," she accused Ondelle and let go of the necklace.

"In what way?" Ondelle tilted her head, distracted by something.

"I didn't get any true message from the whisper light. It didn't speak to me at all."

"I do not recall saying that you did." Ondelle said and held up her hand before Brigitta could respond. "Quiet."

Confused, Brigitta reached back into her memory of the farewell ceremony. For something that had happened so recently, it felt like seasons in the past. She couldn't reconnect the events. Nauseous from the unfamiliar air, she sat down on the steps.

The winds of her argument scattered. The elements were confused inside her. She tried to locate her water strength, but she was in too much pain and couldn't concentrate. Finally, she muttered, "Well, you tricked them, at least. You led them to believe something that isn't true."

Ondelle shot a stern look at Brigitta. "You would do well to remember that I am your High Priestess. I do not have to explain myself to you or any other Apprentice."

Brigitta closed her mouth tight to keep more words from escaping. Something about the elements in Noe affected her emotions. She could feel them poking around just under her skin. She looked down and counted to ten. When she looked back up, Ondelle's face was turned toward the top of the hill. It took Brigitta a moment to hear the distant rushing sound coming from the other side. Water.

"How are your wings?" asked Ondelle.

Brigitta stretched and fluttered them a few times. They ached, but they worked. She nodded at Ondelle, still angry.

"Come, then."

Brigitta trailed after Ondelle up the hill, although it was difficult to get her wings to function properly. It reminded her of when she flew in the heaviness of the Dark Forest. The elements didn't get along there either. She wondered if the White Forest was the only place left in all of Faweh where the elements cooperated.

Ondelle slowed down, allowing Brigitta to catch up. "The air is unstable. It's affecting our emotions."

Brigitta nodded. "It feels wrong."

"Describe it," suggested Ondelle as they proceeded up the hill, the patches of grass beneath them growing sparser and sparser until the ground was completely bald.

"I have to think about my wings moving through the air, like I'm a toddling faerie again. I can feel it prickling—"

They had reached the top of the hill. On the other side, spread below them at the base of a great valley, was an enormous crater that could fit five Center Realms. Its sides were sloped downward, like a gigantic bowl carved into the rocky earth. From the center of the bowl gushed a thick, violent geyser of water that climbed up the side of the crater, through the valley, and then disappeared into the mountains where Brigitta had met it seasons before.

"The River That Runs Backwards," she whispered.

Mesmerized by the surge of the defiant river, Brigitta and Ondelle stood in awe, staring into the massive crater. On either side of it rose two mountain ranges that toiled north as far as the eye could see. The ranges were inaccessible, with jutting crags above the tree line topped in a strange whiteness Brigitta had never seen before.

Between the mountain ranges stretched the Valley of Noe, a mass of shadows and tangled woods. The River That Runs Backwards sliced the valley, churning itself uphill, where Brigitta knew it would eventually re-enter the earth at Dead Mountain.

She squinted, trying to imagine what the valley had looked like long ago when populated by the Ancients and their kin. She thought about her Auntie Ferna's stories and caught her breath. "Is that where Lake Indago used to be?"

"I believe it is," said Ondelle softly, placing her palms over her heart in reverence. "By the Dragon's breath . . ."

Ondelle suddenly pulled Brigitta behind a fallen pillar strangled with ivy. "Stay here," she said and flew up, hovered above the pillar for a moment, then dropped back down. "Some beasts are moving in the lakebed. It's too far to see what they are."

"What should we do?" asked Brigitta, realizing that they were very much alone against whatever creatures haunted the region, with no idea of where to hide.

"Let's see what kind of beings occupy this land."

They moved down the north side of the hill, close to the ground and as camouflaged into the rocks and debris as possible, until they came to the edge of the crater. They peered down into the bowl. A gust of wind drove a hot, sandy storm into their faces, and they put their hands over their mouths as they squinted.

Dotting the inside of the bowl were dozens of gray-winged creatures. They were pale and skinny and wore ragged tunics with bulky scarves wrapped around their heads to deflect the pelting sands caught in the river-wind. The tops of their heads were oddly flattish and wide. Each one carried some kind of chisel, and a coarse bag hung from a rope around each waist.

The creatures drove their chisels into the lakebed rocks, over and over again, searching for something. One male turned and helped a female stumble back up the side of the crater. When they reached a pile of supplies, the male withdrew a water flask from a pack as the female unwound her scarf. She pulled a wide metal disc from on top of her head. The male poured water into her disc so she could rinse out her eyes. Her face was sallow, her cheekbones sunken, and her eyes crystal white.

"They're faeries!" gasped Ondelle, grabbing hold of Brigitta's arm.

Brigitta stared at them. They couldn't be faeries. They were so small and thin and sickly. Their wings were ragged, papery, and most of all, free from any destiny marks. She stared as they drank, their dull wispy hair blowing in the river-wind.

"But look at them! They're so . . . so . . . awful." Brigitta tried to sense any elemental connection. She shook her head. "They aren't bound to any element. They can't be faeries."

"They have not had the benefits of living in the White Forest. There is no balance here. The poor beasts must not receive an element nor any destiny."

"They were left behind?"

"Or they chose to stay."

Shivers went up Brigitta's spine. She couldn't imagine life without an element. It would be like not being able to touch or taste or see. And what faerie would choose to live like this? They must have been left behind. But why? Had they done something wrong?

The female placed the metal disc back on her head and rewrapped her face. The two turned in unison and chiseled their way back down to the others, digging their tools rhythmically into the rock.

Another smaller female faerie stopped chiseling and called out. Two males knelt down to where she pointed. The river was far too loud to hear what they were saying, but they all nodded in agreement. The two male faeries chiseled beside her until a large portion of rock was loosened. The first faerie dropped the chunk of rock into her pouch, and they patted her on the back.

With a loud cry, a dozen more faeries leapt over the side of the lakebed and shot toward the faerie with the rock. The attacking faeries wore black tunics with circular silver symbols and carried sticks that spat fire. All the chiseler faeries flew to their comrade. They pulled the discs from their heads and held their chisels up, tools now shields and weapons, as another dozen faeries attacked from the other side of the crater.

"Ondelle, do something!" cried Brigitta. "Help them!"

"Which ones? We don't know the cause of this fight."

The chiselers moved into a practiced circular formation, with the rock-holding faerie on the inside and their strongest faeries on the outside.

The attacking faeries shot at them with their firesticks.

The chiselers blocked the flames with their shields. A quick flame shot through their defenses to a chiseler faerie's wing. He dropped to the ground and the formation immediately incorporated him into the protected circle.

A female chiseler leapt up, weapon extended, into the attackers. She swerved at the last minute and sliced an attacking faerie's arm. He, too, fell to the ground, but the black tunic faeries left him there, whimpering in pain. The attacking faeries thrust themselves into the chiselers, whose formation broke, and they scattered. The small faerie carrying the rock got caught in the wind.

"Help!" she cried, swimming through the air and flapping her wings. She dropped her pouch, and it was immediately sucked into the river-wind and lost inside the watery mass.

A larger faerie flew to her assistance, reaching out his hands to grasp hers. They struggled against the river-wind, but it was no use, and they were slowly sucked backward. The larger faerie planted his feet against a rock for leverage, but could not hold the weight of the other faerie and was soon torn off his feet. The other chiselers helplessly watched, dodging their attackers as their friends were pulled away.

Without thinking, Brigitta shot over the side. "No!" she cried as she flew toward the struggling faeries.

A moment later, Ondelle zipped past Brigitta and stopped just shy of the two little beasts, wrapping her left arm around an outcropping of rock and reaching out with her right. "Fly to me! You can do it!"

The two faeries, stunned in the presence of this imposing creature, stopped fighting the wind and were instantly sucked through the air into the violent spasm of water.

Brigitta caught up with Ondelle and reached forward, not wanting to believe that the faeries were gone. But there was no trace of them. Dust spun about, pelting her skin. She ignored the tiny pricks as she stared into the stormy river, horrified.

"There was nothing you could do," called Ondelle over the noise, holding Brigitta back.

Ondelle steered an astounded Brigitta toward the other faeries. All the fighting had stopped. The black tunic attackers and defending chiselers hovered in mid knife-stroke and fire-blast.

Ondelle held up her hand. "Hello. We mean you no—"

The faeries bolted away in all directions, pulling their wounded through the air. In a moonsbreath, Brigitta and Ondelle were alone in the lakebed with only the sound of the rushing river behind them.

"Are you all right?" asked Ondelle.

Brigitta turned and stared into the river where the two faeries had vanished.

"They . . . they just . . . " stammered Brigitta, her whole body shaking.

"I know," said Ondelle, placing her hands on Brigitta's arms and rubbing some warmth into them as she examined their surroundings. "At least they have stopped fighting. We should leave. It is not safe here."

Once they emerged from the crater that had once been Lake Indago, Ondelle decided they should head west into the forest, as opposed to north or east into the forest. The only other choice was back down the hill of ruins, but she said even the tricky elements could tell her that was the southern border of Noe. The western forest was closest and she wanted to get under cover and set up camp for the night.

So they flew west and were swallowed by the dense leaves, which quickly muffled the sounds of the backward river. Brigitta numbly followed her High Priestess, unable to dislodge the image from her mind of the poor little faeries' surprised faces when they disappeared into the angry water.

After several moonbeats they entered a small clearing. Ondelle landed, studying the trees, which formed a circle around them, and the ground, covered in seasons of wild growth.

She picked a branch up off the ground, rubbed it, and then flicked it at the ivy. The ivy half-heartedly obeyed Ondelle's silent command, dancing a bit before flopping back down on itself.

"We will have to do this the hard way," she said, dropping her pack. "Help me clear these vines."

Together they scraped the vines away until a shallow metallic font appeared on top of a petrified tree stump. The dish was empty but shone as if it had recently been polished. They cleared the overgrown area around the font and uncovered a circular stone floor that stretched out to the trees.

"This will do," said Ondelle. She reached into her pack, removed two firestones, and handed them to Brigitta. "Build a fire in the font, and I will create some protection around us."

"Why don't we stay in the trees?" asked Brigitta.

Ondelle looked up into the dark, twisted leaves, vines, and branches. "I don't trust them." She tapped the stone floor with her foot. "This feels safe. It was a sacred place."

"How can you tell?" Brigitta tapped on the floor as well.

Ondelle pointed to the side of the petrified stump, and Brigitta kneeled to have a look at it while Ondelle retrieved a globelight, two thin blankets, and a bottle of dustmist. There was a symbol etched into the stony surface: a circle with a square inside and another circle inside the square.

"I've seen that before," said Brigitta, "in a passageway under the Center Realm. What's it mean?"

"In a passageway under the Center Realm?" asked Ondelle as she shaped a dustmist wall around the perimeter of the stone floor. She stopped working and stood there, hand in mid-wave. "How odd I have never seen it down there before."

Brigitta gathered some dry brush and placed it in the font. She struck the firestones together, but nothing happened. Not a spark. She struck them several more times but still, nothing. "Stupid rocks," she growled and smashed them together again.

"I believe these symbols lead us to the artifact we seek," continued Ondelle as she finished her wall of dustmist.

"What?" Brigitta dropped one of the stones in the font with a clang, the sound cutting sharply through the forest. Something scurried up a tree and another beast flapped its wings and snarled.

Ondelle placed her hands on Brigitta's shoulders. "Try again."

Taking a deep a breath, Brigitta relaxed and let go of all other thought, concentrating on the weight of the stones in her hands and the fire energy within them. She struck them together again. A flame appeared and caught the brush.

"Thanks," mumbled Brigitta as Ondelle pulled a vial of

firepepper from the belt around her tunic.

Tired and hungry and feeling a new weight, Brigitta sat down on a rock with her head in her arms. She pictured, once again, the two little feral faeries being sucked away by the river and how she could do nothing to save them.

"Be careful, I treated the dustmist wall with firepepper." Ondelle spread some moss on the ground and used the last of the dustmist to form a cushion beneath it.

She sat down and opened a container of seasoned gundlebeans. "My own recipe."

For a moment, Brigitta allowed herself to be amused by the image of Ondelle cooking, hair stuck to her face, recipe books scattered, apron stained with trial batches of stew. The image became her own mother, waving her spoon around the kitchen.

Had she really only left the White Forest that morning?

They snacked on the gundlebeans and sucked on some tingermint drops in silence, watching the flames dance inside the font. Brigitta played the events of the day over in her mind, from Ondelle's dramatics in front of everybody in the entire forest, to the painful Blue Spell experience, to that awful attack in the dry lakebed.

"Why didn't you do something to those black tunic faeries?" asked Brigitta. "The little chiseling ones hadn't done anything wrong."

"White Forest faeries are talented healers and artisans. We are not warriors."

"Well, maybe we should teach ourselves to be."

Ondelle didn't argue. She placed the remaining food into her pack and handed Brigitta a blanket. It was surprisingly warm for being so thin. "A gift from Elder Hammus," commented Ondelle. "He has talent with textiles."

It was indeed a well-crafted blanket, and focusing temperature was something she had looked forward to learning, but now it seemed a waste of time. Nothing Apprentices were taught would truly help them survive outside the White Forest.

"Couldn't you have performed some powerful magic to stop them? You're the High Priestess." Brigitta swallowed the lump in her throat that was threatening to turn into tears.

Ondelle handed her a little green leaf. "Have some ceunias. It's been a trying day."

Brigitta took the leaf and eyed Ondelle suspiciously, remembering the controversy about using it on baby Duna. But Ondelle placed a leaf on her own tongue and smiled. Brigitta slipped the leaf into her mouth. Her mind eased and her skin opened to the warmth of the blanket.

"There is no such thing as magic," said Ondelle, packing the remainder of the leaves away. "Not in the sense you imply."

"What do you mean? I've seen plenty of magic. And Hrathgar Evil knew all kinds of terrible sorcery."

Ondelle picked up her globelight and waved her hand across the top to light it. "Was that magic?"

"Of course not. You just lit it with your hand's energy, anyone can do that."

"Yes, but to any beast who has never seen such a thing, who has no knowledge of how globelights work, it is magic."

Ondelle blew onto the sphere and the light disappeared. She handed the globelight to Brigitta, who examined its smooth, round surface. It was flawless. A master craftsfaerie had made it. Brigitta touched it lightly with her pinky, and a tiny perfect dot lit up. She blew it out again.

"One could say that a flower blooming is magic," continued Ondelle, "or that our breathing is magic. Life is magical in that sense, in the absolute miracle of it. But nothing can be conjured without the right conditions, nor can we perform spells that require knowledge we do not have.

"What you call magic is simply knowing how to transform something with that knowledge. You must not become too enamored by so-called sorcery or fear what you do not understand. Anything you witness, you can know."

"Yes, Ondelle."

"You have learned many things these past moons as Second Apprentice, things you did not know before. Things that appeared difficult, perhaps even magical, when you were a child.

"You have become quite the empather, for instance." Ondelle glanced at Brigitta, her signature twinkle in her eyes. "Why don't you lie back and practice on the leaves?"

Brigitta snuggled into the moss, tucking her wings beneath the blanket. She stared up into the trees and watched the leaves flittering in the light wind. One leaf caught her attention. It was greener than the others and whole.

Ondelle lay down next to Brigitta and they listened to the unfamiliar buzzing and howling of the night beasts. Something flew into the firepepper and zapped away with a disgruntled chirp.

"I have kept knowledge from you," murmured Ondelle, as she sucked on her ceunias leaf, "and if this upsets you, I understand." She paused for a moment, gathering her thoughts. "Holding onto knowledge is like holding back a flood. I must feed it to you in trickles to stave off your being drowned."

"You don't think I can handle it," said Brigitta. It wasn't a question; she knew she had proven herself to be reckless and irresponsible.

"I must protect you." Ondelle closed her eyes. "That is all."

The little green leaf shivered on its branch. Brigitta reached out to it and connected to its water energy. The leaf's energy was weak, like a shaky heartbeat. Life is so delicate, she thought. It can be there, and then gone.

She let those thoughts drift away, breathing steadily until she and the leaf were bound. As the leaf, she looked down at the shapes of two faeries lying below, one large and luminous, the other curled into a ball, cheeks wet with tears.

Chapter Eight

reen light. All she could see and feel was green light. It numbed her. Where was she? What was she supposed to be doing? Somewhere inside herself, she knew she had a task, but she couldn't connect with that part of herself. Brigitta, *a voice echoed through her mind,* come back. *The voice soothed her. It was golden and warm and danced through the green. She wanted to go to it; she wanted more of it. Not sure how she was moving, she did. And as she moved forward, the green became less dense, less confusing. She could see other colors now, browns and yellows. Shapes, too . . .*

"Brigitta?" The golden voice was closer.

Everything snapped into place. She was sitting on her moss bed, next to the font, surrounded by forest in the Valley of Noe. It was morning, and she could just make out the strange red-gray sky through the tops of the trees. She wiggled her fingers and toes.

Ondelle sealed up the larger of the two spell seeds and set it down beside her pack. "Very good," she said, opening a small bottle and vial. She began to undo the dustmist wall. With graceful finger flicks, she separated firepepper from dustmist and directed them into their containers. A puff of dustmist lingered between the trees. She directed it with her index finger and a twist of her wrist, but it stayed, suspended in the air. "I guess the forest is keeping some for itself."

She capped the firepepper and dropped down to the moss beds. Brigitta had not moved.

"The zynthia pushed through," she said.

"Yes," said Ondelle, "but you began to recover before I put it away."

"Only because I could follow your voice."

"It is progress." Ondelle helped Brigitta up and collected the dustmist from the moss. "What was magic to you before, you are now understanding through knowledge."

It was true, Brigitta thought. She never would have imagined she could resist green zynthia hypnosis. All it took was practice, learning how to stay balanced using what she knew about energy. She wondered if she could ever learn the secrets of something even more powerful.

"Ondelle, why did you leave your scepter back in the White Forest?" asked Brigitta, suddenly remembering being caught in its force. "Doesn't it contain powerful energy? Couldn't you have used it against the attacking faeries?"

"The scepter must stay in the White Forest. It was a gift from the Ancients. We would not want it to fall into the wrong hands."

After their morning meal, Ondelle and Brigitta flew east back toward the old lakebed. As they broke through the trees and faced the rocky crater and the raging northbound river, Brigitta was once again reminded of the poor little beasts they had discovered there.

"What are we going to do about those left-behind faeries?" she asked.

"First things first, Brigitta," said Ondelle. "And one thing at a time."

She took off her pack and removed a scroll. She rolled it out on a rock and pinned it in place with some small earthen weights she removed from her belt. It was an ancient map, but the drawings and symbols were familiar to Brigitta.

"Is that Gola's map?" she asked, moving closer.

"No, this map was drawn by Chevalde of Grobjahar. At least we assume it was. It was inside one of her books."

"The one with the rhyme?"

"Yes." Ondelle traced her finger down through the Valley of Noe to Lake Indago, represented by a fading blue-green patch. South of the lake was the hill they had appeared on the day before, labeled Lake Hill, and beneath that lay the Southcoast Forest. There was a symbol on the hill, a circular shape with a square inside it and another circle.

"That's the same symbol as before," said Brigitta, studying the map more carefully.

To the west of Lake Indago was the Valley Forest and past that a mountain range labeled Western Range. To the east was more forest, the Valley Plateau, and then the Eastern Range. The Valley Forest surrounded Lake Indago on the north as well.

"Western Range? Valley Forest? Lake Hill? For such wise beings the Ancients had no imagination."

Ondelle laughed and tapped the round symbol with her finger. "If this symbol is the key, we should go back to the hill and look around. The object could be hidden in all that overgrowth."

"Ondelle," said Brigitta, pointing to the blue-green patch, "Gola's map has the River That Runs Backwards drawn on it. This one has Lake Indago." She pointed to the northern part of the map. "And Gola's has an hourglass symbol in the middle of the White Forest, this one doesn't."

"Brigitta, I am appalled by my own lack of curiosity. I should have studied hers more closely." She stepped aside and motioned with her hand. "Go on. What else?"

"Well, Dead Mountain is called Dragon Mountain on your map. The Sea of Tzajeek has the same serpent running through the name. But that circle and square symbol, Gola's map doesn't have one anywhere on it. I'm positive."

"The maps were drawn on two different occasions . . ." Ondelle furled her brow.

"Before and after the Great World Cry," Brigitta finished Ondelle's thought.

"Before and after the elemental faeries moved to the White Forest," added Ondelle.

"Well, the ones that got moved, anyway," said Brigitta quietly.

She thought about the escape her ancestors had made generations ago. She didn't know why it hadn't occurred to her before, but how exactly did they all get to the White Forest? She had assumed the Ancients were so powerful they had just transported thousands of faeries by Blue Spell. But if they were that powerful, why did they have to abandon their home in the first place?

"I don't think that sacred object is on the hill any longer," decided Brigitta. "I think it was moved. Maybe to keep it safe from—"

Ondelle held up her hand to silence Brigitta, cocked her head, and listened. Her eyes grew wide, but before she could utter a warning, dozens of faeries zipped down from the trees, surrounding them, shields up and daggers drawn. They wore the same ragged tunics as the chiseler faeries.

A young male faerie emerged from the swarm. He was taller than the rest, as tall as Brigitta, with long thin wings, more golden than gray, and deep crystal blue eyes. Brigitta stared. She knew that face.

He wore a blue tunic that matched his eyes. The others hovered behind him as he examined Ondelle and Brigitta, their glares doing nothing to mask their fear.

Ondelle extended her hands, palms up, to show that they were empty. "Hello—"

Before she could finish her sentence, the blue-eyed faerie slapped a long black strap against Ondelle's outstretched arms. The strap immediately wound itself around her wrists and tightened like a thin constricting snake. From behind them, two faeries slapped straps against her wings, and the bands wound themselves around the tips, drawing them together and preventing flight.

Brigitta was so startled that she didn't have a chance to move before they strapped her own wrists and wings. "Hey!" she cried, twisting against the bindings.

The taller faerie boy pulled the straps tight and then snaked them together in the palm of his hand. "A bad-tempered stranglewood vine," he warned. He looked her in the eyes, his dark hair plastered against his forehead. "Don't struggle, and it won't separate your hands from your wrists."

"My faerie kin, there is no need for such bondage." Ondelle's voice was steady.

She looked into his crystal blue eyes, and his composure flittered. Brigitta could tell Ondelle was trying to empath his thoughts, but he shook her off and stared back, his mental walls solid. Ondelle's face brightened in surprise.

He stuffed the map into Ondelle's pack and threw the

pack over his shoulder. "Bring them," he said to the smaller white-eyed faeries, whose minds were not as trained as his. Fear emanated from them, made them jittery like dancing flames, which Brigitta knew also made them dangerous.

Chapter Nine

The sickly faeries prodded Brigitta and Ondelle from behind with their shields as they all stumbled down the narrow path. It was overgrown with thorny ivies and roots that burrowed in and out of the ground like rugged sea serpents. Bushy spider nests hung between the thick branches that criss-crossed overhead. The crystal blue-eyed boy flew behind them, barking orders at the scouts in front.

Brigitta's heart pounded so hard it scattered her thoughts. Something washed over them and Ondelle's voice echoed in her head. *Transform your mind. I should not be able to enter this easily.*

"Breathe," Ondelle said out loud. "Remember what you know."

Brigitta had been learning transformation from Elder Adaire; she just needed to alter her thoughts. She allowed them all to appear, the anxious and frightened ones, and then saw them as leaves in a stream. As the thought-leaves floated away, she filled the space left behind with water energy. She glanced at Ondelle, whose expression was one of calm amusement. Brigitta tried her best to imitate that expression.

They traveled for about three moonbeats until they came to a tunnel in a large tree that spanned the path. The tunnel was guarded by a female and male faerie, both slightly taller and more muscular than the other faeries, both wearing dark blue tunics, and both with crystal blue eyes.

The blue-eyed faeries nodded at one another as Brigitta and Ondelle were pushed into the tunnel. The High Priestess had to duck to avoid hitting her forehead against the trunk of the tree. When they emerged from the tunnel, they were standing inside a menacing circle of lifeless trees.

The trunks of the trees were stiff and wide and had grown so closely together they formed an impenetrable wall. The wall grew high around them until it came to a structure at the top that blocked out the sky. Little light filtered through, and it took a moment for Brigitta's eyes to adjust. As they did, she grew more and more ill. Something was horribly wrong with this place. She sensed Ondelle stiffen beside her.

Part way up the tree in front of her, there was a thick metal bar connecting it with the next tree. And where the bar had pierced the skin of each tree, the bark was infected and stained with ooze. She looked from one tree to the next and it was the same. At different heights, the bars held the trees together so that they could not bend or fall. It looked as though someone had thrust the bars into the trees while they were young, imprisoning them, so that they would grow this way.

Brigitta and Ondelle were pushed toward one of the trees. It was cracked up the side, providing an entrance near the base. The crystal blue-eyed faerie boy pointed into the dark opening.

"Inside," he commanded as he hovered beside them.

Ondelle studied his face. "What is your name?"

He stared back at her, trying to match her gaze, but his eyes began to twitch. He glanced down at Brigitta, then back to Ondelle, who smiled.

"Jarlath," he growled. "I am your Watcher."

"And Jarlath, what is this place? Where are we?" Ondelle asked the questions so softly and sweetly that Brigitta could feel his mental wall melting away.

Four older faeries dropped down from the branches, startling Brigitta. She hadn't noticed the numerous cracks in the tree trunks, with a crystal blue-eyed faerie posted at each one. Watching them.

"Queen Mabbe wants to see them as soon as possible," grumbled the largest one, whose wings were less golden than Jarlath's, but longer and thicker.

"Yes, Watcher Dugald," said Jarlath. "You heard him." He shoved Ondelle and Brigitta into the crack.

They stumbled inside and the crack sealed behind them. It was pitch black. Brigitta could only feel Ondelle next to her.

"You're in the Hollows," a voice whispered from beside them.

Brigitta jumped and moved closer to Ondelle.

"Face me," said Ondelle. "Hold up your arms."

Brigitta did so and felt Ondelle rotate her wrists around Brigitta's. The bonds loosened and they both sighed in relief.

"Turn around so I may reach into your pack."

Brigitta turned around and Ondelle rifled through her supplies. A moment later, a light emerged from the center of the trunk, and there was a collective gasp. Ondelle held Brigitta's globelight in a loosely bound hand, illuminating six trembling faeries, four wearing black tunics and two in tattered brown. The faeries' hands and wings were bound with stranglewood vines and their faces were bruised. One black tunic faerie's lip was torn and bleeding. Blood dripped down onto his tunic, staining the silver symbol on the front: a circle with a square inside of it, and another circle.

Brigitta raised her hands to point out the symbol, but Ondelle intercepted the motion and pulled them back down.

"I am High Priestess Ondelle of Grioth and this is Second Elder Apprentice Brigitta of Tiragarrow." Ondelle's voice was soft and warm. "We come from the far north, from a place called the White Forest."

The faeries stood motionless, mesmerized by the purity of the globe's light and stunned by the imposing presence of the woman holding it.

"We are your kin." Ondelle gestured toward them.

The faeries looked at one another.

"Your lip is torn," continued Ondelle, "my healing salve is in my pack, which Watcher Jarlath has taken." She reached out to the injured faerie. "But, if you allow me, I can still ease your pain."

The faerie with the torn lip stepped closer. "So, it's true," he managed with a trembling voice, looking up at Ondelle with wide eyes. She started to speak, but he lurched forward and spat in her face. "The Ancients abandoned us after all!"

Rage fuelled Brigitta and she was about to lash out, but Ondelle held her in place and calmly wiped the bloody spittle from her cheek.

"That is what we would like to find out," she said. "We have lost contact with the Ancient Ones. We were never told that faeries were still living in the Valley of Noe."

"Liar!" Another black tunic faerie stepped forward. She was thin and dirty. Her feet were bare and her left foot was missing two toes. "You have used up all your sorcery and have come to take ours!"

Before Ondelle or Brigitta could respond, there was a loud howling from above. The other faeries seemed unconcerned when the sound came rushing down toward them. They all stood perfectly still with eyes closed.

"Close your eyes!" yelled Ondelle over the noise.

Just as the howling wind hit them, Brigitta shut her eyes tight. The howling spun around the inside of the trunk and became a thick rope of air, winding about them. Brigitta felt herself lifted up off the ground. The band tying her wrist to Ondelle's pulled taut again, cutting into her skin, and she cried out in pain. A moment later the wind stopped.

Brigitta opened her eyes as she was yanked forward by the wrist straps. She stumbled into an enormous burl that twisted wickedly as it rose, growing more and more narrow until it became a dark funnel above them. From the darkness of the funnel, a chain extended on which hung a large chandelier made from thorny branches. The ends of the branches were capped with large bird talons.

Before she had time to ask where they were, she was yanked forward again by a hook on the end of a staff held by Watcher Jarlath. Another Watcher yanked Ondelle forward with his staff hook, and a third shepherded the others out of the trunk.

The burl was large but suffocating, as there was no natural light. The smoke from the candled chandelier snaked through the branches before climbing up the chain and disappearing into the darkness. The rest of the decor looked as though it had been excavated from a ruin. The floor was strewn with faded rugs, and broken pieces of pottery sat in the crevasses of the walls. Two cracked white columns stood across the room. Each column was topped with a rusty cage overflowing with bones. A Watcher holding a hooked staff was posted next to each column.

Between the columns, in a rounded enclave that had been polished smooth, sat three carved chairs with legs that mimicked the burl's twisted design. In the center chair sat the oldest, ugliest faerie woman Brigitta had ever seen. What hair she had left sat like cobwebs on her white scalp. Her face was a maze of wrinkles and spots. Her pupils were clouded over and her nose and ears were stretched long from gravity and time. Her back was stooped and her deformed hands held a scepter topped with more bird talons clutching a black orb. Her wings were ashen and peeling. The only attractive thing about her was her tunic, which was an intense shimmering blue with bold yellow stitching, the brightest thing Brigitta had seen since landing in Noe.

"All honor Queen Mabbe! True leader of Noe!" shouted the Watchers at the pillars.

Two more Watchers moved into the room and sat on either side of the elderly faerie. They wore the standard Watcher garb, except their tunics had bright yellow stitching around the sleeves and neck. One of them was Dugald, the surly male who had been sent down to meet Jarlath. In his lap he held Ondelle's pack. The other Watcher was a female, equally dour, with a large tear in one of her grayish-pink wings. They both looked better fed than any of the other faeries.

The female leaned over and whispered into Mabbe's ear, who nodded, staring out over the burl. She stood up, which didn't alter her height, and rapped her scepter on the floor.

"Just because I'm blind doesn't mean I can't see," she cackled, widening her eyes and sniffing the air like some four-legged beast.

The two captive faeries with brown tunics fell to their knees and bowed. The four black tunic faeries scowled at Mabbe, who snorted, "Your insolence is noted."

"My wise Sister," bowed Ondelle, "we have come—"

"Silence!" Mabbe pointed her staff at Ondelle, the clouds in her eyes darkening like a storm.

A black frog-like tongue shot forth from Mabbe's scepter and into Ondelle's mouth. Just as fast, the black shape retracted from Ondelle's face, struggling and bulging with something in its grasp. It snapped back across the room and into the scepter. Ondelle tried to speak, but no sound came out.

"I will keep your pretty voice while you listen to me." Mabbe reached to her right and the surly male placed Ondelle's pack in her hand. She turned the pack inside out and spilled the contents onto the floor, waving her hands over the items and sniffing the air. "These are items of sorcery." She poked through them with her scepter. "It's against the laws of my Queendom to carry such items."

"One hundred seasons in the Colony!" shouted Dugald, and his female counterpart sniggered.

"I've never sensed you before," said Mabbe, snaking her head through the air. "You've never lived in the Hollows. Were you sent from Croilus?"

"She's not one of ours," spat the torn-lipped faerie.

Mabbe swung her scepter toward him and cocked her head, eyes dotting around as she located him across the room. "Any faerie captured from Croilus's tribe receives life in the Colony for traitorous activity!"

She bobbed her head, and one of the Watchers grabbed the torn-lipped faerie from behind. "I may take pity and lighten your sentence," Mabbe continued, "if you have anything of interest to tell me."

"That large one sent two Hollows faeries into the Mad River yesterday!"

Mabbe's eyes stormed over again, and Brigitta swore she could see lightning bolts behind the gray clouds. "So, that was you who lost my two diggers, was it?"

"No!" exclaimed Brigitta. "We were trying to save them!"

"Liar!" spat the torn-lipped faerie. "The tall one swooped down and sent them to their deaths!"

"She was trying to steal your sorcery sands," another Croilus faerie added, and the rest of them nodded.

"But, but . . . " stammered Brigitta, "they were the ones who attacked your faeries, not us! They had sticks that spat fire."

"I'm afraid you're outnumbered," said Mabbe, "unless there is someone who will speak on your behalf?" She raised her eyebrows and smiled, exposing teeth that had rotted into points.

Brigitta glanced around the room and spotted Jarlath near the entrance to the tree. He gazed back at her, expressionless.

"I thought not." Mabbe gestured, and three Watchers each grabbed a remaining Croilus faerie. "I will consider this information, but you'd better spend your night thinking about what you know of Croilus's activities if you want to impress me."

On his way out of the burl, the torn-lipped faerie shouted back, "She came from the far north! The Ancients left us behind, and now they've come back for our sorcery!"

Mabbe froze with her hand in the air, her gaze softening. For a brief moment, the storm in her eyes slowed, the clouds parted, and a sliver of blue moon flickered in her right eye. A smile spread across her face, and then she cackled, raising the storm in her eyes once again.

"Bring me your pack," Mabbe pointed her scepter at Brigitta, and the strap holding her wrists to Ondelle's loosened and fell to the floor. Brigitta stumbled forward and removed her pack. As she did, her hourglass necklace slipped out from under her tunic. She tucked it back inside as she dropped her pack onto the floor.

"Wait!" Mabbe screeched, hands clawing the air. Brigitta faced the ugly faerie as she stepped closer and pointed at Brigitta's chest. "That necklace, too!"

"No!" Brigitta clenched her hand over the necklace through her tunic.

Mabbe scowled and stung Brigitta in the arm with the tip of her staff, then flicked the hourglass out of Brigitta's tunic again. She lunged for it, then screeched and retracted her hand, smoke rising from her fingers.

She swiftly smacked Brigitta across the head with the stone on the end of her scepter. Pain shot through Brigitta's skull as she fell to the floor. Ondelle rushed to her side and caressed Brigitta's head where the stone had struck her, warming the pain away. Ondelle mouthed an explanation to Mabbe, gesturing at the necklace.

The Queen pointed her scepter at Ondelle and the black tendril shot in and out of her mouth once more, replacing her voice. Ondelle drew her breath.

"The necklace has been spell-cast, she cannot remove it," she said as she helped Brigitta to her feet.

"Perhaps if I remove her head first?" cackled Mabbe. Her Watcher pets guffawed from their chairs.

"It would do you no good. It will deflect the energy of all but the rightful owner." Ondelle tapped the necklace with her pinky finger and a little puff of smoke spat off of it. "You have no need to fear the necklace; there are no harmful uses for it."

"I fear nothing," Mabbe growled, pointing her scepter back at Ondelle. The black tongue extracted her voice once again. The decrepit faerie straightened herself up as far as she was physically able and returned to her chair. "If you are lying, your little companion will be punished."

Legs slung over the armrests of their chairs, the Watchers at her sides lounged as Mabbe contemplated her prisoners. She pointed at Brigitta, "One hundred seasons for your items of sorcery and another one hundred for your unfortunate attitude."

She moved her attention to Ondelle and sent her a vicious smile. "Life in the Colony for murder."

Brigitta was about to protest, but Ondelle held her back and shook her head.

Leaning into her chair, Mabbe put an arm around the female Watcher. She stroked her check affectionately with her bony thumb. "Veena, what of those last two?"

"Found sleeping during harvest time," Veena reported.

"Brand them and let them go with a warning. I'm feeling generous." Mabbe waved her scepter to dismiss them.

The two little Hollows faeries stood up and bowed over

and over again. Their Watcher herded them toward the entrance, and they scraped and bowed their way from the burl. "Thank you, Great Mabbe. Long life to the true leader of Noe."

"My faeries love to gossip," said Mabbe after they had disappeared into the trunk of the tree. "News of the murdering and thieving faeries from the North will spread. I'm afraid you won't make many friends during your stay." She mock pouted at them and then cackled. She raised her arms in the air, and the straps snaked up from the floor, wrapped themselves around Brigitta's and Ondelle's wrists, and pulled taut.

Pointing to the items on the floor, Mabbe turned to Dugald, "Bring these to my room." She stood once more and smiled wickedly, "Watcher Jarlath, take our visitors on a tour of the Colony."

Jarlath and the Watcher guard to his right pulled Brigitta and Ondelle backward by the wrist straps with their hooks.

"What about her voice?" asked Brigitta as she stumbled away. "Give her back her voice!"

"She'll get it back," said Mabbe, "after I hear what it has to say." She snickered, petting the black stone that held Ondelle's voice as she shuffled into the alcove and disappeared.

Chapter Ten

The Colony was higher up in the circle of bound trees that made up the Hollows. An opening in each trunk in the circle led to a large mesh prison cell that extended out the back over the forest.

The ground of the Colony was built similarly to a White Forest village-nest, with layers and layers of twigs, bark, earth, and mud. The canopy was thick above, but portions of daylight still shone through and Brigitta was relieved to see the sky again, even if it was reddish-gray.

As Jarlath and the other Watcher led Ondelle and Brigitta through the Colony, faerie prisoners shot them nervous glances while they pounded, sifted, and sorted through piles of rocks similar to the one the chiselers had found in the lakebed. One faerie stood up with some miniscule grains between her forefinger and thumb. She showed them to a Watcher guard and then dropped them into a tube that disappeared into the ground.

A cry came from behind them. Near the entrance to the Colony, one of the Hollow faeries who had been sentenced to branding was lying face down over a log. When a Watcher pulled him up, there was a large X burned into the top of his right wing. The branded faerie glared at Brigitta so viciously that she turned away.

"You will work with the sifters," Jarlath said, "to make up for the sorcery sands you lost in the Mad River."

"You know as well as I do that we didn't lose those sands," growled Brigitta, shifting her strapped wings. "It was the Croilus faeries who attacked your faeries, not us."

The Watcher leading Ondelle was a skinny, pale thing with large hands and muddy-colored wings. He stopped in front of one of the prison trees and before Brigitta realized what was happening, he pushed Ondelle inside. Jarlath continued walking, pulling Brigitta along.

"No, wait," she said, tripping after him, "where are you taking me?"

From the next tree, six bedraggled Croilus faeries emerged, led on a single chain by a straw-haired female Watcher. None of the Croilus faeries had wings. A chill went up Brigitta's spine. Wingless faeries? She had never heard of such an awful thing.

When they reached the following tree, Jarlath pushed Brigitta inside. There were two cages in the near-dark, with a Hollows faerie huddled in each. He opened the door to the cell that extended out the back of the tree and thrust Brigitta forward. He locked the door, poured some water from a pail into a cup, and placed the cup on the floor of her cell.

Brigitta kicked the cup, and water spattered all over Jarlath.

"That was unwise," he said. "That was your daily ration." He put the pail back in the corner.

"Please, Jarlath," pleaded Brigitta, gripping the bars of the cell, "we only came here to find out how to get back in touch with the Ancients. We had no idea there were still faeries left in the old land. We haven't hurt anyone."

"A sentence from Mabbe may only be overturned by Mabbe," he said and left. The faeries inside the trunk shrunk back in their cages. Brigitta's cell was much bigger than theirs, and she supposed she should be grateful for that.

"Ha!" she shouted and rattled her cage. They'd been two suns in Noe and their situation was already hopeless. She couldn't live in this miserable place for sixty season cycles. This wasn't happening.

A desperate laughter burst from some place inside her. The laughter soon turned to tears and she ran to the back of the cell, stretching as far out as she could to get a glimpse of Ondelle. But she could only see the back of the next cell due to the curve of the trees.

What was wrong with her High Priestess?

"Why haven't you defended us?" she demanded. "I promised my parents you would keep me safe!" Brigitta shook the bars and cried.

She heard a squeak to her right and swung her head in that direction. In the back end of that tree's cell an elderly faerie with an X burned into her right wing and a slash burned into the other clung to mesh bars, holding herself up off the ground. She was a sinewy thing, with short white hair that stood straight up on her head. She gestured toward the floor and Brigitta looked down. Her prison cell floor was one giant trap door with a vine attached to the latch. If anyone pulled the latch, Brigitta, without the use of her wings, would plummet through the trees to the ground far below.

She slowly backed into the trunk as she studied the vine, which stretched out into the trees and terminated at a hut on a small platform where two Watchers stood talking. Not knowing how she could have missed it before, she now saw dozens of these platform huts. They were surrounded by Watchers.

Once she was safely inside the trunk, Brigitta sunk to the ground and pulled her knees up to her chin. She spotted a small stone next to her foot and stared at it for a long while. Then, she took a shaky breath and dropped all thoughts except for stone thoughts. She felt its coolness and let it wash over her. The heat of her anger dissipated as she became still with the stone.

Holding that quiet stoneness, she sent a tendril of energy forth, mind-misting as Elder Fozk had taught. In her mind she moved with the mist out through her prison-tree and down the path. She moved with it through Ondelle's tree to her High Priestess, who sat on the floor against the wall.

As Brigitta's energy settled beside her, she could tell how solid Ondelle's wall of defense was. She knew it was important to prevent any harmful beasts from getting inside, but how come Ondelle wouldn't let Brigitta in?

She felt her balance slipping and she let go of those thoughts and allowed her cool stone energy to drift, waiting for any sliver that could be an opening. Then, she felt it, the slightest crack. Focused and calm, Brigitta slipped into Ondelle's mind.

Mabbe's screams slammed into Brigitta and she felt Ondelle's energy push them away. Heart pounding, she gasped and opened her eyes. She was back in her own cell.

She slumped down to the floor and lay there. Ondelle was fighting for her thoughts and Brigitta may have just ruined her concentration. But even that thought didn't alarm her as much as what she had just felt while she was in Ondelle's mind.

Her High Priestess was afraid.

Wake up, faerie, a voice called.

Brigitta pulled herself awake. Jarlath was staring down at her with those crystal blue eyes, face up against the cage. She knew those eyes; she knew that face. That was it!

Brigitta leapt up so quickly that Jarlath dropped the tray he was carrying, and it clattered on the floor. He did not bend to pick it up, caught in the intensity of Brigitta's gaze as she moved toward him.

"I know you . . . " she whispered, reaching out through the mesh.

Jarlath, too, moved closer, as if hypnotized.

She cupped the side of his face with the palm of her hand. Both of them breathed together as a thousand voices entered the room, speaking all at once. Jarlath pulled back and the voices stopped. Brigitta blinked, once again aware of the room.

"What was—"

"Shut up!" Jarlath hissed. "Just shut up!" He fumbled as he retrieved the tray and the bits of food scattered on the ground. He threw all the pieces through the bars. "There, that will teach you."

The other two caged faeries watched this display as they gnawed on meager bones.

"Be careful of that one," growled Jarlath, "she has tricky mind sorcery."

The faeries kept staring.

"Look away!" commanded Jarlath, and the faeries grabbed the rest of their food and turned around. He gripped Brigitta's cage and whispered fiercely, "You don't know me. Got it?"

"I saw your face in a vision," insisted Brigitta, voice low.

"Really? And did your vision warn you of this place?" he asked.

Brigitta shook her head.

"Not much good then, was it?"

Before Brigitta could answer, the skinny Watcher who had taken Ondelle stepped into the tree. Jarlath straightened up.

"Mabbe wants to see this one," said the Watcher, pointing to Brigitta.

Brigitta sat on a stool at the front of the burl. The contents of her pack lay on the floor mixed with Ondelle's.

"Leave us, Watcher Jarlath," said Mabbe, hunched in her carved chair. "I will send for you."

Jarlath gave a small bow and left.

"Your companion's voice has been uncooperative. Amusing, but uncooperative."

"Ondelle is a powerful priestess." Brigitta smirked at the cloudy-eyed faerie woman. So, Ondelle had managed to keep Mabbe out of her head after all.

Mabbe laughed. "Obviously not powerful enough. And underprepared, I'm afraid."

She waved her staff at the triple lyllium suclaide.

"Bringing sweets on your journey?" Mabbe cackled and pointed to the globelight and herbs. "Some light and some simple remedies?" She gestured over the blankets, firestones, map, the gifts from her poppa and Himalette, and the two spell seeds. "Useless, useless, useless . . . but these are quite interesting. What are they?"

She tapped the two spell seeds with the end of her scepter, then looked up into Brigitta's face and smiled with her pointed teeth. Brigitta could smell her putrid breath, but her smile was also strangely inviting. A glint of light caught Brigitta's attention and she looked up into Mabbe's eyes, where the clouds had parted. The orange Lola Moon appeared in one eye and the Great Blue Moon appeared in the other. They were beautiful, alluring.

"You can tell me, dear," Mabbe's smile broadened. "I can keep a secret."

Brigitta felt herself smiling in response. Yes, she could trust Mabbe. There was no reason to lie. She opened her mouth to speak, but somewhere in the back of her mind she knew it was a trick. She slapped her hand over her mouth.

Whatever she spoke had to be the truth. She knew she couldn't lie. She fought the words back, but they were too strong. Wait, she remembered, don't fight. Relax. Give some up. Let Mabbe think it was flowing with no resistance. She released her thoughts into the water energy and allowed only some words to emerge, like handing Mabbe a cupful of her momma's tea from a larger vat.

"They are seed pods," said Brigitta. She smiled brightly, impressed with herself.

"Oh, how nice," purred Mabbe. "What kind of seed pods?"

Brigitta allowed another thought to flow from her lips. "Seed pods from Gola," she said, giggling.

"And who is Gola?"

"Gola is an old tree-woman. She's my friend."

"I see," said Mabbe with less patience in her voice. She picked up the smaller of the pods and held it to Brigitta's face. A cloud drifted back over the Lola Moon in her eye. "What's inside the pod?"

"Gola made a potion to give me courage!" exclaimed Brigitta, practically giddy with excitement.

Mabbe dropped the spell seed on the floor. "Useless!" She kicked the other one across the room and into the wall.

Brigitta shook her head. All the giddiness disappeared.

Mabbe rushed at Brigitta, eye clouds storming. She sniffed and pawed the air. "Why are you here?"

"We just came to save our forest," stammered Brigitta.

"The forest of the Ancients!" screeched Mabbe.

"Our forest," Brigitta replied. "The White Forest. The Ancients are gone."

"Gone? Gone! Where did they go?"

"We don't know. That's why we came here."

"Ha! Fools after all!" Mabbe cackled and danced wildly about the room, knocking the globelight across the floor. She suddenly stopped.

"Young faerie," she approached Brigitta with open hands, "all I want is to rule in peace. But my little faeries are weak, you see, unable to care for themselves." Mabbe tapped on Brigitta's stool with her scepter. "I would like to make you a deal."

"What kind of deal?" asked Brigitta.

"I will allow you and your *powerful* priestess to return

home, unharmed, and you will never enter my forest again. But first, you must do something for me."

"What?"

Mabbe made her way back to her chair and sat down. "You have seen how Croilus attacks my defenseless faeries. I need to be able to protect them, do I not? You will go to Croilus and retrieve his sorcery sands."

"You mean steal them?"

"It is not stealing to get back that which rightfully belongs to me!" Mabbe struck the ground with her staff, and a lightning bolt shot through the clouds of her left eye. She calmed herself again with a long breath and smiled as she exhaled.

"You will think of some way to acquire them. I don't care how. You're a smart one." Her smile broadened. "If you do not return in three suns' time, I will remove your High Priestess' wings and keep her voice forever."

Remove her wings? Brigitta pictured the wingless Croilus faeries she had seen in the Colony. She clenched her fists. "I'll need my belongings back in order to do so."

Mabbe tapped her scepter against a metallic gong in front of the alcove. Jarlath entered the room, and Mabbe motioned for him to retrieve the items strewn across the floor.

"If you try to trick me in any way," Mabbe sent Brigitta her biggest smile yet, "I promise that your voiceless and wingless High Priestess will be thrown into the Mad River."

Jarlath and Brigitta stepped through a hollow in one of the trees and out onto a platform. He spun her around and removed the lashings on her wings.

She sighed in relief and stretched her body. "Oh, thank the moonbeams!" she exclaimed.

"Can you fly?" asked Jarlath. "Are they all right?"

"I can fly higher and faster than you," said Brigitta.

"But you'll stay with me," he said, "or your friend might lose her wings."

"Yes, of course," said Brigitta.

"Then let's go."

"I need to see Ondelle first."

"We should leave straight away."

"Please, Jarlath," said Brigitta, "she needs to know where I've gone. What if I don't come back? That could happen, right?"

Jarlath narrowed his eyes. "Very well, but make it quick."

They flew up through the trees to the Colony and darted through a split in one of the trunks. They landed inside and startled three malnourished faeries sifting piles of broken rock. All of them had slashes branded on their wings and two had tears in them caked with dried blood.

"I don't know how you can live with yourself," said Brigitta.

"You don't know anything about me or how we've had to live these many seasons," spat Jarlath as he led her to a fenced area.

Inside the pen was a pile of long slender branches. A small group of Hollows and Croilus faeries were stripping fibers from the branches and soaking them in a barrel of thick liquid. More faeries were pulling the strips out of the liquid, setting them in rows to dry, and pulling long thin strands from the dehydrated ones.

"What's this?" asked Brigitta.

"They're making material for clothing," said Jarlath, pointing to the far side of the pen where faeries were weaving the strands into cloth.

Ondelle stood among them.

"Don't you have Clothiers? Faeries born with that talent?"

"They only serve the Queen and her staff. The Colony takes care of everyone else. They harvest the folyia branches," Jarlath waved his hand toward the tops of the trees, "make the cloth, and sew the tunics. It's a good system."

"Forced labor is not a system." Brigitta started across the pen, then stopped when she spotted Ondelle's right wing. It was tarnished with a branded line that cut into her golden High Priestess marking. Brigitta's throat constricted with anger.

Huddled over one young weaver, Ondelle was guiding her hands on a loom, showing her how to be in rhythm with the machine. The little faerie looked absolutely terrified by Ondelle but managed a small smile as her hands started to perform on their own. Even under the worst of circumstances, thought Brigitta, Ondelle put herself in the service of others.

Suddenly, Brigitta didn't want to talk with Ondelle any longer. She was ashamed. All she had been thinking about was how miserable she was when every faerie around her had no other life than this. She contemplated leaving the pen, but it was too late. Ondelle had sensed her. She straightened up as Brigitta and Jarlath approached.

"May we be alone?" asked Brigitta.

Jarlath looked suspiciously from Brigitta to Ondelle,

who smiled warmly at him.

"Mabbe has her voice, so she can't even talk to me," said Brigitta.

Jarlath grunted and moved down the fence to speak with another Watcher.

They both kneeled, and Ondelle took Brigitta's hands in her own. Brigitta relaxed her mind as Ondelle's gaze penetrated hers.

"I made a deal. Mabbe is going to let us both return home. I just have to go to the other tribe, to Croilus, and get her stolen sands back."

Ondelle quickly glanced down to where the hourglass lay under Brigitta's tunic. Was she asking Brigitta to empath her? Grabbing hold of the hourglass, Brigitta let go of all her frantic thoughts and allowed them to drift away. They transformed into black feathers on the wind, twisting and dancing. Mesmerized by the feathers, she followed them, further and further until . . .

Brigitta, Ondelle's voice whispered in the vastness of her mind. A protected vastness, as if they were the only two faeries in the world. *You must return to the White Forest.*

No, echoed Brigitta's voice. *I have to get the sands for Mabbe or she'll hurt you.*

It does not matter what happens to me any longer. Do as I say.

But what about the artifact? Don't we need it to save the forest? Maybe there's a way to trade something for it?

Do not chance it. And trust no one about the artifact.

Then we'll find it together, after Mabbe releases you.

Do not fool yourself. Mabbe will never release me, Brigitta, and I am weakened. You must not risk your life. It is too important. You will leave and tell the Elders what you know. That is a direct order—

No! Brigitta snapped back into her own mind, the coldness of the Colony shocking her skin. Ondelle's eyes looked down at her like moist shadows. She looked much older than Brigitta remembered, and tired.

"No!" Brigitta repeated out loud.

Jarlath and the other Watcher turned at the noise. Jarlath patted the Watcher on the arm and headed toward them.

"Even if I could leave you behind," she whispered to Ondelle as Jarlath approached, "I wouldn't know how to return, I don't have the power."

Yes, you do, mouthed Ondelle, dropping her gaze to the hourglass necklace.

Brigitta's hand went to her chest and she recalled the flash from Ondelle's scepter and the blue energy that had enveloped her in front of the Hourglass of Protection. Brigitta now understood what Ondelle had done. Not only had she spell-cast it so no one, not even her, could remove it, but she had also created some kind of spell that could get Brigitta home.

Ondelle let go of Brigitta's hand, leaving something in it. She glanced down at her palm. The words *Blue Spell* were shaped out in strands from the stripped bark.

Jarlath grabbed them both by the arms and hauled them up. Ondelle's message fell apart as it floated to the ground.

Something sliced into Brigitta's thoughts as Jarlath pulled her away. It was Ondelle, forcing her way into her mind. *All you have to do is let me go—*

"No!" Brigitta called, transforming her thoughts to a heavy rain to drown out Ondelle's words. "I won't go back without you!"

"That's enough!" snarled Jarlath. "Don't make it worse for yourselves."

"I'll get their stupid sands and come back. I promise."

Ondelle's eyes misted for a moment and then hardened again as Jarlath pulled Brigitta out of the Colony.

Chapter Eleven

Brigitta glanced at the moody boy flying beside her, his breath heavy, struggling to keep her pace. Even with his larger Watcher's wings, Jarlath was no match for her. She smirked as she slowed down. It might not be wise to demonstrate just how strong she was, even though she was tempted to show off.

He sprung up over a branch and then dropped back down low to the ground. He might be a weaker flyer, but he did have good technique, she admitted to herself. If he had been a White Forest faerie, she guessed he would have been a Fire Faerie. There was definitely a heat about him. His long, slender body was more muscular than his peers. She wondered what his colors would have been, if he had been bound to the element of Fire. Perhaps he'd have wings and skin tinted red and gold.

He was different than the other Watchers in small ways. His hair was thicker and darker, his eyes more intense. He noticed things as well; he paid attention. He would have had the destiny markings for a Life Task requiring cleverness, she thought, like a Potion Master, if he had been visited by the Ancients at birth.

After several moonbeats they broke past the forest perimeter surrounding the old lakebed, and Jarlath stopped. He scanned the landscape in all directions.

"We don't want to be here at night," he said and frowned as he watched the river spouting up from the earth. "There's a nasty pull today."

Brigitta could feel the force of the river-wind from where they stood. It was stronger than the previous day and the waters wilder. "Where I come from, we call it the River That Runs Backwards," she said.

"That name is too kind."

Jarlath set off again, following the tree-line, stopping every few moments to look around and listen. Brigitta looked too. No faerie chiselers from the Hollows were in sight, nor any of the Croilus faeries. They were alone. She wondered if she could overpower Jarlath and leave him tied up somewhere. Then she could go back and rescue Ondelle.

"If you are considering an escape, may I remind you of Mabbe's promise," he said dryly.

"You mean her threat," corrected Brigitta, although she knew he was right. She could not risk Ondelle's life. She had no doubt Mabbe was capable of murder. No, she was going to have to think of a way to trick this Croilus faerie. She wondered how close she could get to him.

"How are we going to get into Croilus's palace?" she asked. "And how will he receive me when I show up?"

"Shhh. Not here."

Jarlath stopped near a fallen tree, and Brigitta stopped behind him. He took a few more nervous looks around and then whistled.

There was a rustling from inside the tree, and a female Watcher appeared. She was about Himalette's age and thin, but muscular, like Jarlath. Her eyes were the telltale crystal blue of a Watcher, and her wings, though not as golden as

Jarlath's, were unblemished. She had a kind face, pink from the cold, and braided sand-colored hair.

"Any sign of Croilus's brood?" asked Jarlath.

"Not today," the young faerie said, approaching Brigitta. "It's been unusually quiet."

"Thistle," Jarlath gestured, "this is Brigitta . . . of the White Forest."

"Wow," breathed Thistle, and she bowed slightly.

Brigitta looked from Thistle to Jarlath and back to Thistle again. Could there possibly be a friendly faerie in these woods?

"Let's go, then," said Jarlath. "We're running out of light."

Brigitta followed the faeries silently as they flew through the woods northwest of the river. The forest was much thinner than around the Hollows, but the trees were covered in a moist sludge from the constant mist. The branches had mossy stalactites, some as long as Brigitta's arm, from seasons of dripping cold river water. As they dove around the hanging forms, Thistle reached out and broke one off. A tinkling of smaller icicle shapes dropped from above and landed, almost musically, on the branches below.

"We call this the Greencicle Forest," she said, waving her mossy cone.

"*You* call this the Greencicle Forest," Jarlath said as he rounded a slick boulder and turned uphill. "To everyone else it's called the Rivermist."

Greencicle Forest, mouthed Thistle, and Brigitta had to laugh.

"Is this the way to Croilus?" Brigitta asked Jarlath.

"Not exactly."

"Then let's go *exactly*! I don't have much time to get

those sands." Brigitta stopped flying and hovered in the air.

"You are not in charge." Jarlath stopped and crossed his arms across his chest. A greencicle broke off from a branch above him and nailed him on the shoulder. "Ow!" he cried as it dropped to the ground. "Blasted birdsong!"

"Language!" Thistle cried, then began to giggle. "Oh, Jarlath," she reprimanded him, "don't be such a mossbottom."

She fluttered to Brigitta, "You can't go to Croilus right now. You'd never make it at night. It's not safe." She broke her greencicle in two, handed the bottom half to Brigitta, and then licked her own a few times before biting off the tip. Brigitta gave hers a tentative lick. It tasted like cold, salty moss.

They continued until the trees broke away, and they were faced with a sheer cliff that extended west and disappeared into the mist. It looked as if the foot of the valley had sunk in some violent cataclysm, perhaps when the River That Runs Backwards was born. To the east, the cliff continued for several moonbeats until it crumbled into another part of the forest. Dividing the cliff, the River That Runs Backwards chugged uphill, spraying moisture across the entire valley, creating fleeting rainbows in the setting sun.

"It's beautiful," Brigitta murmured.

"Yeah, until it sucks you down into it. Come on." Jarlath moved along the side of the cliff.

Thistle grabbed Brigitta's greencicle-free hand and led her along. "Be careful of falling rocks," she said. "The Mad River sometimes makes an earthshake." She wiggled her body to demonstrate what shaking earth might look like, which made Brigitta laugh once again. The laugh echoed strangely off the cliff, as if mocking her, and Jarlath turned to glower at them both.

They came to a large portion of the cliff that had broken away and slid down, leaving a mass of boulders and scree at the base of the slump. They stopped for a moment and Jarlath examined a log that had six pits carved into the top. Four pits had white stones in them, and Jarlath placed two more white stones in the empty pits before disappearing into a crevasse that had been created by the slide.

Thistle pulled Brigitta into the crevasse, which was barely wide enough for them to open their wings. They flew up until they reached the top of the area that had broken free, then turned right, flitting over the fallen boulders littering the split in the mountain. They dropped down, soaring between the rocks, until they came to the entrance of a natural stone fortress created by fallen boulders that had gotten stuck between the cliff and the slump. The inside was completely hidden from above.

Thistle made a grand gesture into the cave. "We call it the Secret Palace."

"*You* call it the Secret Palace," said Jarlath. "The rest of us call it the Gathering Place." He continued into the rock cavern.

Thistle whispered to Brigitta, "Secret Palace."

Brigitta decided she liked this young faerie and, to spite Jarlath, would call the forest and the fortress anything Thistle wanted.

A moment later they came to a flat rock near a fire pit with several smaller rock seats around it. A fire burned in the pit, casting haphazard shadows around the cavern. The roof and floor were entirely made of fallen rocks. It looked like something had purposefully laid the boulders in this manner to make a home for rock dragons.

"Is it safe?" Brigitta asked Thistle.

"Oh, no one else in the Hollows or at Croilus knows of this place. We're certain of that, otherwise . . . "

"No, I meant," Brigitta gestured at the boulders balanced around them.

"Oh, um—mostly safe, I think. No sliverleaves or nightwalkers at least."

Before Brigitta could ask what sliverleaves and night-walkers were, four more Watchers emerged from the rocks and joined them at the fire pit. Two males wore black tunics with the round symbol of Croilus and another female and a small boy wore the blue tunics of Mabbe's Watchers.

"Brigitta, this is Ferris and Jarlath's brother Roane," said Thistle, pointing to the girl and small boy. "They're from the Hollows." She motioned to the other males, "And Devin and Zhay from Croilus."

All together they were a strange band of beasts. Zhay was slightly smaller than Jarlath, with much paler crystal blue eyes, long ragged white hair, and jaundiced skin that was so papery it looked as if one could poke a hole through it with a finger. His muddy green wings were tough and calloused compared to the rest of him.

The other Croilus faerie, Devin, was a little younger and more pleasant to look at. He had darker features, with brown tones to his wings and skin. His hair and eyebrows were more gray than brown, but a neglectful gray, not the wizened gray of old age. The top half of his left ear was missing.

Slightly taller than Devin, Ferris stood protectively at his side. She had peculiar green-tinted skin covered with dozens of tiny straight scars that shone silver where the skin had healed. Three of these scars marked her face, one across a brow that left a small silver streak of eyebrow hair.

Ferris's green-gray wings were oversized for her small body and also covered in strange silver scars, almost like destiny markings, and what looked to be a large bite off the end of her right wing. She had striking hair, like the burst of a sunset, all reds and yellows and oranges.

The smallest faerie of the bunch, Roane, hid behind Thistle, wrapping his fists in the back of her tunic. He had the palest eyes of them all, with just a hint of blue, but they were too large for his baby face. His dark hair was soft like a girl's, with long lashes to match. His skin and wings carried gold tones like Jarlath's, and as he turned shyly away, Brigitta noticed a branded X on the end of his left wing that made her heart ache.

They all mumbled nervous greetings to her. Thistle, oblivious to the tension in the air, broke her greencicle once again and handed half to Roane. They sat down in front of the fire.

Brigitta dropped next to them and tossed the rest of her greencicle in the dirt beside the fire. As it melted, the faeries continued to stare at her until she could not stand it any longer.

"Why are you all here together?" she asked. "Aren't you sworn enemies?"

Devin, Ferris, and Zhay took seats around the pit.

"We are of like minds," said Jarlath, gathering up a pile of twigs stacked against the rock wall.

"Mostly like minds," said Zhay, correcting Jarlath. "But none of us believes either tribe is ruled fairly." He placed some dry leaves into the fire.

"So, what, you're some kind of rebels?"

They looked around at each other. Even Thistle's friendly face turned anxious.

"Something like that," said Jarlath, carrying the twigs to the pit.

"If you're afraid I'm going to give you away, don't be," said Brigitta. "I have no loyalties to either tribe."

Brigitta wasn't sure how much her word meant to these so called rebel faeries, but she felt the tension in the cavern dissipate as Jarlath and Zhay built up the fire.

"Is it true you come from the home of the Ancients?" asked Devin.

"Well, this is really the home of the Ancients," Brigitta pointed out. "At least it was a long time ago."

"I've never seen one," said Ferris, crossing her scarred arms across her chest. "What are they like?"

"I've never seen one either," admitted Brigitta. "They're ethereal. And they don't live with us elemental faeries in the White Forest."

"Where do they live?" asked Thistle.

"They live in the ethers, bound to the fifth element," Brigitta automatically repeated from her numerous lessons. "At least that's what I've been told. I've never actually spoken with one."

Zhay snickered. "Sounds like a pile of bird drop to me."

Brigitta turned on him, "What do you know? You've never been to the White Forest. You haven't seen how they've protected us all these seasons." She didn't know why she felt the need to protect the Ancients, since she had her own doubts, but she didn't like his accusatory tone.

"Why are you here, then?" asked Zhay.

"Because we've lost touch with them," confessed Brigitta, "which puts us in danger."

"They deserted you just like they deserted us," snorted Jarlath, snapping a twig in two and flinging both halves into the fire.

"You don't know if they deserted us," said Thistle as she hugged Roane to her chest.

"Then why are we still here and not in this amazing White Forest?" asked Jarlath.

"I don't know, but we can't trust what Mabbe tells us," reasoned Thistle.

"If you've never seen an Ancient," yawned Devin, snuggling himself into Ferris, "how do you know they exist?"

"Because of my element and my destiny markings," Brigitta pointed to the dark green symbols on her wings. "Only an Ethereal, an Ancient One, can create a destiny marking."

"So the Ancients brand you with your tribe symbols?" asked Zhay.

"They're not brands," she said. "The destiny markings mean that some day I will sit on the Council of Elders. But right now I'm just a Second Apprentice."

"And everyone in your tribe has an element?" asked Thistle.

"Everyone is bound to one, yes, but every once in a while some are born with two elements, like Ondelle. Everything about the White Forest, the Great Hourglass, the bound elements and destiny markings, has been designed by the Ancients to keep it safe and in balance." Brigitta looked around at all the rebel Watchers. "Haven't you ever been told the story of the Great World Cry?"

The faeries stared out at her blankly. Thistle shook her head.

"You know what I think?" asked Jarlath. "I think these Ancients stole all those elements from Noe, took a bunch of traitorous faeries north, and left us here to rot."

"You can't believe that's true," said Brigitta.

"Too bad we can't ask one to find out."

"They didn't desert you and they haven't deserted us," Brigitta insisted. "They'd never do that. We just have to figure out why they've stopped giving destiny marks and dispersing the spirits of the dead."

Everyone froze and stared at each other. Roane moved over to Jarlath and he took him into his lap.

"Dispersing your spirits?" whispered Thistle, breaking the silence. "You mean ascending the dead?"

"I guess so," said Brigitta, confused as to why they suddenly looked so frightened. "What happens here when a faerie dies? Is their spirit *ascended* as you say?"

"They used to be," said Jarlath, choosing his words carefully, "according to the older members of the Hollows. But now . . ."

"We throw them into the river," finished Ferris.

"You what?" exclaimed Brigitta, horrified. "What happens to their spirits?"

"Usually the spirits go after them into the Mad River," said Devin. "But sometimes, well, they stick around."

"Nightwalkers," said Thistle, and everyone shivered.

"But how can you just throw the bodies into the river?" asked Brigitta.

"You'd rather we let the birds tear them apart and leave us the remains?" spat Ferris. Devin put his arm around her shoulders and squeezed.

Roane began to whimper and buried his face in Jarlath's tunic. Jarlath shot Ferris an angry look.

"Sorry, Roane," said Ferris quietly.

Everyone grew silent and sullen. Brigitta didn't think she was getting anywhere with these rebel faeries. At least, nothing was getting her closer to stealing Mabbe's sands back . . . or finding the sacred item.

"So, this Croilus faerie," said Brigitta, changing the subject, "he named the palace and his lands after himself? Isn't that a little conceited?"

"That's the kind of ruler he is," said Zhay.

"And that's his symbol on your tunic?" she asked Devin, trying to sound casual.

"More like an obsession of his," said Devin, looking down at the front of his tunic and tracing the symbol with a finger. "The Purview, he calls it. It's supposed to be some great tool of sorcery."

"Yeah, and it's probably just as much mythic bird drop," laughed Zhay.

"No, I bet the Ancients took that with them, too," Jarlath pointed out.

"It's not in our forest," said Brigitta. "I'm sure we'd have seen it."

"Is that why you're going to Croilus?" Devin asked. "To find this Purview?"

Brigitta paused. Ondelle had said to trust no one about the artifact. But that was before they knew there was anyone to trust.

"No, she's going to steal all of Croilus's sands," said Jarlath before Brigitta could answer. "She has to," he added quickly, "or Mabbe will kill her High Priestess if she doesn't."

"Mabbe will kill her High Priestess anyway!" shouted Zhay. "You can't leave Croilus defenseless!"

"Defenseless?" Ferris stood up and poked Zhay in the chest. "Whose tribe is attacking whose? Besides, where did he get all those sands in the first place?"

Zhay pointed to Brigitta. "She's going to ruin all our plans."

"What plans?" asked Jarlath. "All we do is argue."

"Yeah, and besides," added Thistle, "maybe she can help us?"

They all turned their crystal blue eyes to Brigitta, and she saw their hopes and their fears reflected there. Could she help them? Could she even help herself?

Brigitta stared into the fire, mind and body numb, as Thistle prepared a meal of strange looking roots inside a battered pot. Roane handed her ingredients as he sucked on the remains of his greencicle.

"Tell us about the White Forest," said Thistle, looking up from her stew.

Brigitta's home and her family seemed so far away. Any description would be muddled, like trying to piece together a dream. Her eyes lit up and she reached into her bag. She pulled out the little pouch containing Himalette's song drop.

"I think this will tell you better."

Brigitta backed away from the fire. She removed the silvery droplet from the pouch and dangled it between her finger and thumb. All the Watchers, even Jarlath and Zhay, admired it as it sparkled in the firelight.

"It's so pretty," said Thistle.

"What's it do?" asked Ferris.

Brigitta let the song drop fall to the rocky floor. It tinkled as the tiny silver object shattered. She felt a slight breeze as her sister's voice flew through the air around them:

My home is in the trees of white

They keep us safe both day and night

Where faeries play and sing and dance

And eat suclaide at every chance

So they can dream of clouds above

And pick blossoms to their heart's delight

Softer and sweeter than Brigitta remembered, Himmy's voice floated through the air around them. Roane played at trying to catch it. Everyone else cocked their heads as they listened.

When I was young I wished I would

Have the very best gift I could

Like Momma makes the finest stew

And Poppa invents a thing or two

As Briggy is marked to lead our kin

I will sing throughout our wood.

"Do you have any more?" asked Thistle as the final quiver of Himalette's little voice faded. Roane nodded with excitement.

"I'm afraid not," said Brigitta. She swept the little silver pieces into her hands and placed them into the front pocket of her tunic. "That was my sister's voice. She was destiny-marked as a Song Master. It was her first song drop." She sniffed back tears of pride as she pictured Himalette gleefully casting the drop with her song.

"When you say marked," asked Jarlath, "you mean you must do what the Ancients command?"

"It's not a command; it's a destiny."

"But you have no choice," said Jarlath. "You must perform this destiny."

"The Ancients are wise, the destiny is . . . " Brigitta searched for the right words to explain, "the destiny is appropriate."

Jarlath folded his arms across his chest, unconvinced.

"You heard the song. Himalette wished to be a Song Master and she became one. She's happy."

"Are you happy?" asked Devin. "With your destiny, I mean."

"My destiny—I'm," struggled Brigitta, "I'm different. I can't explain."

"Sounds just like having to be a Watcher," said Jarlath. "I didn't choose to be bigger and have blue eyes and hear—"

The others looked fiercely at Jarlath.

"I didn't pick to be this, and I'd rather not have anyone, especially not some invisible Ancient, telling me what to do." Jarlath sat down and scowled into the fire.

Roane turned to Brigitta, pointed to her pocket, and then held out his hand. She retrieved a piece of Himalette's song drop and placed it in his palm. He stroked it with a finger and then looked up at her with teary eyes.

"What?" asked Brigitta. "What's wrong?"

"Roane doesn't speak," said Ferris.

"Mabbe took his voice away," said Thistle.

"Oh, yeah," said Brigitta, "I could see why you'd think life here is much better than in the White Forest."

"I didn't say it was better," argued Jarlath.

Brigitta reached into her bag and took out a piece of triple lyllium suclaide. "This will help," she said to Roane. "You eat it. My momma made it. It's the best suclaide in all our forest."

Roane put the treat in his mouth and shut his eyes as he savored it. Brigitta handed out pieces to everyone. Jarlath reluctantly took one and nodded as he sucked on it.

Brigitta popped one into her own mouth. "We'll all have sweet dreams tonight," she said, though she doubted any of them even knew what a good dream was.

Zhay took first watch as the rest of them settled into sleep. Brigitta found herself nestled between Thistle and Roane, who had suddenly decided not to leave her side.

Devin and Ferris retired farther away, snuggled under one of Brigitta's White Forest blankets and sighing as they stroked the soft material. Jarlath tended the fire, ready to take second watch when Zhay's shift was done.

"Are you scared about going to Croilus?" asked Thistle.

"Right now, I don't know how to feel," said Brigitta. "The thing is, I need a plan. I don't know enough about this Croilus faerie."

"Devin will help."

"And Zhay?"

"He's all right," said Thistle. "He and Jarlath are kinda

bitter. They've both lost family in the Sorcery Sand Wars. Jarlath's sister . . . Well, she didn't have enough Watcher blood according to Mabbe, so she was made to dig at the Mad River. Then one day . . . "

Roane squirmed uncomfortably at Brigitta's side.

"Oh, I'm sorry Roane," said Thistle. "He doesn't like to hear about what happened to her."

"It must be hard growing up in such a dangerous place," said Brigitta, fingering the pieces of Himmy's song drop in her pocket.

"But you and Ondelle know magic, right?" asked Thistle. "You can help us?"

"There's no such thing as magic," Brigitta murmured to herself.

Chapter Twelve

Brigitta awoke early the next morning and ventured out of the fortress to where Ferris stood guard. They sat next to each other on top of a boulder, facing into the valley, where they could see down into the old lakebed. The valley mist glowed in the morning light and slowly breathed in and out, caught in the changing winds of the River the Runs Backwards. They sat in silence, listening to the buzzing morning beasts. A small brown scaly creature slithered across the broken cliff wall. Its two long tails twitched as it spied the faerie girls.

"Scat!" cried Ferris, throwing a rock at the beast.

The creature hissed, then opened its maw and spat a black substance onto the boulder beneath their feet before disappearing into a crack.

"You can eat them in a pinch," said Ferris. "Except the head. It's poisonous."

"Thanks for the tip." The thought of eating any creature in Rivermist did not appeal to Brigitta. She doubted even her mother could make the creepy thing appetizing.

"How did there get to be two kinds of faeries? How come there are Watchers and the other ones?"

"Lesser faeries, Mabbe and Croilus call them," said Ferris. "According to Mabbe, she created Watchers."

"How?"

"Using the sorcery sands." Ferris picked up a stone and chucked it against the wall. It clattered on the rocks as it bounced down through the crevasse. "A long time ago, she wanted to create a band of stronger and wiser faeries. She used up a bunch of the sorcery sands to do it. She sometimes calls us her *children*." Ferris laughed at this idea.

"Then one of them, Croilus, rose up against her. About fifty season cycles ago he stole her sands and took some faeries with him. We've been in the Sand Wars ever since."

"Croilus is a Watcher, like you?"

"Croilus is mad, like the river."

The strange scaly creature stuck its head out of the crack, and Ferris threw another rock at it. "He's the reason we can't ascend our dead any longer and are trained from birth to keep our minds closed. He was always listening to the—" Ferris stopped and tucked her knees under her chin.

"The what?" Brigitta asked.

"Shhh!" Ferris hissed, looking behind them at the entrance to the fortress. "It's nothing. Forget it."

Brigitta lowered her voice. "If you want me to stop him, you've got to tell me."

Ferris gripped Brigitta's arm so tightly it hurt. "They drove him mad, the voices that spoke to Croilus," she whispered fiercely. "Every Watcher can hear the voices, and before Croilus rebelled they somehow used the voices to ascend the dead. But now we're all trained to block out mind sorcery. We are put to death if we even speak of the voices." Ferris dropped Brigitta's arm.

"But your friends wouldn't tell anyone, would they?"

Ferris only shut her mouth and shook her head.

Brigitta thought about when she touched Jarlath's face

back in the Colony. She had heard the voices, too, and had almost given him away. She had almost gotten them both killed.

And now she had to somehow trick this "mad" Croilus into giving her his sands. If Watchers could block out empathing, getting close to him wasn't going to do any good. She had to find something more powerful to use against him.

Just then, a ray of sun broke through the gray, sending a flash sparking over the horizon. It danced on Ferris's greenish skin, the hard silvery scars catching the light.

Ferris saw her looking and wiggled her arm. "Devin thinks it's pretty how they shine. He says it's hypnotic."

Hypnotic. Brigitta stopped Ferris's arm. "Have you ever heard of green zynthias?"

🌒

Thistle dished out a red berry mash for breakfast. Roane fluttered about, topping each bowl of mash with some of Ondelle's herbs.

Meanwhile, Brigitta displayed her supplies on the boulders, and the others gathered around to examine the items.

"Such sorcery!" exclaimed Devin.

"Hardly," said Brigitta. She pointed to two small canisters. "The firepepper and dustmist may come in handy, but this," she picked up the larger spell seed containing the zynthia, "this is our strongest weapon."

"Your zyntha's inside there?" asked Ferris.

"Zynthia, yes. And if they've never seen one before, neither Mabbe nor Croilus could fight its hypnotic power.

That takes training to do."

"So Zhay and I pretend to have captured you," said Devin, taking his bowl of mash from Roane, "and you offer this zynthia as a gift to Croilus and use it on him?"

"Exactly."

"And then what?" asked Jarlath.

"Then we take his sands. Mabbe has promised to release Ondelle if I bring them to her."

Zhay burst out laughing. "Yes, and you can trust what Mabbe says."

"I didn't say that," said Brigitta, "but she thinks I believe her. That gives us some time."

"For what?" asked Zhay.

"To figure out how to deal with her. I haven't gotten that far yet." Brigitta looked around at their skeptical faces. "But at least Croilus will be out of the way."

Zhay muttered to himself as he extinguished the fire.

"Do you have a better plan, Zhay?" Jarlath asked.

"Isn't this why we're here?" said Ferris. "To get rid of Croilus and Mabbe."

As Zhay continued to putter around the fire pit, everyone else grew excited about the prospect of leaving Croilus incapacitated. Brigitta packed the spell seed with the green zynthia, along with the firepepper, dustmist, and globelight. She left the rest of her belongings behind a rock, making sure the suclaide was well-hidden from Roane.

"Ready," she said to Devin and Zhay.

They said their goodbyes and flew from the fortress, over the fallen boulders, and back down into the crevasse. When they reached the bottom, Zhay dropped to the log with the pits.

"Hey, there's seven log stones," he said.

"Yeah," Devin said, grinning, "I added a pit for Brigitta this morning."

"What is that?" she asked.

"A message system." Devin pointed at the log. "If you're in the Gathering Place, you put a white stone in your spot. When you leave, if you don't know when you'll be back, you leave it empty. If you plan to be back within a sun or two, put a black stone. If there's trouble, put red. Don't go to the Gathering Place if there's a red stone in your spot."

He pointed to the pit on the far right. "That one's for you."

Brigitta picked up a black stone and placed it in the seventh pit. Devin laughed and placed one in his pit as well.

Zhay shook his head. "Come on."

The three faeries traveled east until they arrived at the River That Runs Backwards, then turned south to follow it, keeping a safe enough distance to avoid its pull. A moonbeat later the banks of the river were high enough that they could cross.

"Don't look down," advised Devin. "And be quick."

As they crossed over, Brigitta focused on the far bank and not the dizzying waters that threatened to suck them under. She was more than relieved when they reached the other side.

With Zhay in the lead, Devin and Brigitta followed him southeast until the forest broke away, and he landed on a bald hill overlooking an enormous overgrown arena. Toppled statues and pillars littered the landscape along with crumbling walls and fountains. Everything was covered in a thorny purple ivy.

In the middle of the ruins stood a plateau supporting a stone palace, gray and crumbling but for the shimmering center structure topped with an immense dome. The brightness of it contrasted with the dull shades of the valley.

There were no other faeries in sight.

Zhay examined the sky. The clouds were thicker and darker than the previous day. He held out his hand for a moment. "Think it's going to rain?" he asked Devin.

Brigitta looked at him, puzzled, but Devin wrinkled his brow and studied the sky. She glanced up as well. The clouds were heavier than White Forest clouds and unfamiliar. She wondered if she could even empath them. "Why does it matter?" she asked.

"If it starts to rain, even a little bit, fly to whichever side of the arena is closest and do not stop," said Devin. "The warwumps come out whenever it rains."

"What's a warwump?"

"You don't want to find out," said Zhay. "Give me your pack."

"Why?"

"Because Croilus will punish us for allowing you inside with it."

Devin nodded in agreement, and Brigitta handed her pack to Zhay.

He gestured to Devin, "Make it look like we're escorting her, one ahead and one behind."

Devin leapt into the air and began to fly over the ruins. Brigitta followed across the littered landscape.

"Don't touch the ivy," Devin warned. "The thorns are vicious and the vines unpredictable." He pointed to a few larger pillars only half smothered by the nasty plant. "If you need to rest, do it as high as possible."

She looked down as they flew. The land was tiered, so that it descended slowly as they flew toward the center, and crumbling buildings poked out under dirt, debris, and writhing ivy.

Devin turned and hovered, gesturing to the ruins below them. "A long time ago, this is where all the Ancients lived."

"Not in the trees?"

"Croilus says they had visitors from all over Faweh and had to host them here."

She contemplated the enormity of the ruins. There must have been thousands of visitors to fill this arena. It was obvious no one had occupied the space for a very long time. "And the palace up there?"

"Where the High Sages and their families lived. Where the World Sages met."

Zhay snorted and gestured over his shoulder. "Yeah, and all the lesser faeries had to live in the Hollows."

"In the dead trees?" said Brigitta. "Why would they live in that horrible place?"

"I guess they weren't good enough to stay with the Ancients," said Zhay.

"Who told you all this?"

"Croilus," Devin said, then shrugged.

"I don't believe him," said Brigitta. "The Ancients exist to protect us."

"Then why did they leave so many of us behind?" Zhay asked and then waved them toward the plateau.

There were at least a dozen Croilus Watchers patrolling the base of the plateau. As they approached, Devin and Zhay took positions on either side of Brigitta and held her arms. Watchers observed them curiously as they made their way to an opening in the plateau, but no one confronted them. A silver staircase ran up through the opening. At the base, the staircase was about as wide as her cottage in Tiragarrow, and it grew narrower and narrower as it reached the top.

The thorny ivy had crawled partway up the stairs. A Watcher sat on the steps above three lesser Croilus faeries, supervising as they pushed the ivy back with firesticks. The lesser faeries stopped and gaped at Brigitta as she passed overhead. A tendril of ivy grabbed one's leg as he was distracted, and he cried out in pain. The others stabbed at the ivy with their sticks, fighting it off as it dragged him down the stairs, thorns caught in his skin. The Watcher stood up but did nothing to assist.

"The ivy!" Brigitta called out and turned to help.

"Leave them!" hissed Zhay, pulling her along.

"But—"

"We can't interfere with another's task," whispered Devin. "It's not allowed."

"But that's ridiculous!" Brigitta said as she watched helplessly from the air.

"It's Croilus's way." Zhay pulled at her again. "Survival of the fittest."

Brigitta glanced over her shoulder as they flew up the length of stairs, relieved when the faeries managed to pull their friend free. They reached the top and glided through the crumbling sections of the palace. Frightened lesser faerie eyes watched them from windows and doorways, pulling into the shadows as Brigitta fluttered by.

Past the ruined walls, they entered a courtyard and

landed in front of the most beautiful structure Brigitta had ever seen. It shone into the dark air like a star. A dozen columns supported the center structure, on top of which stood a giant dome. The building was pure white and opened like arms from its domed center.

"How come..." Brigitta's voice trailed off as she noticed several little white figures darting about the columns. The longer she watched, the more of them she saw flitting in and around the palace. "What are those things doing?"

"Who, the sprites?" asked Zhay.

"Sprites?" Brigitta was dumbfounded. She stepped closer, and sure enough, the little pale-haired, pale-skinned, white-clothed flying beasts were sprites. They were smaller than the ones in her forest, and she'd never seen such ghostly ones before, but they were definitely sprites. "How in Faweh did you get them to—to—*work*?"

"What do you mean?" asked Devin. "They don't do anything else. They never stop."

"I think they've always been here." Zhay looked at the sprites as if for the first time.

It didn't make any sense to Brigitta, but there wasn't much about Noe that made sense, she thought, as they flew up to the center building. She passed a little sprite methodically polishing a column as if under some kind of green zynthia hypnosis. For a moment, Brigitta swore she could see through the wispy beast. Its eyes never left its task.

Everything was painfully clean in the courtyard. Brigitta was afraid she'd leave dirty footprints on the beautiful surface and was surprised when she turned to look and there were none. The open arms of the structure were corridors that led up to the center dome. The corridors had ceilings, but no walls, and were supported by more columns. Along the corridors, silver benches invited non-existent guests to relax, and in the middle of the courtyard sat a dry silver fountain.

Something poked at her side, and she turned to find Devin with a grim expression. He nodded to an older Watcher entering the courtyard.

"Stay here," said Zhay, who fluttered over to the guard, showed him Brigitta's pack, and pointed to her. The guard and Zhay slipped around the side of the building.

It was strangely quiet. The only movements were the eerie sprites, polishing and polishing. It was far too lovely to be so empty. The loneliness of it stung Brigitta's heart.

"Why didn't Mabbe choose to live here?" she whispered.

"Because Mabbe is clever," Devin whispered back, "and Croilus is vain."

There was a metal clang, and Zhay pushed open a pair of enormous silver doors between the centermost columns. Devin flew Brigitta to the entrance and they stepped inside. Zhay shut the door behind them and everything went dark.

As they stood there, shapes slowly appeared. It was dingier inside the domed structure. There were rotting tapestries, dusty floors, and scavenged shelves. They moved through a curved passageway until it opened up into a cavernous room with four sections of stone seats. It was shaped like the Center Realm grandstands, but was not at all festive. The dome above was covered with seasons of grime, so that little light shone through.

In front of the tiers of seats sat another silver platform with five carved chairs of varying size and shape. On the far right was the largest chair, which was squat and wide. Next to it sat a chair that was slightly larger than an Elder's chair. On the far left was a tall slender one, and next to that, one with a high seat and an attached footstool. In the middle was a high-backed chair carved in, of course, more silver.

Brigitta gasped and clutched Devin. "This must be where the High Sages—"

"Quiet!" snarled Zhay, startling Brigitta, who had forgotten for a moment that she was their prisoner.

The older Watcher stood at the base of the platform.

"Here, hold this," said Zhay, handing Brigitta's pack to Devin. Instead of flying down to meet the other Watcher, he walked down the steps, which were spaced too far apart to do so with any grace.

As they waited for Zhay to reach the other Watcher, Devin squeezed her hand and pulled away. A chill went up Brigitta's spine as she suddenly grew nervous. Her heart pounded in her chest for a moment before she could calm herself again.

When Zhay made it to the bottom, the older Watcher gestured and Zhay cleared his throat. "Oh, great leader Croilus," he called. "We have captured a faerie who claims to have a gift for you."

They stared up at the domed ceiling.

"She says it is a magical gift, Croilus of Noe," he continued, "and requests your presence."

The cavernous room was still and quiet as if holding its breath.

"Guess he's not interested," grunted the older Watcher, cracking the silence. He twirled his firestick. "Bind her wings and take her to the—"

"The Ancient Ones wish to bestow a gift worthy of you!"

yelled Brigitta up at the dome. Croilus was vain, Devin had said.

A moment later, there was a flash, and a large Watcher appeared above them in the air. He dropped down and settled into the silver high-backed chair. He was wearing the most ridiculous robe Brigitta had ever seen. It was thick and purple and longer than his body. The arms flared out into huge poofs of delicately spun lace. Brigitta would have burst out laughing if it weren't for his maniacal crystal blue eyes upon her. The rest of his face was pale and sharp and firm. He wore a silver wreath around his bald head.

Zhay and the older Watcher kneeled in front of him.

"Oh, great leader Croilus," said Devin, voice wavering. "We were patrolling the lakebed and found this faerie." He nudged Brigitta down the steps.

"I knew it!" cried Croilus gleefully. "You've finally come!"

"I'm not sure what you mean, sir," said Brigitta as she descended. "I am Brigitta of the White Forest. I came here on a mission of peace to bring you greetings and a gift from the Ancients."

"Enough! I know why you are here!" wailed Croilus, standing and getting caught in his robe. "You have come to steal my sorcery sands!"

"Why would I do that, sir?" laughed Brigitta. "We have a gigantic hourglass full of sand in the White Forest. We have so much sand we dance around it in celebration."

Croilus stared down at her as she approached the platform. His gaze did not affect her. He had no power to enter her mind. Perhaps she could fool him after all.

"As a matter of fact," she pulled her hourglass necklace from inside her tunic, "I have some right here in this miniature hourglass. Every faerie born in the White Forest is given their own hourglass full of sand, there is so much of it."

"You never told us that," accused Zhay.

Croilus flashed a staff at Zhay and a bolt of red shot out and hit him in the chest, knocking him off his feet. "I did not say you could speak."

Zhay writhed in pain and struggled for breath. "Many . . . apologies . . . sir."

Croilus pointed his staff at Brigitta and smiled wickedly. "You can have the sands. I won't be needing them anymore."

Devin and Zhay exchanged confused glances.

"Now where is this gift?" he asked, pounding the floor with his staff.

"Watcher Devin has it, sir," Zhay pointed to Devin, who held up Brigitta's pack.

"Bring it to me!" Croilus ordered.

Devin stepped up to the platform and held up the pack to Croilus, who snatched it away. Devin dropped to his knees and bowed his head.

Croilus reached hungrily into the pack and pulled out Brigitta's globelight.

"That's just a light to guide my way," said Brigitta.

He dropped the globelight to the floor and dove into the pack again, pulling out the firepepper and dustmist.

"Those are spices," said Brigitta. "It's the large seed pod."

Brigitta approached and Croilus readied his staff. "Stay back, faerie," he said.

He stuck his hand into the pack once more and pulled out the bottom of the bag. "There's nothing else! What's the meaning of this?"

"No, it can't be!" she cried. "There was a sorcery seed! It was a gift from the . . . from the Ancients."

"It's true, there was a sorcery seed. She showed it to us," said Zhay, crawling to his knees.

"Yes!" exclaimed Brigitta. "They both saw it."

"Then Watcher Devin must have stolen it for himself." Zhay pointed at Devin.

Both Devin and Brigitta whirled around to face Zhay.

"No . . . no . . ." stammered Devin, waving his arms in defense. "I didn't take it!" He turned to Brigitta. "It wasn't me!"

"He had her pack, sir," said Zhay, getting to his feet, "and she showed us the pod inside it."

Croilus sent such a flare out to Devin from his staff that it knocked him across the floor and into the first set of stone seats, where he smacked his head and was still.

"Devin!" cried Brigitta, and she turned to run to him.

Croilus jumped from the platform and landed in front of Brigitta, staff pointed in her face.

"But he's lying!" Brigitta pointed to Zhay.

"Silence!" he seethed. "If Watcher Devin wakes, he will bring me this sorcery seed. If he doesn't wake, you'd better hope that you can find it. I've waited far too long for this."

Croilus motioned to Zhay, who grabbed Brigitta by the arm. Before she had a chance to struggle, Croilus flung his staff in her direction. A fiery force struck her in the legs, and they buckled under her. She fell forward to the floor, legs burning. For a second, she thought she would fall flat on her face, but Zhay stopped her just in time and set her down.

She wanted to strike out at him, but her legs pained her so badly that she couldn't speak. The pain intensified, as if a fire grew inside of them, making her dizzy. Immobilized, she lay on the floor, wondering if Devin was still alive.

Chapter Thirteen

A pulse of pain beat through her legs as Brigitta awoke next to Devin on the cold floor under the dome. She didn't remember passing out. She tried to stretch out, but her arms, legs, and wings were restrained. It was quiet except for the sound of Devin breathing. So, he was alive.

Wondering if they were alone, Brigitta relaxed and tentatively misted her mind out, shaky at first, but finding balance quickly. She was getting better at it; Elder Fozk would be proud.

She sensed someone at the back of the room, but she couldn't tell who. Reaching farther, she felt the tattered fabrics and cold stone furniture. After a breath, her mind continued across the room, up the stairs, through the rounded passageway, and out into the courtyard. She could sense the fluttering of the sprites, but what she felt was like the opposite of energy, as if the essence of the sprites had been drained, leaving unconscious and empty shells.

She drifted among their steady rhythms, misting higher and higher, floating up into the sky. The thick fullness of the clouds met her and pulled her in. She faltered for a moonsbreath, surprised at their strength, but relaxed further into her breath and allowed her mind-mist to mingle there. Steady and focused, her vision shifted, and she was gazing down onto the ruins. Something impossibly large shifted under the ivy deep inside the earth.

Zhay crouched down in front of her, and her mind snapped back. "Tell me how to open the spell seed, and I'll help you escape," he whispered.

"What do you want with it?" growled Brigitta.

"The same thing you do. To stop Croilus."

"So you can take his place?"

Zhay moved closer to Brigitta's face and took her chin in his hands. "My father died in the ivy, my mother was swallowed by the Mad River, and my sister taken by the warwumps. Croilus does nothing to better our lives."

"So then help us," Brigitta said, "for them."

"And set everyone free, like Devin and the rest want?"

"Of course!"

"What do you think would happen if these faeries were left to rule themselves? They've never been free. It would be a complete mess. There would be six warring tribes instead of two. More faeries would die." Zhay let go of her face. "But they will follow the one who defeats Croilus."

"And why should you be the one to lead them?" asked Brigitta.

"They couldn't have worse than Croilus." Zhay leaned back and shook his head. "That's the crazy thing. Everyone hates him, but they fear losing their leader more than they fear for their own lives."

"Watcher Zhay!" a voice called from across the room, and Zhay's eyes grew panicked. "Croilus wants to know if you have any knowledge of this faerie light or these spices. One appears to have burned his skin."

"Get my pack back for me and I'll think about helping you," Brigitta hissed.

Zhay stepped over Brigitta. A moment later she heard him and the older Watcher talking in low voices behind her. Devin's eyes fluttered and opened. He stared at Brigitta, confused.

"Shhh. Don't let them know you're awake," whispered Brigitta. "Close your eyes and keep still."

Devin closed his eyes, and Brigitta scooted a little closer. "Zhay took the spell seed but blamed you. Croilus wants you to lead us to it."

"How can I do that?" whispered Devin.

"I want you to pretend to know where it is," she said. "Now, tell me about these warwumps."

❦

Brigitta and Devin hovered in the air, facing the ivy-ridden arena surrounding the plateau. They were linked together by a silver chain. Zhay and five more Watchers hovered in the air behind them with firesticks.

As part of Brigitta's plan, Devin had told the older Watcher the sorcery seed was hidden in the arena. Zhay had tried to protest, but more Watchers had entered with orders from Croilus to find the seed. He had no choice but to go along with them.

Zhay moved closer and spoke quietly to Brigitta. "I don't know what you're up to, but you'll only get yourselves hurt."

"Don't talk to us, you traitor," growled Devin. "I should have known you couldn't be trusted."

"I only wanted what's best for all of us," replied Zhay. "Don't say I didn't give you a chance. You can't blame me for this."

Zhay moved back into the Watcher formation, taking position in the half circle around Devin and Brigitta.

"Well?" she turned to Devin. "Show us where you hid the seed!"

Devin gave Brigitta an uneasy glance. "This way," he said softly before flying off across the ivy.

As she took off, Brigitta made note on which shoulder Zhay carried her pack. Getting it would be tricky, but she had the element of surprise. And fear. She looked up at the sky and was pleased to see the Watchers do the same. The clouds were thick and dark in the red-gray sky. Manipulating them would be difficult to do while flying.

She pointed to a tall pillar sticking out of the ivy. "Can we land there please?"

"What's wrong?" demanded Zhay.

"I'm feeling weak from Croilus's attack," said Brigitta. "I just need a moonsbreath to rest."

She wavered in the air and Devin took hold of her, but his wings were not strong enough to support them both. He led her to the pillar, and she pretended to catch her breath. Zhay and the other Watchers buzzed around them.

"What's going on?" whispered Devin.

"I'm fine," whispered Brigitta, "just be ready."

Brigitta took a deep breath and stretched out her arms and wings. She settled her mind and body, letting go of everything but cloud energy. Just like at Green Lake, she said to herself, then let that thought go, slowly and carefully drifting up. She bounced around a bit and then was looking down from a great height, passing over the arena. Everything was far below her as she drifted. Once she was balanced, she swam along with the clouds, feeling for moisture, feeling—

there! A wide expanse of heaviness, like a bladder about to burst.

"All right, that's enough!" barked Zhay, nudging Brigitta with his stick. "Let's go."

With her eyes, Brigitta directed Devin toward the rain clouds. The color drained from his face as they flew, and Brigitta pulled on the chain to keep him going in the right direction.

Zhay, weary himself, flew around and stopped in front of them. "We didn't fly this way today. This can't be the right place."

Brigitta and Devin hovered in the air, silver chain swaying between them. She gave Zhay a big smile. "Oh, this is exactly the right place."

Gripping her hourglass necklace, Brigitta concentrated with every ounce of water energy she could muster. Zhay's voice dropped away. Someone prodded her back, but she ignored it and held her necklace as the clouds reformed, graying as they grew denser.

"We're going back!" Zhay's voice cut into her concentration.

She opened her eyes and looked at Devin, whose face was so terrified she felt guilty for what she had asked him to do.

"I've had enough." Zhay turned to the other Watchers. "Let Croilus deal with them."

The Watchers gathered around the other side of Devin and Brigitta as she touched Devin's arm and nodded. He nodded back, shaking with fear.

"What was that?" one of the Watchers cried out.

"Did you feel that?" called another.

Brigitta felt a drop on her head. A large, wet, oily drop.

"Rain!" cried Zhay. "It's going to rain!"

There was another drop and another and before they knew it, the clouds had opened up, and it was pouring down on them.

"It worked!" laughed Brigitta over the torrent of water.

Zhay and all the other Watchers buzzed around in a panic. Brigitta snagged her pack from Zhay's shoulder. He turned to take it back, but she flew out of reach, dragging Devin with her as the rain pounded harder.

With an anguished cry, Zhay sped toward the outer edge, and the other Watchers took off toward the plateau, leaving Devin and Brigitta alone in the middle of the ruins. As the rain came down, she felt heavier and heavier. Her wings were soaked in oily wetness. The rain was like mucus.

"Follow me," she said to the wet and trembling Devin.

The ground rumbled beneath them, the ivy shook, and the earth caved in. Brigitta grabbed Devin's arm and flew up as hard and fast as she could. The rain had coated her wings so that they slipped in the air. She struggled with him as she flew.

Devin snapped out of his daze and began to pump his wings as well. They flew up together, away from the thunderous sounds. "I—I—I can't fly this high," panted Devin. "I'll never make it."

"Just do it!"

Brigitta glanced down as an enormous black beast burst up through the earth. It was limbless and hairless, like a worm, but with a hard shell and a beakish mouth that took up a quarter of its body. Another sprung through the ground, and they both opened their mouths and flung themselves about wildly. Their screams were deafening. Brigitta and

Devin hovered just out of reach. Four more warwumps burst through the ruins, their mouths wide enough to swallow a cottage.

"Can you hover by yourself for a moment?" yelled Brigitta over the sound of the rain and screams.

She let go of Devin and removed the dustmist and the firepepper from her pack. She poured out the dustmist so that it settled beneath them, like a thick floating carpet, and sprinkled the firepepper into it. It was a sloppy job, with holes in the pattern, but it would have to do.

She floated up a little higher, pulling Devin with her. She made another thick carpet of dustmist and sprinkled the remainder of the firepepper inside of it.

They hovered together, Brigitta supporting Devin as best she could, watching as warwump after warwump burst through the earth. One stretched up toward them, and Devin closed his eyes and cringed. The warwump hit the firepepper cloud and immediately shrank back down.

"We're safe up here!" Brigitta squeezed Devin, who opened his eyes, surprised he had not been swallowed.

They watched as the beasts thrashed about beneath them, jaws open wide. Their enormous bodies undulated as the rain streamed down into their mouths. There was a desperation about them, and Brigitta slowed her thoughts to catch a hint of warwump energy. Instead of feeling anger or meanness, as she would expect, she felt only relief.

"They're thirsty, that's all!" exclaimed Brigitta, and then she laughed. "They don't eat faeries. At least not on purpose. They just come for the rain."

"Brigitta," said Devin, as he began to falter. "I can't . . . "

Brigitta refocused on the clouds as she held her hourglass

necklace. She pulled and pulled on the water energy, gathering it back up. Slowly, the rain began to subside, and the warwumps became less frantic. As the rain stopped, the gigantic worms retreated back into the earth.

Devin, sopping wet with oily rain, fluttered about erratically while Brigitta gathered the dustmist and firepepper. The air was not cooperating and kept holding back. The chain yanked at her waist as Devin slipped lower. Fearing he would completely exhaust his energy, she gave up on collecting the rest and pulled Devin away from the pepper heat. They descended back down to the arena. The earth and ivy were already closing in over the warwump holes.

There was synchronicity in the Valley of Noe after all, she thought, even if it was a dangerous place for faeries. She led Devin toward the outer side of the arena, away from the directions that Zhay and the other Watchers had sped.

By the time Brigitta and Devin reached the edge of the lakebed, Mabbe's afternoon chiselers were packing up to return to the Hollows. They watched from a safe distance behind an outcropping, pounding a rock on the silver chain that bound them. They had decided to take the long way around the lakebed to the Gathering Place, hoping to surprise Zhay, assuming that's where he had gone. They didn't know what else to do.

"How did you end up with Mabbe's rebel Watchers?" asked Brigitta as she pounded on the chain.

"I was on duty, making my rounds, when I spotted

Ferris," said Devin. "She was poking through some ruins on the other side of the hill."

"But weren't you sworn enemies?"

"Mabbe and Croilus are enemies, and we fight for them to survive," said Devin, "but when I saw Ferris, I just sort of forgot who I was. I didn't even bother to hide. I just stood there, staring at her like an idiot."

"Was she, you know, scarred like that?" asked Brigitta.

"Yeah, they were like silver jewels glinting in the light." Devin smiled at the memory, then turned to Brigitta and grinned. "Of course, she gave me an earful that first time. Then we started meeting every few moons in secret. She told me of a Watcher named Jarlath who had once saved a Croilus faerie from a gargan."

"A what?"

"Big ugly spider."

"Don't you have any nice furry animals in Noe?" asked Brigitta, breaking through one of the chain links. "Or perhaps some dimwitted grovens? I haven't even seen any birds."

"We have birds," Devin shuddered.

"As pets?"

Devin looked at Brigitta as if she were insane.

"Never mind." Brigitta watched as the last of the Hollows faeries left the lakebed.

"We do have chygpallas," said Devin. "Children like them. I'll show you one sometime."

"What about Zhay, when did he join up?" asked Brigitta.

"He tracked me out to the Gathering Place. I thought we were as good as dead, but he swore he was on our side. Jarlath never trusted him. I shouldn't have either."

"I think they're all in the woods," said Brigitta. She pulled apart the mangled chain. "Let's go."

As Devin stood up and brushed himself off, Brigitta took hold of his arm. "I don't know what we'll find at your Secret Palace. We need to be ready to fight or fly."

"Yeah," Devin said grimly and leapt into the air. "I know."

It was nearly dark when Brigitta and Devin made it to the slump in the cliff. The message log was no help; every pit was empty. Brigitta pulled out her globelight and rubbed it, and Devin was momentarily mesmerized by the purity of the light. She honed the light down by rubbing it again so that it shone a narrow path in front of them.

The two faeries made their way through the crevasse in silence. They flew around to the back of the slump, over the boulders that hid the entrance to the fortress, and slipped inside. It was empty and there were no embers in the fire pit.

"No one's here," Brigitta whispered, shining her light into the cracks and corners. She pulled her belongings from behind the rock where she had hidden them. "Zhay didn't bother with my things."

"Maybe he was in a hurry?" Devin knelt down by the fire pit and sniffed the air. "It hasn't been lit today."

There was movement and something heavy flew at them. Devin grunted as he was knocked backward onto the ground.

"Show yourself!" called a voice from the rocks.

"It's us, Brigitta and Devin!" said Brigitta, shining her globelight on her face.

"Brigitta!" Thistle came flying out from the darkness and careened into Brigitta, hugging her tightly and knocking the globelight from her hand.

"Thistle!" Jarlath emerged, shading his eyes as the beam of light hit his face. "It could have been a trick."

Roane leapt out and scooped up the globelight, shining it about the cavern. The light landed on Devin as he groaned from the floor.

"Jarlath, you idiot!" cried Brigitta, escaping from Thistle and fluttering to Devin. "You could have hurt him."

"Leave him alone!" commanded Jarlath. "He's a traitor!"

"For the Blue Moon, he's not a traitor." Brigitta eased Devin up off the ground. "He helped me escape."

"We were fooled by Zhay," growled Jarlath. "How do you know he's not fooling us as well?"

"I know," said Brigitta.

Thistle moved to help her set Devin on a rock. They both checked him for damage.

"Zhay was here. He took Ferris," said Thistle.

"What?" cried Devin, wobbling to his feet. Thistle gently pushed him back down onto the rock.

"We couldn't stop him. He had one of those firesticks in her face," said Thistle. "He pretended to be injured, said something about you being captured, so naturally Ferris went to ask him what happened."

"No!" Devin grabbed Brigitta's tunic. "We have to go back for her!"

"We can't risk it," said Jarlath.

"He said he'll give her back if Brigitta tells him how to open the sorcery seed," said Thistle.

"See?" Jarlath said. "Ferris is safe for now. He needs that

seed to defeat Croilus."

"We need to get the seed *and* Ferris back," said Brigitta as she watched Roane flashing the globelight on the rocks, casting shadows on the rugged walls. She glanced at the four weary faeries. "We need to get help."

"We've got to get out of here, too," said Jarlath. "It's not safe."

"I'm not going anywhere without Ferris," said Devin.

"Ferris is gone," said Jarlath.

"But if she escapes, she'll come here," Devin pointed out. "This is the only place she knows where to find me."

Jarlath was about to protest, but Brigitta stopped him. "He can't go back to Croilus, and he can't go with us to the Hollows."

"Who says we're going back to the Hollows?" asked Jarlath.

"I'm going back to the Hollows," corrected Brigitta. She gathered up her remaining belongings and reached out for the globelight. "I'm going to rescue Ondelle."

Roane reluctantly handed her the light, and she motioned for him to step back. She slammed the globe onto a rock and it broke into six even pieces, like little slices of the Great Moon. She rubbed one of the slices with two fingers and handed the bright shard to Roane.

Brigitta, Thistle, Jarlath, and Roane flew silently through the crevasse, each carrying a shard of glowing globelight.

"I don't feel right about leaving Devin back there alone," said Thistle.

"What if Ferris does manage to escape?" said Brigitta. "It's better that someone's left to meet her."

As they exited the slump and approached the trees, Brigitta dropped down to the message log. She placed red stones in her own and Devin's spots. "That way Zhay will think we never made it back," she reasoned.

Jarlath nodded at her cleverness as she rose. "Stay behind me," he warned. "There are reasons we don't go into the forest at night."

They flew carefully through the trees, Jarlath and Thistle with shields up, Brigitta and Roane between them. Annoyed with their slow progress, Brigitta was about to ask if they could pick up the pace when Jarlath stopped and hovered in the air.

"Shhhh!" he commanded, even though no one was talking. "Hide your lights!"

They all hid their shards in their tunics and listened. A moment later, there was a rustling, then what sounded like hundreds of little humming beasts.

Brigitta peered into the trees. "What is—"

"To the ground!" Jarlath dropped to the forest floor, and Roane and Thistle followed with frightened squeals.

Brigitta hesitated and several small dark shapes darted past. A moment later something seared her right wing and another stabbed the back of her hand. She dropped to the ground and Jarlath pushed her down, covering her with his own body. Roane whimpered beside her where Thistle was protecting him with her arms.

The humming increased as a swarm of the small creatures flew overhead. Brigitta tried to see what was going on, but Jarlath firmly held her in place. He lowered his own head to the ground next to Brigitta's. "Keep your face down," he said, so close she could feel his breath in her ear.

After a while, the forest grew quiet again, but the faeries remained still, listening. Brigitta turned to face Jarlath and caught his crystal blue eyes off guard. They stared at each other and in that moment a thousand voices began to whip through the air. Jarlath leapt up and wiped himself off. The voices disappeared.

Brigitta stood, pondering what had just happened. It reminded her of the first time she had sat in an Elder's chair. She had been overwhelmed by voices.

She reached out to Jarlath and a sharp sting coursed from her right wing to her shoulder, down her arm, and into her hand. She cried out and grabbed her hand. It was marked with a thin slice of blood. Looking over her shoulder, she saw a thin slit in her wing that went right through the center of the eye glyph. Both cuts were the same size and shape as the numerous scars that dotted Ferris's face and body.

Thistle got up and helped a frightened Roane to his feet. "They'll heal right away," she said, "but the poison stings for a few moons."

Brigitta nodded and thanked Faweh that she had only been sliced twice by the nasty things. "Sliverleaves," she murmured staring into the darkness. "Poor Ferris."

They stayed close to the ground the rest of the way to the lakebed. When they burst through the trees, a glowing landscape greeted them. Through an opening in the thick clouds, the two moons shone down, the little orange moon tagging after her big blue sister.

"It's lovely," said Thistle. "I had no idea."

They landed and stared in awe. The moons were bright

and nearly full, but still could not penetrate the dense clouds. They could only shine through the opening, casting an eerie beam down on the valley, spotlighting the lakebed. The River That Runs Backwards churned madly in the light, more ominous than in the day. And in the crater, scattered around the bowl, tiny sparkles danced, caught in the moon rays.

"Those sparkles. It's the sorcery sands!" Thistle pointed into the enormous bowl. "The moons could lead us right to them!"

Brigitta moved forward and Jarlath grabbed her arm. "It's too dangerous."

Thistle nodded and Brigitta sighed. They all looked on, hungrily, as the ancient sands twinkled.

As they stood there, the clouds closed up and the moonslight disappeared, along with the sparkling sands. If it weren't for the little slices of globelight, it would have been pitch black.

Exhausted, they decided to rest against some fallen logs. It was bitterly cold. Brigitta pulled out her two White Forest blankets. Thistle cuddled up to Brigitta, and she wrapped a blanket around them both. Jarlath and Roane did the same. Night beasts croaked and buzzed, and the rushing of the river continued in the background.

"We have to figure out how to get in and out of the Hollows," said Brigitta.

Jarlath snorted. "I'm not convinced we should go back at all."

"I'll make you a deal," said Brigitta. "You help me rescue Ondelle, and we'll make sure Mabbe never harms anyone ever again."

"Don't make promises you can't keep."

"Jarlath, what else can we do?" asked Thistle. "Isn't this what we've been waiting for? Isn't this what the voices meant when you—"

Jarlath grabbed Thistle's arm so forcefully she gasped. "No, it isn't," he hissed. "They didn't mean anything."

She lowered her eyes. "I'm sorry."

Brigitta glared at Jarlath, and Roane stared up at him with his big sad eyes. He let go of Thistle and placed his hand on Roane's head.

"No, Thistle, I'm sorry," he said. "I shouldn't have listened to them, and you shouldn't have listened to me."

He pulled Roane close and gave his little brother a hug. "I got us all in over our heads."

They sat in silence and huddled into the blankets for warmth.

"How many more of your secret clan are there?" asked Brigitta.

"Thistle's mother is servant to Mabbe," said Jarlath.

"Who else?"

"There are no others," admitted Jarlath.

"Not yet," added Thistle.

"The seven of you were planning to overthrow Mabbe and Croilus yourselves?"

"Six. Zhay was a traitor," Jarlath reminded her.

"So, there's no one else who can help us?"

"Brigitta, you have to understand," said Jarlath, "what we're doing, even mentioned in jest, is punishable by death."

"The Watchers are too scared; the lesser faeries are too weak," said Thistle.

"How many Watchers are there?" asked Brigitta.

"A hundred and fifty, maybe more," said Jarlath.

"Do you know them all by face and name?" asked Brigitta.

"Not entirely. Some I see every few moons, some I see once a season, if at all." Jarlath leaned forward into his beam of light. "Why?"

The clouds broke open again, and the moonslight cascaded down into the lakebed. The glittering sorcery sands taunted them.

Brigitta's gaze went from the lakebed to Jarlath's hip, where he wore his dagger. Was it sharp enough to chisel petrified sands?

"Don't even think about it," muttered Jarlath, leaning back against the log. "You'd be invaded by nightwalkers before you even reached the sands."

"I thought nightwalkers were just your non-ascended spirits?" she asked, remembering the sensation of Jorris's undispersed energy in the lower chamber of the Hive. Skin-tingling and unpleasant, yes, but not dangerous.

"Nightwalkers can invade your mind!" said Thistle. "And take over your body!"

"Who told you that?" laughed Brigitta. "Do you know anyone whose mind was taken over by a nightwalker?"

"Well, no," said Thistle, "but Mabbe says . . ." She trailed off, as if contemplating the likelihood that Mabbe ever told them the truth.

Brigitta grabbed her dustmist canister and stood up, tucking the blanket around Thistle. "You know what I think?" She emptied the dustmist into the air and spread a tight, thin wall around the curious faeries, the best she could manage, having lost much of it in the sky above the warwumps. "I think you Watchers have your own kind of sorcery, but Mabbe is so threatened by it that she makes you fear it."

"Or punishes us for talking about it," offered Thistle.

Brigitta stepped back and held her hands in the mist. Using a transformation technique, she focused on the reflectivity of the water energy, creating a makeshift cloak. It was almost effortless, and she was impressed by her own skill. Maybe she was more relaxed. Or perhaps just getting used to the elements in Noe. She slowly twirled her fingers to finish the job, until her right hand stiffened and pain shot up her arm to the tear in her wing. She gritted her teeth as she stepped through.

"That will keep you mostly hidden," she said to the others, trying to shake off the pain. "Douse your globelights if you hear trouble. The light shines through a bit."

"Wait! Where are you going?" cried Thistle.

"Mabbe wants sorcery sands; I'm getting sorcery sands. Jarlath, loan me your knife."

Chapter Fourteen

Against Thistle's pleading, Brigitta struck out alone across the stretch of land that led to the dry lakebed, telling the others that if she did not return before sunbreak to go back to the Hollows without her. The moonslight guided her to the edge of the bowl. She studied the River That Runs Backwards, feeling its powerful draw. No slipups, she told herself. Not this time.

She fluttered over the edge and down the inside of the bowl. The pull of the river-wind increased. Jarlath was right; at night the river was stronger. But she knew water, she told herself. She and water had an understanding.

"Remember me, Mad River?" said Brigitta. "You almost ate my sister once."

She dropped down closer to the lakebed where the air was calmer. She'd have to walk, as her wings weren't strong enough to fight the river's pull. The inner bowl was steeper than she remembered. She grabbed onto an old root sticking out of the side, but it broke away in her hand, throwing her off balance. She steadied herself before continuing, vowing to be more careful.

As she descended, she scanned the lakebed for balanced sands. Sorcery sands, she corrected herself and almost laughed out loud. These naive faeries thought everything was magical.

Hush, she scolded herself. She wasn't any better than they were, Ondelle would say. She pictured her High Priestess assisting the little weavers in the Colony. She was going to save Ondelle, find the Purview, and leave this place. Except she had promised she would help get rid of Mabbe. And rescue Ferris.

"First things first," she muttered. "And one thing at a time."

Most of the sands at the top of the bowl had been gathered, as there were few sparkles remaining in the moonlight. The rest were closer down into the bowl, closer to the river, where fewer faeries had tread.

She spied a little vein of shimmering sands down to her right. She looked up at the moons, nearly across the break in the clouds. As fast as she could, she raced around the side of the bowl, flitting her wings to help her scramble across the rough surface. When she was directly above the sparkling sands, she descended, keeping an eye on the shifting river.

As she clambered down, the wind pulled harder and harder. It picked her up by her wings, and she skidded down until her feet hit a protrusion in the rocky bed. She pulled her wings in tightly and dropped all the way to the ground, grabbing hold of the outcropping until she could get her bearings. The vein of sorcery sands was only a few steps away.

She crawled toward the bright specks, her right arm and wing stinging with the poison of the sliverleaf cuts.

"Hagspit," she swore. The sorcery sands were too scattered about. With the knife in her left hand, she carefully chiseled around one cluster of sands, hoping the vein was deep. As she chiseled, her hourglass necklace began to warm.

"What?" Brigitta asked her hourglass sands. "Do you

recognize your kin?"

Her skin suddenly prickled. A dark shape shifted in the periphery of her vision, and she glanced up from her work. Nothing was there.

"Just the spirits of the dead," she murmured to herself and went back to her task. "Nothing to get excited about."

She chiseled as quickly as she could around the vein. It was a good sized chunk of rock, but she had no idea if it contained enough balanced sands to appease, or at least fool, Mabbe. She tucked the knife away and pulled at the loosened rock. Just as it broke free from the lakebed, the moons disappeared in the clouds, and the world went black.

She held the rock in her left hand and reached into her pocket for her shard of globelight with her right. Pain shot from the wound in her wing to her fingertips, and the shard slipped from her hand. She reached after it, but it was gone.

The river sounded louder than ever in the dark, and she could feel its pull. She looked up and the sky was impossibly black. Maybe she could move the clouds herself. She tried to feel the cloud energy, but she was too disoriented. As she sat there, unable to see an arm's length away, she felt a movement, then another, on either side of her. She couldn't tell how far away the beasts were, but she could tell that they were large. She began to wonder if undispersed spirits really could invade her mind and body in Noe.

Suddenly very afraid, she turned to go back up the way she came. Using the incline of the lakebed as her guide, she crawled as fast as she could while holding onto the rock. Then she realized she had left the knife behind, but there was no going back.

Her hand landed on something scaly. It slid out from

under her and she felt a claw strike out against her arm. She shrieked and leapt up, fluttering away from the beast. She tried to fly forward, but the river-wind was too strong. She fought to keep control of her wings. The rock slipped from her hand and tumbled into the darkness.

Brigitta struggled with all her might, but the wind was too strong. She felt herself weakening, her strength used up.

"No!" she cried into the darkness, tumbling backward.

A moment later, her body, then her head, struck something solid. The impact knocked the breath out of her, and everything blurred.

The object moved.

"I've got you now," a deep voice growled.

The hulking beast began to trudge forward as Brigitta blacked out.

❦

Brigitta felt the warmth of a fire and smelled the comforting aroma of toasted mushrooms. It must be a new recipe of her momma's, she thought, smiling to herself.

She opened her eyes to dancing flames and snuggled into the blanket wrapped around her. The thickness and weight of it were unfamiliar. It smelled like wet sand.

"You're awake," a low female voice broke the silence.

Brigitta turned her head to find a large gray beast kneeling over her. A baby rock dragon! She gasped and tried to sit up, but her head was too dizzy.

"It's all right, little faerie," said the beast, blinking her double eyelids, "you're safe."

Brigitta froze in confusion, her memory scattered.

162

Where was she and how did she get here?

The beast tilted her head, concern in her eyes. No, she wasn't a rock dragon at all. Her skin was like armor and covered only with a few brown straps that held a large pack across her back. Her body was thick and round, with sturdy pillars for legs that ended in webbed claws. Her head was small for the rest of her body, flattish and triangular, narrowing into a single horn above her lip.

"I'm Abdira," she said and nodded her head toward another beast on the other side of the fire. "He's Uwain."

Brigitta slowly righted herself and looked at Uwain, a darker, slightly larger version of Abdira. He had two horns, one above his lip and one above and between his eyes. He grunted at Brigitta.

"He's much friendlier than he looks," said Abdira. "Are you hungry?"

Brigitta sat up, trying to remember what had happened and how she had gotten from—where had she last been? "Where—how—" she began.

"There, there." Abdira handed her a wooden bowl of steaming mushrooms. "Have some hrooshka. It'll warm your insides. This place is horribly chilly."

Brigitta took the bowl and stared into the steamy mushrooms. Her head was so fuzzy she didn't know if she had come from a dream or was having one now, but she did have a sense that she was supposed to be doing something important.

"You smacked yourself pretty good. We're sorry about that." Abdira smiled, and even though there was something a bit reptilian about it, it was a trustworthy smile.

Brigitta nipped tentatively at a spoonful of mushrooms.

They were meaty and soft and cooked perfectly. As she lifted her spoon again, pain shot through her hand and up to her wing. She dropped the spoon and stared at the back of her hand. A shiny silver scar shone on her skin. She looked up at her wing. In the middle of the dark green destiny marking, through the center of the eye glyph, was another thin silver scar. The haze lifted and she remembered where she was, and that before she lost consciousness, she was hurtling toward the River That Runs Backwards.

"The sorcery sands!" she exclaimed. "Ondelle!"

The two beasts exchanged looks.

Brigitta handed the bowl back to Abdira. "I have to get back to my friends."

Abdira pushed the bowl back again. "There is time. You need strength. Eat first."

Uwain grunted again, and Brigitta looked back and forth at the gray beasts. Abdira nodded at Uwain, and he slowly sat forward and cleared his throat.

"When you are called by whisper light," he began in his low gruff voice, "and know it through the fate of kin, you'll travel back to times of old, and serve to balance all again."

Brigitta nearly dropped the bowl of mushrooms. "Where did you— how did you— that's a faerie prophecy!"

"It's a Nhord prophecy as well," Abdira said.

"It's no prophecy," corrected Uwain, "it's a promise. A promise from the Nhords to the Ancient Ones."

"To the Ancients?" stammered Brigitta. "But who are you? Are you from Noe?"

"No," Uwain said and waved his webbed paws vaguely to the north. "We're from far away."

Abdira leaned in closer. "We're here to serve."

164

Uwain stood up. He wasn't much taller this way, with his stumpy pillar-legs. "Born to serve the destiny that awaits."

"That's right," agreed Abdira. "We are here to serve. Service is our highest endeavor."

Brigitta's head was spinning, and not just from her concussion. What in Faweh did these Nhord beasts have to do with any of this?

"But why did you come here?" she asked.

"For you, dear." Abdira smiled down at her. "We came here for you."

Uwain placed a web-clawed foot over the fire and stamped it out, saving one long stick as a torchlight, which he secured to his harness. Abdira hauled her large frame off the ground, and the three of them began their journey across the edge of the crater. The River That Runs Backwards spouted wildly in the distance. The moons were long gone, and the clouds were blacker than ever.

Brigitta mulled over what she had learned from the Nhords. For hundreds of seasons, passing the promise from generation to generation, two Nhords had always served as Sentries, waiting for a whisper light to open the Purview and give them what they called a "knowing" of where to go.

"Go forward, into the Purview, your destiny awaits?" asked Brigitta and the two Nhords grunted. "That's the only instruction you were given?"

"Simple words are best," said Abdira.

"Well, it's not much to go on."

"We're here to serve," Uwain repeated for the umpteenth time.

"And this Purview brought you here?" Brigitta asked.

"You stepped into it and appeared here?"

"Yes," confirmed Abdira, "and, hopplebuggers, it was a strange sensation!"

"Strange and uncomfortable," agreed Uwain.

"You didn't use Blue Spell to get here? No other magic?"

"Nhords have no magic," Uwain said. "Wisdom prevails over magic," he added, as if automatically repeating some Nhord adage.

"We did have our rings," Abdira added, pulling a ring from a small pouch on her strap. The crystal gem sparkled off of Uwain's torch. "A gift from the Ancients."

If this Purview was some quick way to travel, Brigitta thought, admiring the shimmering jewel, could anyone use it? Did she have to have this "knowing" or just the whisper light?

Brigitta stopped and the Nhords stopped with her. She had thought Ondelle simply made the whisper light disappear, but she had really put it into her necklace. Ondelle had hidden the whisper light and then protected it with that spell. Which meant she hadn't trusted Brigitta with this knowledge, but more importantly, it meant Ondelle must have known they could get through with it. Did this mean they could both get back home? Could the rebel faeries come with them?

Her excitement grew as the seeds of a new plan were planted in her mind. She rushed forward as a dark thought passed. Once the Purview was open, would Croilus or Mabbe be able to use it as well?

As Brigitta approached the dustmist wall, fading in places so that there were moments of light and shadow, she made a decision. She would tell the rebels all about the Purview. They trusted her, and she needed to trust them.

She passed through and found Roane asleep under a blanket. Jarlath and Thistle were whispering so intensely over their shards of globelight that Brigitta's entrance startled them.

"Brigitta!" Thistle flew to her and hugged her. "We were so worried. I was about to go search for you. Where did you get that blanket?"

Brigitta looked down at Abdira's blanket just as the two Nhords appeared. Jarlath and Thistle shrieked in surprise.

"It's all right," Brigitta assured them. "They're friendly. Abdira and Uwain, this is Jarlath, Thistle, and the sleeping boy is Roane."

"We're here to serve," said Abdira and Uwain, bowing slightly.

"They say that a lot," Brigitta said as she sat down.

Jarlath and Thistle stood with mouths gaping as the two Nhords plopped themselves down behind Brigitta.

"They saved me from getting sucked into the river," said Brigitta. "They came from across the ocean." She leaned forward. "They came through a Purview."

Thistle and Jarlath slowly sank back down to the ground, eyes wide with disbelief, as Brigitta explained all that had happened at the river. Thistle wrapped her arms around herself as she listened, and Jarlath, for once, was stunned into silence.

"I think it could be our way home." Brigitta took Thistle's hand. "A way you could come with me. And I think I know how to open it."

"You think?" Jarlath crossed his arms over his chest.

"Jarlath!" exclaimed Thistle. "We could take my momma and Roane and Ferris and Devin and leave this place!"

"Don't get your hopes up," Jarlath warned. "If it doesn't work she can go back to the White Forest and forget all about us, but we'd be traitors. We'd have to run away, and you wouldn't last three nights out there." Jarlath gestured to the world around them.

"We came through a Purview," said Abdira matter-of-factly.

"We don't even know where it is!" cried Jarlath. "We don't even know where to look for it. Croilus has been searching for seasons and hasn't found it yet."

"First, we rescue Ondelle. If anyone can find it, she can."

Brigitta took hold of her necklace as everyone sank into silence, contemplating this new information. She had to think of a way to sneak into the Hollows. Ondelle had said to leave without her, but she wouldn't. She hadn't even let Ondelle tell her how. And even if she had Blue Spell in her necklace, Brigitta didn't know how to use it. Only Ondelle and the Elders and the Ancients knew—

The Ancients!

She looked into Jarlath's eyes. She remembered her idea about the voices.

"Give me your hands," she said to Jarlath.

Jarlath hesitated, and then held out his hands, palms up. She took them, and a shock of warmth shot up her arms and rested there.

"You've spent your entire life blocking out these so called mad voices," said Brigitta. "I don't think they're mad voices at all. I think what you hear are echoes of the voices of the Ancients."

Jarlath pulled his hands back, but Brigitta held them firmly in place. "Listen to me, it makes sense," she explained. "It's the only way Croilus would know so much. Because he listened to the voices. It's why Mabbe stopped the ascensions, because she was afraid you'd listen too.

"And I think it's part of why I'm here," said Brigitta. "Finding you, bringing you back with us through this Purview, reconnecting with the Ancients . . ."

"I don't know," Jarlath murmured.

"I think Mabbe has made you distrust the Ancients so you wouldn't leave."

"We are loyal to the Ancients," Uwain added in his gruff voice. "Many sand cycles ago, long before our grandparents' memories, we Nhords visited with them in the Valley of Noe."

"And how did their ancestors get here?" Brigitta asked. "Look at them, they couldn't have flown or swum. It must have been through these Purviews."

Jarlath's eyes softened as he contemplated Brigitta's logic.

"The Ancients left a message with the Nhords. They were sent here to help—to *serve* us. If the Ancients were as bad as Mabbe says, why would they do this?"

She concentrated on his crystal blue eyes. "Please, you have to let your mind go. I need to get inside."

Jarlath looked, for the first time since she had met him, truly frightened. Thistle encouraged him with a smile.

He nodded and took a deep breath. When he exhaled, his body heaved relief, as if it had been carrying a heavy burden for a long time and had finally set it down. His grip loosened and the energy flowed between their hands until they were connected with a band of it, warm and vibrating.

169

Voices ghosted around them. Thousands of echoes filled an eternity of space. She felt Jarlath withdrawing, but Brigitta held him in place.

"It's all right," she murmured. "Just keep looking at me."

She concentrated on her hourglass and let go of all thought that this idea of hers wouldn't work. That it was too dangerous. That she would lose her way back. Shhhhh, she thought, focus and use everything you know.

She was going to get to the Ancients through empathing Jarlath.

You are mad, she thought, and let that go. She watched the thought float away on a wave of blue light. The voices seemed to emanate from the light. She glided into the wave of light, and it lifted her.

Her body felt electrified by the voices. Then they were resonating within her and around her at the same time. She was part of them and it was beautiful. It was safe. She had never felt so at peace. She could stay there. Yes, stay there forever.

Do not forget yourself, Ondelle's warning broke in from somewhere inside her. *Anchor yourself.*

An anchor. She had used her hourglass. But she wasn't holding her hourglass. She was holding Jarlath's hands. And his hands were holding –

She was looking back on herself, through his eyes. She felt an odd mixture of feelings. There was fear and hope. There was anger and sadness.

Now what? Jarlath's thoughts reverberated in her mind.

She concentrated on the wave of voices. They were weak, she realized, pulling away. There were so many of them that they sounded loud and powerful, but they weren't. She got the sense that if she used their energy, it would weaken them still. But she had no choice.

From the part of her that was now one with Jarlath, she concentrated on her hourglass. She had no idea how much energy it would take; this wasn't anything she had been taught. She let go of that thought as she invited the Ancients to join her. All connected—the hourglass, Brigitta, Jarlath, and the Ancients—she stated her intention: transformation. She wanted to become like one of them.

For a brief moment, her body went numb and her mind blank. Then, as quickly as it had happened, everything returned to normal. She let go of Jarlath's hands.

Thistle's mouth dropped open and her hands went to her own face. "Your eyes," she whispered.

Brigitta looked over her shoulders to her wings. The destiny markings were gone, and her wings were now a grayish green, but the silver scar remained at the top of her right one.

"I don't believe it," said Jarlath.

"You look just like a Watcher!" exclaimed Thistle.

"Exactly," Brigitta said and lay back, completely exhausted, onto Abdira's foreleg.

Chapter Fifteen

The Nhords left just before dawn. It had been decided that they would stay on the south side of the hill overlooking the lakebed, above the area where Ondelle and Brigitta had appeared. They were a bit too obvious to travel through the forest with the band of faeries.

"We will hide ourselves," agreed Uwain, "until we are needed."

"Hide yourselves?" laughed Brigitta. "That I'd like to see."

"So you shall," said Abdira as the two beasts trudged away without so much as a goodbye.

"Your new friends are a little strange," pondered Thistle, "but I like them. I'm going to call them the Huggabeasts."

Jarlath groaned. "The Huggabeasts?"

"Yeah," said Thistle, "they're beastly, but you still want to hug them."

"Why do you always have to rename everything?" he asked.

Thistle shrugged. "We have to make some kind of fun in this world, Mossbottom."

"I agree," said Brigitta. "Mossbottom."

Roane awoke confused, yet amused, by Brigitta's disguise. After a meager breakfast, they all discussed their plan. They had to get Ondelle away from the Colony and into the Hollows where Thistle's mother could hide them all until nightfall, when they would escape. Jarlath would distract Mabbe by giving her a detailed report as to what had happened with Croilus, including a lengthy story about how he had been captured and had only escaped because of the rain calling forth the warwumps.

"I'll tell her I left you there with a reminder of your deal," he concluded. "Technically, you still have another sun to bring back the sands, Brigitta."

"You shouldn't call me that," Brigitta said. She thought for a moment. "Call me Narine."

They waited until the first shift of chiselers had gone down into the lakebed, and then they made their way to the Hollows. They found a hiding place behind an uprooted tree, where they could spy on the entrance.

"Wait here until the last chiselers get back," Jarlath whispered. "I should be able to speak with Mabbe before then." Jarlath put his arm around Roane's shoulders. "If anything goes wrong, Roane will come out instead, and you will leave immediately."

Brigitta resisted the urge to say that Jarlath couldn't tell her what to do.

"How will you get a message to my mother?" asked Thistle.

"Bird drops," swore Jarlath, "that's right."

"You won't be able to speak with her?" asked Brigitta.

"Not likely. Mabbe doesn't like her guards to socialize with the servants. It makes her suspicious."

"I'll go up and talk with her," suggested Thistle.

"No," insisted Jarlath, "I don't want to leave Brigitta alone out here."

"Can Roane get to her? He's not suspicious."

"Sure, but—" he gestured to Roane's silent face.

Brigitta reached into her pack, pulled out Mousha's greenish-brown disc, and waggled it. "Use this."

Roane screwed up his face at the smell.

"What is it?" Thistle asked, holding her nose.

"It's a, uh . . . vorple blat. An invention of my poppa's," said Brigitta. "Where will we meet her?"

"In the Kitchen Cozy," said Thistle. Off Jarlath's look, she added, "She'll know what that means."

Brigitta held up the vorple blat and whispered into it, "Meet Thistle in the Kitchen Cozy after dinner." She balled up the rubbery disc and handed it to Jarlath. "Have him throw it at her."

"Throw it?" Jarlath asked as he took the stinkball.

"Make sure she's alone and near a wall. When it hits the wall, it will repeat my message three times, but that's it."

"Your poppa is a genius," said Thistle as Jarlath wrapped up the ball and placed it in Roane's pocket.

"Yes, he is."

⚜

Brigitta and Thistle flew high into the trees toward the Colony. Thistle was much stronger than she looked and wasn't even breathing heavily when they reached the top. They were about to step into the nest-like grounds when Thistle put her arm out.

"Your disguise," whispered Thistle. "You're too . . . grand."

A full head and shoulders taller than Thistle, and definitely better fed, Brigitta hunched down and pulled her wings and stomach in.

They didn't see Ondelle on the grounds, so they marched over to her prison tree. There were two Watchers posted outside.

"Watcher Thistle and I have been instructed to bring the large faerie woman to Mabbe for questioning," said Brigitta, giving her iciest glare to the smaller Watcher.

"We need her there in a moonbeat or she'll have all our wings," growled Thistle, and Brigitta nearly laughed, surprised at the ferocity of the little faerie's voice.

The two Watchers looked at each other.

"I've never seen you before," said the larger of the two.

"We've been transferred from patrol to Mabbe's guard," said Brigitta.

"From night patrol," added Thistle, gesturing to Brigitta's scarred wing.

"Is she well-restrained?" asked Brigitta. "I hear she knows powerful magic."

"I checked the bindings myself," the Watcher said.

"We'll see about that!" spat Thistle. "Hand me the key and step aside."

He handed Thistle a key, and she and Brigitta stepped inside. In the mesh cage, Ondelle sat alone, cross-legged, against the inside of the tree. She appeared to be asleep, but Brigitta knew better. She opened her intense eyes as Brigitta approached.

"Ondelle of Grioth," whispered Brigitta, "this is Thistle of Noe."

Thistle gave a small bow as Ondelle rose. The little Watcher looked up in awe at the incredibly tall faerie with black eyes and bright gold markings on her fiery wings.

"We're here to rescue you," Thistle said.

Ondelle reached through the cage and touched Brigitta's face with her bound hands. Brigitta wasn't entirely sure Ondelle was glad to see her, but she could sense her High Priestess wasn't at all surprised.

She could also sense something else. Ondelle's energy was weak.

Thistle unlocked the cell and unbound her feet. "We'll have to leave the hand and wing bindings for now."

They led Ondelle past the Watcher guards and into one of the transport trees. This time, Brigitta was prepared for the journey through the trunk. She closed her eyes as the howling began. The wind surged around her and wrapped her in a blanket of air, tightening and pulling. A moment later, all was still again.

"This way," whispered Thistle.

She guided them out of the trunk and right into another Watcher. Thistle gasped and then recovered. "Watch where you're going!" she growled and pushed past, yanking Ondelle with her.

They continued through the passageway and then slipped silently around a corner. They stopped and listened for a moment.

"You're like two people," whispered Brigitta. "I didn't know you had it in you, Thistle."

"It's easy. I just pretend I'm Jarlath," she said, giggling.

"Where are we?" asked Brigitta.

"Near the servants' burl." Thistle turned and removed the rest of Ondelle's restraints.

Ondelle heaved a sigh and stretched out her wings. They were enormous, reaching across the entire passageway. She pulled them back in and thanked Thistle with a pat on her arm.

They continued quickly, turning another corner, until Thistle held up her hand for them to stop. She looked both ways, twice, down the passageway.

"In here," she finally said, moving a chunk of wood aside and slipping into a narrow crack in the burl.

Brigitta struggled into the crack and was surprised that Ondelle could fit at all. Ondelle replaced the wood behind her, and they squeezed themselves through the gap.

"We're both going to get stuck," Brigitta said.

"Just a little farther," Thistle replied.

A moment later the crack opened up into a mini-burl, a small natural chamber. There was just enough room in the dimly lit space for the three of them to sit down. As Brigitta's eyes adjusted to the darkness, she noticed drawings on the inside of the walls. Seasons and seasons' worth of a child's artwork, faded with time.

"Momma hid me in here to keep me out of trouble," whispered Thistle. "I used to ask too many questions."

"I know someone like that," said Brigitta.

There was a scraping noise as something heavy was dragged across a floor. The wall began to move. A large piece of the burl fell away, and standing in the light was a round faerie woman.

"Oh, lola!" she cried, and for a moment, silhouetted in the light, Brigitta thought she saw her own mother standing there in her cooking tunic.

Granae reached into the wall for her daughter. She was an older version of Thistle, a little paler, much larger, but unmistakably kin. Her crystal blue eyes were faded but shone with delight as she held her daughter.

Brigitta choked back tears, hearing Granae use the familiar pet name. She recovered by stepping out of the chamber and helping Ondelle do the same. When Ondelle emerged, Granae gave a deep bow.

"Momma, this is Ondelle, High Priestess of the White Forest, and Brigitta, Second Elder Apprentice."

"I heard stories of stunning visitors from the north."

Ondelle smiled sweetly and gestured to her mouth.

"Yes, a shame," said Granae, "a vile practice of Mabbe's."

Brigitta looked around the kitchen. It wasn't nearly as homey as her momma's, but it was large and functional. The handle of the heavy wooden door was barred with a sturdy chair. There were jars of strange roots and herbs, mostly green-gray, pots and bowls in rows along the wall, a large vat bubbling away, and a table in the middle piled with an odd assortment of vegetables. She looked back at the hole in the burl and the shelving that had been pushed aside to expose it.

"You got our message," said Thistle.

Granae pulled the vorple blat out of her pocket. "Roane nearly scared me out of my skin when he threw this thing at me."

The stench of the vorple blat was not disguised by the aroma of the food. Brigitta took it from Granae and quickly wrapped it up in a cloth and tucked it into her bag.

"And no one else heard it?" asked Brigitta.

Granae shook her head as Brigitta's stomach growled.

"Oh, shame on me," cooed Granae, "you must be famished."

Granae piled some meaty nuts onto a tray, as well as

three steaming bowls of the stew she had brewing, while Thistle and Brigitta relayed their recent adventures. Granae nearly dropped the bowl of stew when Brigitta mentioned the warwumps.

"You called the rain?" she asked, amazed. "You called the warwumps?"

Ondelle's eyes communicated the pride she had in Brigitta, and Brigitta shrugged, cheeks red under her gaze.

Granae touched Brigitta's wings. "And you used magic to transform yourself?"

"She called the voices," Thistle whispered.

"Shhhhh!" Granae hissed, eyes panicked. She looked behind her as if someone might be listening.

"We're all going to sneak away tonight along with Jarlath and Roane," said Thistle. "Gather your things, Momma."

"Oh, no, lola, the outer realm is no place for an old faerie like me." Granae lifted the tray and carried it to the chamber in the wall.

"Then we'll come back for you," said Brigitta, "when we've figured out a way to get home."

"Please," said Granae turning to Ondelle, desperation in her voice. "Please, just take my Thistle and go back to your forest. Don't risk your lives for me. You may know sorcery, but Mabbe has too many guardians and no mercy."

"I won't leave you, Momma," said Thistle, tears forming in her eyes.

"Lola, you're too sweet for this dark world," Granae said. "I need you to have a better life than this."

Thistle buried her face in her mother's tunic. "We'll get rid of Mabbe, you'll see."

"You know, I've thought of poisoning Mabbe many

times," said Granae, putting her arms around Thistle, "but if I failed and she found out, she'd get to me through my daughter. That's how she works."

Ondelle nodded and took Granae's hand. Something knowing passed between them. If Thistle would be punished for Granae's rebellion, surely Granae would be punished for Thistle's.

Like I would have been, thought Brigitta, if Ondelle had attacked Mabbe. She looked at her High Priestess with a new understanding.

Granae ushered them back into the mini-burl. "I'll let you know when it's all right to emerge. For now, you'd better stow away."

The three scooted into the nook, Thistle giving her mother a tearful hug before climbing back inside. They sat down to eat as Granae closed up the hole and pushed the shelving back in front of it.

After their meal, the three faeries spent a cramped evening in the Kitchen Cozy as Thistle alternated between crying about leaving her momma and swearing to return for her. Brigitta offered up the last few pieces of suclaide to help calm the young faerie. Eventually, they drifted off to sleep with the comforting aromas of Granae's kitchen seeping through cracks in the burl.

In the middle of the night they were awoken by the sound of the shelves being slid away. They blinked their eyes into the light when the burl opened. It was Jarlath and Roane. Roane looked up at Ondelle with such wide eyes Brigitta thought they would pop right out of his head. Jarlath signaled for them all to keep quiet as he led them from the kitchen into the passageway.

"What happened with Mabbe?" whispered Brigitta.

"My report seemed to appease her," Jarlath whispered, "although she doubts your success with Croilus."

"Has anyone reported Ondelle missing?"

"I haven't heard a word about it," Jarlath responded.

"Mabbe either doesn't know or doesn't want anyone to think there's been an escape," said Brigitta. "We have to get out of here regardless."

"We'll stick to the servants' burl and exit out the north window," whispered Jarlath. "We'll have to slip past the Watchers posted around the Hollows, which wouldn't be so difficult except for . . . " Jarlath glanced at Ondelle.

Ondelle stood out from the rest of them like the shining Palace at Croilus. She would never blend in with the Watchers, even with gray skin and crystal blue eyes.

"We'll just have to be quick," whispered Brigitta.

"And stick to the shadows," added Thistle.

They made it to the end of the passageway and flew out a small window. It was cold outside. Only a few lanterns shone from the dark like yellow eyes. Jarlath turned and handed a vine to Roane, who handed it to Brigitta.

"We can't risk any lights. Take hold of the vine so we can stick together," said Jarlath.

Brigitta passed the vine to Ondelle and Thistle. Jarlath dropped straight down through the trees, and Roane followed. Brigitta felt the tug of the vine and fell in after them. She let the vine lead her down and around several trees, branches tugging at her hair and tunic.

They landed at the base of an ancient tree. Jarlath pulled on a branch and the bark parted, leaving an opening in the trunk.

"This leads to one of the sky farms." Jarlath gestured for the others to enter the tree. "No one will be there at night."

"Jarlath," said Thistle, "we're not flying above the forest, are we?"

"It's the only way to avoid the night patrols." Jarlath closed the trunk, and all light disappeared.

"But, Jarlath!"

A slice of globelight lit up in Jarlath's hand, illuminating Thistle's frightened face. Brigitta lit another shard and handed it to Ondelle, then lit another for herself.

"What's wrong with flying above the forest?" asked Brigitta.

"The birds," Thistle shuddered. "They feed at night."

Roane frantically pulled on Jarlath's tunic.

"It'll be fine!" growled Jarlath to Roane.

Thistle and Roane looked unconvinced.

"Would you rather be taken back to the Hollows?" he asked. "Because we all know how that will end."

He flew up through the tree, and the vine yanked Roane from his feet. Brigitta followed, then Ondelle and Thistle. As they fluttered up, the trunk grew narrower but still left plenty of room to fly. Brigitta let her finger slide along the inside of the trunk, thinking that finally something was going right and that maybe they would all be safe in the White Forest soon.

They broke through an opening in the top of the tree and into the night air. The clouds were scattered above, and the stars shone down reassuringly. Everyone let go of the vine, and Jarlath wound it in his hands. They landed on a solid field spread across the tops of the trees.

"Wow," said Brigitta, "I've never seen such a thing."

"The sky farms are the only way our crops can get enough light . . . " Thistle's voice trailed off as a *craw* sounded in the distance.

The field stretched out for a great expanse in front of them, row upon row of grasses and herbs and roots and vegetables. There were even whole fruit trees. Brigitta reached down and touched the field. It was earth.

"Dirt!" she exclaimed, letting it slip through her fingers.

"What else would we grow things in?" asked Jarlath. "I suppose in your forest everything grows in the air itself?"

There were two more *craws*, this time closer. Roane grabbed Brigitta's hand, and Thistle held her breath.

"This way." Jarlath took off over the field as two shadows darted from the trees.

Everyone followed silently, the *craws* growing more distant as the faeries flew past the farms.

"We'll stay over the forest, then drop down outside the lakebed and meet up with your friends."

"The Huggabeasts," said Brigitta.

Thistle laughed nervously.

The air that high was strangely light, very different from below. Below the trees, Brigitta's wings felt as if they were slogging through stew. Up above the trees, it felt like the air wasn't heavy enough, and she had to flutter her wings twice as fast to stay afloat. She watched as Thistle and Roane struggled to fly.

"They need to rest, Jarlath," said Brigitta, rushing to catch up with him.

"There's no place to land now," said Jarlath through labored breath. "The branches are too weak."

Roane started to tremble, his wings working frantically.

Ondelle slipped under Roane and caught him on her back. He held on and pulled in his wings.

"Not much farther," huffed Jarlath. "Keep—"

There was a loud cry, and a dozen black-winged creatures erupted from the trees, *craw-crawing* in a frenzy. Their red eyes gleamed in the moonlight as they descended upon the faeries, talons extended. Thistle screamed as one attacked her wing, pulling at it with its long beak.

Brigitta swatted at the bird with her shard of globelight, striking the back of its solid head. It let go of Thistle and turned in the air, screeching. It was almost as big as Roane, with mottled black feathers, and as it opened its beak in distress, Brigitta saw that the ugly creature had teeth.

Two more shot after Jarlath. He dropped into the trees and yanked off a branch, swatting at the beasts. Three attacked Ondelle, and she managed to strike one with her fist, sending it plummeting into the trees. With her wing injured, Thistle collided into Ondelle, and Roane slipped off her back, falling through the air. He tried to catch himself, but he was too tired and the air too thin.

"Nooo!" cried Jarlath as he dove after him.

The other three followed, and Brigitta managed to grab Roane's arm just before he hit a thick branch. They tumbled through the air, catching on the trees as they fell. Jarlath grabbed Roane's other arm, and they all steadied themselves. Ondelle swooped down beside them, leading a whimpering Thistle, whose left wing was badly torn.

The faeries quickly descended and landed heavily on the ground. They all sat there, catching their breaths. Ondelle placed her hands on Thistle's wing, and she stopped crying. Brigitta scowled at Jarlath as he checked Roane for damage.

His arms were scraped and his tunic ripped, but he was not seriously hurt. Jarlath gave a satisfied nod.

"Well, we're past the guard perimeter of the Hollows," he said. "We can stick to the forest from here."

Ondelle gestured to Thistle's wing.

"We're not going anywhere until Thistle and Roane are rested," said Brigitta.

"We're not safe here," said Jarlath.

"Do you want to get us all killed!" hissed Brigitta.

"Not as much as you want us all to get caught!"

"Don't be an idiot!" shot Brigitta.

Ondelle placed one hand on each of the faeries' shoulders and shook her head.

"Stop it, you two," said Thistle. "It's fine. I'm fine."

Jarlath's crystal blue eyes narrowed, and Brigitta glared back at him. She and Ondelle turned to double check on Roane, who was staring past them with terror in his eyes.

They all followed his gaze. A sickly colored Watcher stood between two trees, grinning at them. He gestured at Jarlath with a dagger. "I see traitors run in your family, Watcher Jarlath."

Jarlath straightened up to his full height and drew his own dagger. "I see ugliness runs in yours."

The Watcher snorted and pulled out a shield. He gestured to Ondelle. "There's a big reward for this one's wings, you know."

Jarlath stepped forward with his shield up. "Is there now?"

"Thought we wouldn't realize she was missing?"

"I was betting you were as stupid as you were repulsive."

Just as Jarlath stepped forward for a fight, eight more

Watchers descended from the trees with an immense net, knocking them all to the ground and ensnaring them. The ugly Watcher looked down at Jarlath and raised his dagger over his head.

"No!" cried Brigitta as she struggled to free herself.

The Watcher plunged the knife into the ground next to Jarlath's face. "You're lucky the reward is doubled if I bring you traitors back alive."

Chapter Sixteen

It seemed like every Hollows Watcher was stuffed into Mabbe's burl, glaring at the captured faeries with their crystal blue eyes. From along the walls, three rows deep, they surrounded the prisoners, who sat together in a circle in the center of the floor, hands and feet bound. Mabbe meant to make examples out of them.

With Ondelle behind her, Brigitta could not see her High Priestess. She leaned back to feel her warmth, to get some kind of strength, but in her despair, she could no longer focus her energy. She remembered Gola's courage potion, but there was no way she could reach it, since her pack now lay at the foot of Mabbe's chair.

It didn't matter any more, she thought, all was lost.

"So!" Mabbe exclaimed, her gruesome face appearing in front of Brigitta, wrinkles wrapped around her sharp-toothed grin, cloudy eyes wild. She cocked her head and sniffed the air so close to Brigitta's face she could see the dark pores on the end of her nose.

"Interesting. I underestimated you, faerie. How do you like being a Watcher? Are you interested in joining my clan?" Mabbe cackled and gestured to Dugald and Veena, who howled along with her.

"You're crafty, but not very smart." Mabbe turned serious and the clouds of her eyes slowed. "You don't keep promises very well, do you?"

"Only promises to my High Priestess and the Ancients." Brigitta stuck her chin out defiantly.

"Yes, the Ancients, who abandoned you." Mabbe gave an exaggerated pout. "Just like they abandoned all the others." She waved her scepter to the faeries around the room. "The Ancients promised to protect us all, and what did they do? They forgot about us!"

Mabbe nodded for her two companions to approach. They stepped down from their chairs and glided to Ondelle, lifting her away from the others. In one fluid motion, Dugald sliced Ondelle's hand bonds, pushed her to her knees in front of Brigitta, and held her in place.

Mabbe held out her hand, and Veena placed a long white dagger in it. She reached down and placed the tip of it against Brigitta's cheek. It was ice cold.

"One thing you'll learn about me, Watcher Brigitta, is that I always keep my promises."

Mabbe twisted around and brought the dagger down. Brigitta screamed as one of Ondelle's beautiful red wings dropped to the floor.

In shock, Ondelle swooned as Brigitta struggled with her bonds. The hourglass necklace burned into her chest, her head grew dizzy, eyes burning with tears. No, no, no, this couldn't be happening! She could feel Roane trembling on one side of her and Thistle gasping for breath on the other.

Mabbe picked Ondelle's wing up off the ground and fanned the air with it a few times. "A fine addition to my collection!" She shrieked with delight and tossed it to the crowd.

Despair flooded Brigitta as Ondelle collapsed in a heap

at Mabbe's feet. She forced herself to look at the injury, but Ondelle wasn't bleeding.

"No blood," she whispered.

"It's a frore dagger," Jarlath said. "It freezes the wound."

"Pick her up," Mabbe directed her two Watcher companions. They dragged Ondelle up off the floor and placed her in front of Brigitta again.

Ondelle lifted her head, her black eyes as wild as Mabbe's. The look pierced straight to Brigitta's heart, and something stirred deep within her.

"Shall I spare her life?" pondered Mabbe, tapping the dagger against her own lips. The clouds of her eyes parted, revealing a full orange and a full blue moon.

"Death to the sorceress!" called a male Watcher from the back of the room, and the other Watchers shouted agreement.

Gathering her strength, Ondelle straightened up to her full height. Wings or no wings, she was the tallest faerie in the room. She looked around and the room grew silent as each Watcher came under her gaze. Then, she dropped down and grabbed hold of Brigitta's hourglass necklace.

Smoke rose from between Ondelle's fingers. The smell of burning flesh filled Brigitta's nostrils as Ondelle held her in place with her black moon eyes.

A whoosh of air burst from Brigitta's lungs, forcing her mouth open. *"And she who calls it by its name, who knows it by its forest kin, will travel back to times of old, and make the balance right again."*

Brigitta had no idea how the words formed in her mouth. Somehow, someone was speaking through her, as her, but the energy felt as if it belonged to her. Belonged, and didn't belong, like a long lost part of herself had returned.

"Treachery!" screamed Mabbe. "Myths from those Ancient fools!"

Brigitta's body and wings began to tingle. She looked down at her arm and saw its natural color return. She arched her head and witnessed the Elder symbol reemerge, the eye with four markings representing the four elements, a silver scar marring the glyph on her right wing. The markings shone brighter than ever before in the dusky burl.

The air whooshed back inside her, spreading throughout her body and limbs as if they were hollow branches. She felt a surge of new energy, and everything around her grew crisp and clear. Dull colors had more sharpness to them, and she could sense every faerie holding his or her breath. She could even see the specks of dust floating in the air.

Ondelle leaned back and opened her burnt and blistered palm. Everyone burst out at once in confusion.

"Quiet, all of you!" demanded Mabbe, lightning flashing in her eyes.

A voice reverberated in Brigitta's head, and she turned to Mabbe, who froze under her gaze. "*I'm back*," said Brigitta in a voice not her own. And then, without thinking, she laughed.

"No," uttered Mabbe, the clouds of her eyes quieting. "Impossible."

Ondelle bowed to Brigitta, deeply, her hair almost touching the floor.

The scepter and knife fell from Mabbe's hands and clattered on the floor. She reached out, gnarled hands trembling.

"Narine?" she whispered.

Head clear, Brigitta now saw Mabbe as she once was: a frightened Noe Valley faerie girl hiding out in the Hollows. Hiding from the Ancients when the world burst forth in its Great Cry.

In a sudden rage, Mabbe picked up the frore dagger and attacked Ondelle, slicing off her other wing. Ondelle once again fell to the floor, and Brigitta's heart tore open as she and the other captive faeries watched in horror.

Ondelle's shoulders shook, and a burst of energy darted from her lips and went dancing about the burl. The Watchers dodged it as it came at them. Mabbe screamed in frustration and drove the dagger into Ondelle's side.

Before Brigitta could react, four lesser faeries and two Watchers burst into the burl. "They're coming! They're coming!" they screamed, fluttering about in a panic.

"What's the meaning of this?" demanded Mabbe, catching one of the lesser faeries by the arm as she wove about the room. The tiny faerie was too worked up to speak. She sputtered for a moment, and Mabbe threw her into the crowd.

One of the Watchers landed in front of Mabbe. "Croilus! Croilus faeries! They're here!" He pointed to the entrance.

A dozen Croilus faeries tumbled into the room through the hollow tree. Several more burst from the enclave. They waved their firesticks, shooting flames at the Watchers along the wall, who barely had time to put up their shields and raise their daggers. Mabbe retrieved her scepter and whacked at two of the Croilus faeries with surprising strength.

Brigitta felt movement to her left. Roane had wiggled an arm free. He started to untie the knot in Brigitta's bonds, but his fingers slipped in his panic.

"Hurry, hurry!" Brigitta said as he struggled with the knot. The knot released and she pulled her arm out as Roane turned to work on Jarlath's bonds.

One of the Croilus faeries knocked the frore dagger out of Mabbe's hand and it clattered to the floor, just out of reach. Brigitta stretched her bound feet out but couldn't get to it. From the floor, Ondelle pushed herself up and with the last of her strength, she slid the dagger to Brigitta, who sliced open her remaining straps. She turned and sliced Thistle free.

"There!" came a voice from the tree. Brigitta twisted around to see the Watcher from Croilus's palace. He pointed his stick at Ondelle and Brigitta. "Bring them! Alive! Croilus wants them alive!"

More Croilus faeries streamed into the burl. Four of them scooped up Ondelle as Mabbe's faeries fought off their attackers. Mabbe pointed her scepter at one of the faeries carrying Ondelle, and a thick black stream snaked out, wrapping around his legs. He let go of Ondelle, and another Croilus faerie took his place.

Brigitta, Roane, Thistle, and Jarlath untangled themselves. Jarlath pushed a Croilus faerie out of the way and he tumbled over, dropping his firestick. Roane picked it up and tossed it to Jarlath.

Brigitta raced to save Ondelle, but Mabbe launched another stream of black, and it wrapped itself around Brigitta's neck, yanking her back as Ondelle was dragged from the burl. In a breathless struggle, Brigitta sliced at the snaky blackness with the frore dagger, and it cut through, releasing her. She lifted the dagger and rushed at Mabbe, but

Dugald intercepted her, grabbing her by the wrist. Stabs of sliverleaf poison pain shot from her hand, down her arm, to her scarred wing, and she dropped the knife.

"Alive, you say?" he bellowed. In an instant he had the frore dagger at her neck.

Firesticks in mid-strike, the Croilus faeries halted.

Jarlath split from his own fight and slipped in behind Mabbe, who spun around and turned her scepter on him. "Well done, my pet," she cooed to Dugald.

"Then we shall take her alive!" Dugald pushed Brigitta into two Croilus faeries, who placed their firesticks at her chest. "And bring her pack!"

"Dugald?" Mabbe turned to him, the clouds of her eyes gathering in a thick wet mass. "No . . . no, my pet . . . not you."

Dugald saluted Mabbe and grinned. "I'm afraid so, my Queen."

In a flash, Dugald and all of the uninjured Croilus faeries backed away and disappeared through the hollow tree, hauling Brigitta with them. She could hear Mabbe's anguished cries as they dropped into the darkness.

Chapter Seventeen

Ondelle was nowhere in sight. Inside the Croilus faerie formation, Brigitta flew with a heavy desperation. Her world was ripping apart. How could her High Priestess have lost her wings?

She glanced at her captors in the hazy morning light, not a friendly face among them. She had no plan, no hope, and yet something drove her on. Something held her together and charged her energy within.

"Narine," she said under her breath. Friend of Gola's, the Ancient High Sage's daughter. That's what Mabbe had whispered. But why?

They must have known each other back in the golden days of Noe, but how was that even possible? That would mean Mabbe was over 900 season cycles old. No faeries, not even Ancients, ever lived that long. Had Mabbe been using the sorcery sands to unnaturally extend her life? Brigitta shivered. Perhaps Mabbe was just an old body held together by bad magic.

The wind felt sharp and cool against every part of her exposed skin. She had thought it was fear that had given her sudden clarity back in Mabbe's burl, but the feeling hadn't left. Or rather, it was like it had always been there and had simply been awoken.

Back in the burl, the air had burst open inside her and

forced her to speak. And then . . . Brigitta searched for something to compare it to, a way to describe how it felt. Then she knew. It felt like the air energy had *merged* with her water energy.

"That's it!" she cried, startling the Croilus faeries.

"Quiet!" commanded Dugald from behind her.

Ondelle had somehow given her all of her air energy. She had no idea how, but she knew it was true. And now that she knew what it was, it seemed obvious. The union of water and air energy coursed inside her. What she had previously thought impossible had been done, and this bit of insight sparked new hope in her heart.

"Why did you betray Mabbe?" Brigitta called to Dugald.

"That old beast plans to live for a long, long time," Dugald snorted. "But someone has to rule Croilus's land when he leaves this place behind."

"Croilus isn't going anywhere until he finds his precious Purview."

Dugald laughed. She could feel the breath of his laughter, she was so in tune with the air now. And she knew what that laugh meant. Croilus had found the Purview.

But he was still here. He couldn't activate it. That's why he was so desperate for the so-called gift Brigitta brought from the Ancients, she realized. He thought it would open the Purview. So, Zhay had managed to keep the spell seed hidden from Croilus.

They broke through the trees, and the massive bowl of the empty riverbed was spread before her. On the south side stood a large regiment of Croilus faeries, Watchers and lesser ones, ready for battle. Behind them sat a stage draped with a black cloth. On the stage, lounging on an ornate couch, was

Croilus in his ridiculous robe. Ondelle lay on the stage next to him, and Ferris was restrained by Zhay on the other side, a nervous look on his pale face.

Brigitta's captors guided her over the lines of faeries and landed in front of the stage, pushing her forward. A dozen firesticks held her in place as she searched for signs of life from her High Priestess. She sensed Ondelle's breathing, though it was weak.

"Ah, Dugald!" Croilus clasped his hands together and beamed. "I knew you were the Watcher for the job!"

"Is this what you wanted?" Brigitta turned to Zhay. "A war between your kin?"

"There has always been war in the Valley of Noe," said Zhay without emotion.

"Oh, do be quiet," snapped Croilus.

"The Ancients didn't abandon you," Brigitta addressed Zhay. "You've been able to hear them all along. That's how Croilus knows about the—"

"I said be quiet!" Croilus stood up and pointed a jeweled firestick at Brigitta.

Zhay stared at her but said nothing, the muscles in his jaw clenched. With her sharpened senses, she could see beads of sweat forming on his brow.

Croilus stepped down from his stage. "There doesn't have to be any more violence, Brigitta," he said, pulling his robe behind him. "You can have your priestess and your Hollows friend." He lifted Brigitta's chin with his stick. "All I want is that gift from the Ancients."

She quickly glanced at Zhay. No wonder he was so nervous, waiting to see what Brigitta would do. If she would give him away. She tried to sense what Zhay was playing at, but his mind was an impenetrable wall.

"You'll hand Ferris and Ondelle over and let us all go?" Brigitta asked.

"Absolutely," he purred and gestured toward the Hollows. "I am nowhere near as heartless as Mabbe. You are even welcome in Croilus if you'd like to stay, right Dugald?" He spread his arms out to Dugald, his lengthy sleeves dragging on the stage.

Fat chance, thought Brigitta. She had one last trick, but it depended upon Zhay's cooperation. "May I have my pack?" she asked.

Croilus motioned for Dugald to hand it over and went back to sit on his couch.

Brigitta pulled the courage spell seed out of her bag and shot Zhay a look that she hoped communicated her intention. They could only pull this off together.

"I'll need some water," she said.

Croilus snapped his fingers, and three canteens appeared in front of her. She grabbed the nearest one and set the spell seed on the platform. "Spin three times in the direction the sun and moons travel," she said as if she were remembering some recent instruction. "One, two, three."

She glanced at Zhay once again, dipping her finger into the canteen. She held the seed on end and lifted her finger. "Then three drops of water on the top of the seed."

There was a kissing sound as the seed popped open. Brigitta tried to look pleased and surprised.

Croilus leaned over expectantly. "Well? Let's see it! Bring it here."

Brigitta climbed the platform and showed Croilus the contents of the spell seed.

"What is that? It looks like a seed full of juice."

"Oh, it's a potion," said Brigitta. "Um, someone drinks it and goes through the Purview. That's how it's activated, I guess." She looked up at him innocently.

"Then you drink it!" he snarled.

"I can't." She leaned closer to him and dropped her voice. "It destroys the body when it goes through the Purview. Is there anyone here you don't mind . . . sacrificing?"

Croilus scanned the crowd. "Pick someone, I don't care."

She nodded toward Zhay. "What about him?"

"Fine, fine," Croilus growled impatiently.

Brigitta approached Zhay and handed him the spell seed. "Drink this." She looked into Ferris's eyes to let her know she was up to something. Ferris blinked back at her.

Zhay took the seed pod and looked skeptically into it. "And go through the Purview?"

Brigitta nodded and whispered. "Do you have the zynthia with you?"

Zhay dipped his head ever so slightly.

"Trust me," said Brigitta as she retreated to the edge of the platform.

"Drink!" demanded Croilus.

Zhay tilted the seed to his lips and drank, then coughed a bit. He shook his head as the courage potion took affect. His eyes widened.

"Well?" asked Croilus, leaning forward, every Croilus faerie leaning forward with him.

"I feel . . ." Zhay put his hands to his head, then grinned. "I feel alive!"

"Excellent!" Croilus spun around and struck Brigitta in the chest with his firestick. She fell from the platform into

Dugald, knocking him to the ground. He picked himself up and then yanked Brigitta to her feet. Pain soared from her chest to her hand to her wing as she tried to catch her breath.

Dizzy from the bolt of fire, she lifted her head and saw Zhay spinning Gola's seed pod on the platform behind Croilus. Brigitta screamed to distract everyone. "I gave you what you wanted! Now let us go!"

"Of course!" Croilus reached for Ferris, knocking the spell seed away from Zhay. He pushed Ferris out into the gathered faeries, and they caught her and passed her along to the steep edge of the bowl. They held her there, suspended.

Zhay looked helplessly from Brigitta to Croilus to the spell seed on the ground. The only sound was from the river, rushing up the other side of the crater.

Croilus laughed and grabbed Zhay as the faeries holding Ferris threw her back and forth between them, taunting her.

From the forest, a wild call sounded and everyone froze. A moonsbreath later, a horde of Hollows Watchers came streaming out, knives and shields in hand.

The faeries on the edge of the bowl dropped Ferris and picked up their firesticks. With her hands bound, Ferris went tumbling into the lakebed as the Croilus faeries reorganized their regiment. Brigitta leapt up to fly after Ferris but was swatted back by three Watchers. One shot at her with a firestick, and she dodged it, gliding to the ground. She buzzed around their legs and headed for the edge of the bowl.

When she arrived, she heard someone shouting in the distance. A dark-haired faerie was streaming like a mad thunderbug around the west side of the lakebed. It was Devin.

"Ferris!" He shouted as he got closer.

As Ferris slid toward the River That Runs Backwards, he swooped under her, catching her in his arms. He kept on flying, struggling with the weight of her, around the inside of the bowl and over the edge out of the fray.

Ondelle! The seed pod! Brigitta turned and flew smack into Dugald. He grabbed her right arm, tripping the poison once again as he brought her back to the platform.

Croilus was seated at his couch, with Ondelle and Zhay at his feet. His regimen stood ready and waiting as Mabbe's Watchers emerged from the forest. The last Watcher out was Veena, and then Mabbe herself appeared.

Croilus's faeries backed toward his stage.

"No!" shouted Croilus, shooting his firestick into the ground in front of them, sending two of his own flying. "Stand your ground! She's an old woman! She's no match for us!"

After Mabbe's Watchers landed on the ground in front of the Croilus faeries, they parted down the center, and Mabbe and Veena made their way through. Scepter in hand, Mabbe strode to the front, then stopped. The clouds of her eyes dark and stormy, she sneered and sniffed at the crowd before her. The Croilus faeries shrunk back in fear.

"How dare you attack my home!" Mabbe bellowed, planting her staff in the ground.

"Did my faeries attack you?" Croilus asked in mock alarm.

Mabbe's lips trembled, and the clouds of her eyes twirled like whirlpools. "I gave you everything!" she wailed. "And you betray me over and over again."

Croilus fluttered off the stage and into crowd. They

made room for him as he landed, Dugald pulling Brigitta through the faeries to him.

"Yes, you did spoil me, didn't you?" admitted Croilus. "But there is only one thing I want from you now." He stepped closer and pointed to her scepter.

She sniffed, snaking her head in the air, then jerked her scepter out of the ground and pointed it at him.

"I'm willing to forgive you, dear Queen, let bygones be bygones, and never bother you again." He gestured to Dugald, who brought Brigitta forward. "I'll even trade this White Forest faerie for it."

Mabbe raised her wiry eyebrows, the clouds of her eyes slowing their swirls. "Now why would I do that?"

"Because I know something about you no one else does."

"You know nothing!" Mabbe glared at Croilus for a moment and then shot a dark stream from her staff. He held up his hand, and the black stream struck it, dissipating as soon as it touched his skin.

"Really, Mabbe," he snorted, "all those sands I stole from you and you don't think I can concoct a simple repellant?"

Croilus, now smug, stepped close to Mabbe. "I know that you have lived for a very long time. Longer than any single faerie here." He spoke loudly, so every faerie could hear. "I know you use the sands to extend your life."

"As do you." Mabbe scowled.

"I know that you have been around since the Great World Cry."

"What does it matter how old I am?" spat Mabbe. "You will return the girl to me at once! I doubt all your faeries have repelling charms."

The Croilus faeries looked uneasily at each other.

Croilus spun around, his robes twirling perfectly as if he had practiced this move in a mirror. "It's not how old you are, dear Queen, it's what you are! You aren't a descendent of the faeries left here by the Ancients. You *are* an Ancient."

All the faeries, both Croilus and Hollows, murmured to each other in bewilderment. A few Hollows faeries stepped away from her.

Mabbe paused for a moment, then the clouds of her eyes parted and the two moons shone out from them. "So what if I am?" She twisted around, scepter pointed out over her Watchers. "They're the ones who abandoned you, not I! I've protected you!"

"No!" shouted Brigitta and she shook herself free. "You weren't abandoned! Mabbe convinced your kin to stay! She's the reason you're still here."

Everyone turned to stare at Brigitta. Mabbe slowly rotated to face her, eyes no longer cloudy, but dark crystal blue. She pulled herself to her full height and stretched her ragged wings. She raised her scepter at Brigitta.

With a primal scream, Zhay lunged from the stage straight for Mabbe, landing on top of her, knocking her staff from her hand. She swiped at him with her long nails and gouged his neck. He fell to the ground bleeding. Several Hollows Watchers surrounded him. Someone shot their firestick toward Veena, and she plunged into Croilus's army. Firesticks went off and daggers flashed. Wings fluttered and screams pierced the air.

Brigitta leaped for the seed pod as both Mabbe and Croilus sprang for her staff. They reached it at the same time and struggled for it, winding themselves up in Croilus's outlandish robes. Brigitta dropped to the ground. Had

Zhay already spun it three times? she thought frantically as the chaos closed in on her. What would happen if he had and she spun it again?

Someone fell into her, and the seed was lost in the fray. There were too many fighting bodies to dodge. She glanced up to the platform just as Jarlath, Devin, Thistle, and Ferris landed. Thistle rushed to Ondelle.

"The spell seed, do you see it?" she shouted to them. "It's down here somewhere!"

Jarlath scanned the ground and then leapt from the platform. He dove into the crowd and came up with the spell seed. Mabbe and Croilus broke through the brawl, still fighting over the scepter. A black stream burst from it and collided with Brigitta's chest, striking her hourglass necklace. There was a popping sound and the whisper light spat forth into the air. It immediately disappeared into the frantic fighting.

"No!" cried Brigitta. "Come back!"

The black stream shot toward her again and she ducked. It lashed out at Jarlath, coiling around him and the spell seed. As Mabbe and Croilus fought, the black stream careened through the air, hauling Jarlath with it.

Behind Mabbe, Dugald charged with the frore dagger and plunged it into her back. In her surprise, she let go of the scepter and spun around to strike Dugald. As she did, Croilus nabbed the scepter for himself. The black stream escaped, out of control, wrapping itself around Mabbe. Waves of voices, the ones she had collected over the season cycles, escaped into the air like a cacophony of ghosts. She looked around wildly, the clouds reforming over her crystal eyes as she was yanked from her feet. The crazed black stream shot over the fighting faeries, carrying Jarlath over the embankment and towing a howling Mabbe along with it.

Brigitta sped through the ruckus after them. As she reached the edge, she saw Jarlath tumbling down the bowl, heading toward the fierce river. She would never make it in time. She fought her way downhill, but the wind picked up, tossing her about.

She was slammed into the side of the bowl by a loud gust. The ground beneath her trembled. It was one of those earthshakes! She held onto an outcropping and watched helplessly as Jarlath spun out of control below her.

The ground in front of him broke away. A large gray shape burst through the earth. It wasn't an earthshake; it was Uwain! A moonsbreath later, Jarlath smacked into the Nhord's armored body and stopped falling. Abdira shot up beside him and shook the petrified sand bits from her horn.

"Thank the Dragon!" Brigitta exhaled in relief. The Nhords might not have any magic or much grace, but they were certainly solid.

One of Mabbe's wings broke free from the black stream, then the other, and she landed against a stone. She thrust up her hands, and her end of the black stream split in two, like a snake's tongue. She held onto the two strands and began to pull Jarlath back up the lakebed. The black streams shifted, and the spell seed fell from his grasp. Abdira stopped it with her clawed flipper.

Brigitta plunged down the lakebed, aiming for Abdira. She dove to the ground and grabbed the seed. Mabbe spread her arms wide and ripped the black stream the rest of the way, down the center, into two separate streams. One still held Jarlath, and the other looped around the seed in

Brigitta's hand. Brigitta held on, summoning every particle of water and air energy in her being, and yanked back. Mabbe, caught off guard, came tumbling forward.

Released from the tension of the black stream, Jarlath fell backward and somersaulted past Abdira. Uwain shot out his flipperpaw and snagged Jarlath by the tunic. Jarlath grabbed hold of Uwain's foreleg as his feet flew out from under him, pulled by the mad river-wind.

Brigitta fluttered her wings frantically to keep from toppling away. She gripped the spell seed, lassoed by the black stream. For a moment, Brigitta could see Mabbe contemplating letting go of the seed and sending Brigitta down into the river. But her face turned curious and instead, she yanked back. Brigitta fell forward, over Abdira's foreleg.

She held onto the seed as the lasso slithered around her fingers, attempting to open her grasp. "I need water!" she called to Abdira.

Mabbe inched her way toward them, raveling the black stream into the palms of her hands, steadying herself with every step against the power of the increasing wind. Behind her, above the edge of the bowl, faerie wings flashed, firesticks flared, and daggers glinted in the light. But the river's rush drowned out any sound of the battle.

Brigitta's grip slipped on the spell seed as Abdira held her steady with one flipperpaw and searched her back straps with the other. Uwain started creeping backward, up the lakebed, with Jarlath desperately clinging to him.

Mabbe grinned as she approached, now in complete control of the black streams. She cackled as she danced her hand around in the air, winding the stream around Abdira's neck.

With a heave, Abdira fumbled a flask from her belt.

The storms of Mabbe's eyes flashed lightning as she approached.

Brigitta flung herself onto the rocky ground in front of Abdira and crouched, using the choking Nhord as a shield.

She hoped for all of Faweh's sake that Zhay had spun the seed completely. She uncorked the canteen, thrust her finger inside and spilled three drops onto the end of the pod. It hissed open.

Mabbe shot her hands toward Brigitta, and the stream wrapped itself around her wings. Poison pain wracked Brigitta's body and paralyzed her right arm. With her left arm, she grasped her hourglass and forced herself to stare directly into the tempest of Mabbe's eyes.

She let go of all thought, all fear, and drifted into the storm.

There was no air! How could there be no air within a beast? How could a thing live and breathe? She inhaled deeply and exhaled, filling the endless space with her own breath. Balancing it for a precarious moment. And with the exhale—

Take the crystal from the seed, her mind spoke inside Mabbe's. *Take the crystal from the seed.*

Mabbe's eyes calmed as she looked down. She reached into the seed and drew out the green zynthia.

"Look away, everyone!" Brigitta called to her friends.

Mabbe gazed into her clawed hands, her cloudy eyes caught by the green light.

The black streams fell from her hands and slithered down the lakebed like slippery worms. Abdira gasped for breath, and Uwain wrapped his whole right foreleg around

Jarlath, dragging him out of the river's pull.

Brigitta struggled to keep her focus away from the zynthia's pull. Her own hand began to tremble; her eyes began to drop despite her efforts. They slowly landed on the crystal as Mabbe's fingers stroked it.

The world around Brigitta began to fade as the zynthia drew her into its spell. *No,* she thought to herself. *Resist!*

Clutching the crystal, Mabbe had frozen in place. Brigitta tried to move, but her body wouldn't respond. The zynthia haze enveloped her, searching for something. Hungry. *No,* something remembered inside her . . . *don't resist. Feed.* She poured forth her water energy like a potion from her poppa's beaker. She poured forth her air energy like a Growing Season breeze.

Brigitta! called a familiar female voice, *Brigitta!*

Where are you? Brigitta's voice echoed in her own mind.

"Brigitta!" It was Abdira, calling to her above the river-wind. "We're sliding backward!"

Brigitta felt Abdira shifting behind her, and she steadied herself with her wings. Mabbe stood in front of her, lost in a trance. Brigitta snatched the zynthia from Mabbe's gnarled fingers and threw it toward the river. Before she could snap her mind clear, Mabbe stumbled after it. Her wings caught in the river-wind and she went tumbling through the air, tossed like a leaf, and was gone.

Uwain and Jarlath humphed themselves to where Brigitta and Adaire sat speechless, staring into the frothy waters. Jarlath reached for Brigitta's hand, and he pulled her to her feet. Together, they lugged their weary bodies up the side of the lakebed, Abdira and Uwain lumbering behind.

Chapter Eighteen

W hen they reached the top they found injured faeries lying about and dozens still fighting in the air above.

Thistle was tending to Ondelle. Devin and Ferris were fighting side by side. Croilus and Zhay were nowhere in sight.

And neither was the whisper light.

Jarlath and Brigitta flew to the platform as Abdira and Uwain nosed their way through faeries. Brigitta sped to Ondelle, where she lay with her head in Thistle's lap. Her body seemed smaller without her magnificent wings and dual elements. Brigitta put a hand on her cold cheek.

"Mabbe is dead!" shouted Jarlath over the battle. "Do you hear!? Croilus has deserted you and Mabbe is dead!"

Several faeries heard Jarlath and looked around. Word spread quickly and the fighting slowed. With bloodied arm and cheek, Dugald fluttered up and scanned the scene. He spotted Abdira and Uwain and backed away.

"Where? How?"

"Taken by the river!" Jarlath pointed to lakebed. "She is gone!"

As the truth settled on each faerie, Dugald's disbelief turned into wicked laughter. He thrust his frore dagger in the air. "To the Hollows!" he commanded.

With only a moment's hesitation, the Hollows Watchers

retreated from the battlefield, pulling their injured tribemates with them. The Croilus faeries dropped to the ground in exhaustion and began to gather their kin.

The color was draining from Ondelle's face. As painful as it was, Brigitta examined the space where Ondelle's wings should have been. Jarlath was right. No blood escaped from the wounds; there were just two smooth scars. She checked Ondelle's side where Mabbe had thrust the dagger. Again, there was nothing but a long white gash.

Jarlath, Ferris, and Devin landed on the platform next to them.

"What's happening?" cried Brigitta. "Why is she shivering like that?"

Thistle touched the gash in Ondelle's side. "It's the frore dagger. She's freezing on the inside. When the cold reaches her heart . . . " Thistle lowered her eyes.

"No! Make it stop!"

"I don't know how," said Thistle sadly.

"Ondelle," Brigitta pleaded, "you still have fire energy left. Fight the cold and stay with me!"

Ondelle pulled at Brigitta's arm and shook her head. Brigitta could barely bring herself to look into her High Priestess' watery eyes.

Ondelle broke into the smallest of smiles. "Brigitta of the White Forest . . . "

Without warning, a well burst and Brigitta was crying. Ondelle looked at her tenderly and Thistle rubbed her back. She cried for her wingless High Priestess. She cried for her exiled new friends. She cried for her destiny-less White Forest kin. And she cried for herself, because she had failed them all.

As confused Croilus faeries tended to each other and murmured amongst themselves, someone brought Brigitta a canteen of water and she helped Ondelle sit up and drink. Jarlath, Devin, Ferris, Thistle, and the two Nhords stood watch over them.

"There must be a way," sniffed Brigitta, "to get us home."

"You will go ... when I do ..." heaved Ondelle, clutching Brigitta's sleeve.

"What do you mean?"

"The spell ... when we left," Ondelle took a deep breath so she could get her entire thought out. "I cast it so that when I died in Noe you would be sent back safely."

"If you died!" cried Brigitta.

"When ..."

"But—" Brigitta looked up at her friends.

Jarlath clenched his jaw, and Thistle's lips trembled. Brigitta had given them hope and Ondelle had just taken it away. How long did she have?

"What about that Purview?" Ferris asked.

"That's where Croilus went with Zhay," said Devin.

"The whisper light! The Purview!" Brigitta's despair grew. She turned to Abdira and Uwain. "Can Croilus get through?"

The Nhords thought about this for a moment. "Does he have a ring?" Abdira asked, pulling hers from the small pocket on her strap and handing it to Brigitta.

She examined the large dark crystal in its setting. "You say the Ancients left this for you?"

"May I?" asked Ondelle, and Brigitta brought it closer

for her to see. She examined it and then fell back. "It's from a scepter . . . "

"Yes!" agreed Abdira. "Split in two, one for each, through generations."

"We guarded them and waited," added Uwain.

Ondelle coughed a few times. "Every Ancient had a scepter . . . like ours . . . infused with the fifth element."

Mabbe was an Ancient. Croilus had her scepter.

"If the whisper light made it to the Purview and activated it," said Brigitta, "Croilus can use the scepter to enter. But where would he go?"

They didn't have time to figure it out. Ondelle was dying and Brigitta had to get her home. There was no way she could move Ondelle without harming her. She'd have to find the Purview and bring it here. If it was moved once, it could be moved again.

She held up the Nhord ring. "If Ondelle and I each wear one of these, we can get back home?"

Uwain removed his ring from a pouch and handed it to Brigitta. "We came to serve," he said with a bow.

Brigitta, Devin, and Jarlath left Thistle and Ferris with Ondelle, who had lost consciousness but was still breathing as Brigitta laid her on the platform's floor.

With her new deodyte strength, Brigitta could cut through the air and easily flew twice as fast as the boys. Her own strength startled her. And yet, the energy felt so comfortable, as if it had always belonged to her.

But she would not keep this air energy, she said to herself. It belonged to Ondelle. She wished she knew how to give it back. Its absence surely had weakened her.

Jarlath and Devin paused when they reached the ruins, habitually checking clouds for rain.

"Come on!" Brigitta insisted. "I'll keep the rain away!"

The two Watchers didn't look convinced, but they proceeded just the same.

As they arrived at the plateau, only a few frightened lesser faeries, but no Watchers, crouched weaponless on the staircase.

Brigitta slowed. "Which way did Croilus go?" she asked. They silently pointed up the stairs, exchanging looks as to why a Croilus faerie, a Hollows faerie, and a stranger would arrive together.

"The battle is over," sang Devin over his shoulder as they flew up the stairs. "Croilus faeries are free!"

The three faeries entered the domed palace quietly and listened.

"If Croilus believed me and took Zhay to the Purview," Brigitta whispered, "then Zhay knows where it is. We just have to find him."

"If Croilus didn't kill him," Devin pointed out.

"Zhay is a traitor," Jarlath growled. "Why would he help us?"

"So we can all get what we want." Brigitta put her hand on Jarlath's shoulder. "He's not evil, Jarlath, he was just doing what he thought best for his tribe."

"Look!" Devin called.

On the floor of the great hall where Croilus had met them were scattered shards of glass. They fluttered into the room and examined the pieces.

"What happened?" asked Brigitta, looking around the room for an object that could have produced so much glass.

"The Purview?" asked Devin.

Brigitta and Jarlath exchanged looks. Had Croilus destroyed it when he entered?

A tiny *tip tip tip* drew Brigitta's attention. To her left, drops of bright red were methodically hitting the first tier of seats. She tracked the drops to the ceiling, where one of the glass panels in the dome was shattered, and Zhay's body lay bleeding across it.

Brigitta dashed to the ceiling, with Devin and Jarlath close behind. It was higher than it appeared from the floor, and as Brigitta rose through the air, the details of the dome started to appear. Holding the glass in place were numerous strips of glazed silverwood, entwined to form strong beams.

Zhay groaned as they reached him, the cut on his arm much less severe than Brigitta had anticipated. They all pushed him through to the outside and then took turns slipping past the broken pane.

A room stood before them, jutting up behind the dome.

It was only accessible from the outside, and only if one thought of checking the backside of the dome. It was small and the outer walls were camouflaged so that no matter where one stood, it looked like a piece of sky or part of the palace. Except for the wall facing the dome, it wasn't a wall at all. It was a large white door, and it was open.

In the center of the room was a round silver hoop, wide enough for two faeries to walk though. Inside the hoop was a decorative square, and then another hoop. Brigitta slowly entered the room and circled the hoop. On its other side, the center wavered like water but reflected like a mirror.

"The Purview," she whispered.

Jarlath and Devin set Zhay down and joined Brigitta.

They all stared into the Purview, and their watery images shone back.

"What happened?" she called to Zhay. "Tell me what happened!"

Zhay moaned, "I couldn't go through. I was too scared."

"But it was just a trick we played on Croilus," said Brigitta.

"I didn't know that!" he cried. "Croilus picked me up and sent me through it!" Zhay slumped down in the doorway, shaking. "I went straight through and shattered the dome glass."

"What's wrong with him!" said Jarlath. "Is he mad?"

"No, it's from the courage potion wearing off. He'll be back to his cheerful self in no time."

Zhay wobbled to his feet. "He came after me— but then— he just disappeared!"

"Keep an eye on him," Brigitta said, and Jarlath went to steady him. "I have to figure out a way to get this Purview out to Ondelle."

The silver ring stood perfectly balanced in the center of the room. It had vine-patterned etchings that moved slowly around the perimeter. They wove in and out of each other, mesmerizing her with their silent steady rhythms.

She was so focused on the silver ring that she didn't notice Devin wandering around the room.

"What is all this?" he asked.

Awakened from her reverie, Brigitta examined her surroundings. Each of three walls was painted with a detailed mural.

To her right, the mural depicted five beings sitting in five carved chairs. On the far right, just like in the great hall below them, was the largest chair. In it sat a hulking armored beast with two horns on its face. In spite of her distress, Brigitta had to smile when she recognized the Nhord Sage.

Next to it sat a hairless creature that was a bit faerie-like in the body and limbs, but its skin was pinky-gray, like an earthworm. Enormous black eyes popped from its bald head, which was capped in shiny purple skin. On the far left was a beast with four arms that came straight down from its neck. It was all limbs and head and looked like it had come from the bottom of Green Lake. Next to that, some kind of maned faun-woman sat with her hooves perched on a stool. All the Sages pointed to Brigitta's right.

In the middle of the Council of Sages was an empty, high-backed, silver chair.

"Where is the High Sage—" Brigitta started to ask, and then she knew. "It's telling us a story."

Jarlath leaned in and Brigitta grabbed Devin. "Look here. The World Sages betrayed the High Sage, who was an Ancient, and he was killed. So no High Sage in the mural. And the other Sages, they're all pointing away to—" Brigitta followed the path of their fingers, or, she thought, whatever you call them. They were directed toward the second panel, to a young faerie girl with green wings bordered in gold. Her arms were lifted and from them flew five fuzzy lights.

"Narine," said Brigitta. She touched the young faerie's wings. "She created the whisper lights that would unlock the Purviews. She asked Gola to watch over them."

In the girl's right hand, she held a scepter. One of the whisper lights had separated from the others and was drifting in front of her scepter, as if flying toward the third wall.

Five silver-blue rings filled the final wall: one in the center, one above and below it, one on either side.

"Five," Brigitta murmured, tugging at Devin. "There are five Purviews."

The rings were drawn just like the symbols in the underground passageway, the map, and the font. A scepter had been painted inside the center one. Inside the other four were two interlocking finger rings with dark gems.

"Just like Abdira and Uwain's," Devin said.

Brigitta snapped back to attention, remembering that she could disappear at any time if Ondelle let herself die. She turned back to the Purview.

"Should we even touch it?"

Jarlath, Devin, and Brigitta contemplated the giant circle of silver.

"I wonder how heavy it is?" Jarlath asked.

Zhay entered, yanked his tunic straight, and cleared his throat. He grasped the ring with both hands and lifted.

"Actually," he said, "it's really light."

Chapter Nineteen

Brigitta and the Watcher boys flew the Purview back through the ruins and placed it on the platform on the side of the hill where Ondelle and Brigitta had appeared in Noe. There it stood on end as it had in the hidden room, vine shapes twisting along its curves.

Now that she had secured the Purview, all her fears returned like a cold rain. Where exactly had Croilus gone? Would traveling through the Purview be too dangerous for Ondelle? What choice did she have, though? Ondelle would die without healing magic, and Brigitta would be drawn home without her.

They returned to the battle scene and the dejected faces of their faerie and Nhord allies. Granae had brought Roane from the Hollows, as well as a full jar of sands she had lifted from Mabbe's chambers while all the Watchers were fighting. A few straggling Croilus faeries spied on them from a distance.

Home. Brigitta and Ondelle were going home.

"I'll come back as soon as I can. We used Blue Spell once, we can use it again. I'll bring the scepter and rings and—"

"Not possible," Ondelle said hoarsely.

Brigitta dropped to her side. "Please, Ondelle, save your strength."

"There are things . . . " breathed Ondelle.

"Shhh, you can tell me after you are well," said Brigitta

"You must know!" Ondelle said with such force that they all stared. "You cannot return . . . "

"What do you mean?"

She lay down again and took a labored breath. "When the Eternal Dragon bestows the fifth element upon the High Priest or Priestess . . . it is limited . . . to the destiny span of that faerie. Once the fifth element is depleted from a High Priestess' scepter . . . the destiny of that faerie is complete."

Ondelle shut her eyes. "The last of the Dragon's gift is in that spell to get you home and shield your necklace."

"What are you saying?" Brigitta cried. "No, no, your destiny is not complete!"

"Brigitta, what I have done to you . . . " Ondelle lifted a finger and traced Brigitta's cheek. "Please, forgive me."

Ondelle's hand dropped to the platform as she lost consciousness.

"Ondelle!" Brigitta buried her face in her High Priestess' hair.

It suddenly made sense. How Ondelle's energy had weakened once they landed in Noe. She had known as soon as she cast that last Blue Spell magic that her life would be over and she would die in Noe. She had paid that price to protect Brigitta. And she had kept this knowledge to herself, because she knew Brigitta would have protested it.

And now, Brigitta was able to go back through the Purview, but she'd have to leave everyone else behind. If she stayed with her friends, Ondelle would die and she'd be spell-cast back to the White Forest alone.

Thistle touched Brigitta's hand, trembling. "It's not your fault."

Devin put his arm around her shoulder. "We know you tried."

She looked up at the Purview, then to the faeries before her. Zhay sat on the edge of the stage with his head in his hands. Both Ferris and Jarlath stood with their arms crossed, not angry, just resigned. Ferris's sliverleaf scars glinted in the fading light. Brigitta looked down at the silver scar on her own hand.

Granae held up the jar of sorcery sands to Brigitta. Abdira and Uwain waited patiently behind her, even after stranding themselves an ocean away from their home by giving up their rings.

A faint *craw craw* sounded in the distance, and Roane grabbed Jarlath's arm. Brigitta looked into Jarlath's bright eyes and held his gaze. Her heart skipped a beat. It was the exact moment, the image from her vision when she had touched Gola's moonstones.

A boy with starry eyes . . . a decision she had to make.

It's not fair, thought Brigitta. I can't leave them! If she took the rings and the sands and left them to fend for themselves, she would be no better than Croilus. But if Croilus had sent himself to the White Forest, would anyone there be able to defend it? *We are not warriors,* Ondelle had told her.

There had to be another way.

"Brigitta?" whispered Granae, holding up the jar. "You'd better leave. It's getting dark."

The straggling Croilus faeries moved closer to the platform. There were only three left, two male and one female, all lesser faeries, and all growing more terrified as the light of day waned.

Roane ran to Brigitta and hugged her waist. She petted

his head, and he held her harder. Jarlath reached over and pulled him back. "Come on, Roane." He smiled sadly at Brigitta as they moved away.

"Oh, no," Devin whispered, pointing toward the lakebed.

On the edge of the lakebed, a few shadowy figures wavered. Brigitta could see the river struggling up the valley right through them. She could feel their presence more than anything, and for a moment she could only see the two of them. Then she saw the rest, seven more, coming closer.

"Nightwalkers!" hissed Jarlath.

Everyone huddled together. Abdira and Uwain stood their ground and growled.

"We must fly!" cried Ferris.

As the nightwalkers approached, smooth and silent, Brigitta noticed glints of blue in the air. She stepped closer to them. They were the spirits of dead Watchers.

"What are you doing? Brigitta, no!" called Granae.

Brigitta waved the faeries back. "It's all right. Trust me."

When the shadows were a moonsbreath away, Brigitta closed her eyes and took hold of her necklace. None of her mentors had ever mentioned how to empath an undispersed spirit, and none had probably ever tried.

Letting go of all thought and fear, Brigitta allowed herself to sit inside her new dual energy. She drifted on a river of wind, which became a tunnel that opened into a fog. The fog was moist but not cold. Nor was it warm. She opened herself to it and it enveloped her.

All echoes of the ether must be called back again, the fog spoke.

What do you mean? Brigitta's voice reverberated through the fog.

We must be dispersed; we are losing touch with the Ancients.

You, too? Brigitta's focus wavered at her surprise, and she rebalanced herself.

If we lose touch with the Ancients, the nightwalkers continued, *we will remain here forever. You must disperse us.*

But how?

A bright light flashed, and Brigitta was looking back at herself and the Watchers behind her on the stage. For that moment, she could not breathe, but before panic hit, she was back in the fog again.

The Watchers can disperse you, Brigitta remembered. *How have Watchers done this? I thought only Ancients could disperse faerie spirits?*

Watchers are descendants of Ancients. Ancients and lesser faeries.

They—what? This sudden insight wreaked too much havoc in Brigitta's thoughts, and she jerked alert in her own body. The Watcher spirits waited in front of her, fading in and out of shadow. Echoes of the ether, they had said. Half-breeds of the Ancients—keepers of the fifth element.

The Watchers weren't created by Mabbe from sorcery sands, they were *descendants* of Mabbe. Her children, she had called them. At some point in time, Mabbe had taken a lesser faerie as a partner.

Brigitta turned and smiled.

"Oh, thank the moons," cried Thistle, pulling Brigitta forward by the hand, "we thought they'd taken over your mind."

"They haven't moved," said Devin, lips trembling.

"What do they want?" asked Jarlath.

"Our help," said Brigitta. She gestured from her

221

bewildered friends to the nightwalkers. "Everyone, meet our way home."

🌸

"It will be a strange journey, but quick," said Brigitta. "Kind of like going up in one of your trees. Hold on tight to Ondelle, Jarlath. And when you get through, you must immediately ask for Gola. She will know what to do. Granae?"

Granae stepped forward. "I was just a girl when ascending the dead was abolished. But I aided my mother in ascending my grandfather. So I hope I've told you all you need."

"Are you sure this will work?" Jarlath looked skeptically at the Watcher spirits, now congregated beside the Purview with them.

"The dispersement, yes," said Brigitta, "my theory about the Purview? No."

"But I guess we'll find out, right?" He smirked at her.

"I could throw you through like Croilus," joked Zhay, but nobody laughed.

Brigitta helped Jarlath and Thistle pick up Ondelle. She checked the Nhord ring around Ondelle's finger. She turned to Abdira and Uwain, a sob stuck in her throat. "There are no words to thank you enough."

The two Nhords bowed slightly.

"It is us who thank you, Brigitta of the White Forest," said Abdira. "Six generations of waiting, and we have the honor of serving you!"

"Born to serve the destiny that awaits," added Uwain gruffly. Thistle was right; they did make her want to hug them.

Jarlath and Thistle stepped up to the Purview with Ondelle. Two Watcher spirits glided up to them, and the color drained from Jarlath's face. Brigitta's theory was that if a Watcher entered the Purview exactly when they dispersed, there would be enough of the fifth element called to send them through.

"If it doesn't work, we'll just step through the ring," Thistle pointed out.

"That's not the part that worries me," muttered Jarlath.

"Remember," said Abdira, "it can only take you where you know to go, so you must know of Brigitta's home as she has described it."

"Picture this," Brigitta held up her hourglass necklace, "only many sizes larger, so large it must be hung between two uul trees."

"Gotcha," said Jarlath.

"Oh, and these," Brigitta pulled the shards of Himmy's song drop from her pocket. "Think about her song. If you can remember it."

"I can," said Thistle, smiling.

Thistle and Jarlath each took a deep breath, the spirits entered them, and they stepped though.

And disappeared.

"It worked!" cried Granae. Brigitta let out a tremendous sigh of relief.

Granae took Roane's hand. "Just like them, okay?"

She and Roane stepped up to the Purview, waited to absorb two spirits, and then they were gone, too. For a moonsbreath, Brigitta saw the lights of the White Forest reflected back at her.

They were safe.

223

Suddenly, Brigitta felt the full weight of her exhaustion. She motioned weakly to Zhay, Ferris, and Devin. "You first," said Brigitta. "I'll follow after I say goodbye to the Nhords and return the Purview to its hiding place."

In all that had happened, Brigitta had forgotten about the three lesser Croilus faeries now curled up with their arms around their knees on the corner of the platform. Zhay was observing them.

He turned back to Brigitta and shook his head. "I'm staying here."

"What? No, you mustn't!"

"I'm staying."

"It's all right Zhay, you can come."

Devin and Ferris stepped forward. "We're staying, too," said Ferris, putting her arm around Devin.

"Croilus is gone," said Zhay, gesturing to the lesser faeries. "Perhaps I can do some good at the Palace."

"And what if Dugald makes trouble?" asked Ferris. "We can't have that."

"Plus we can make sure every single spirit left in Noe is ascended," said Devin, "before they get stuck here."

Brigitta looked into the faces of her new friends. They were serious. "You're sure you want to do this?" asked Brigitta.

"We're sure," said Ferris.

"We've created our own destinies," said Zhay with a grin. "We are now the Watchers of the Purview."

"It's an important Life Task," said Brigitta as tears welled up in her eyes.

A moment later, two Watcher spirits thrust themselves into Zhay. His eyes bulged and he opened his mouth to speak but only gagged.

"What's wrong?" cried Ferris. "What's happening? They're killing him!"

"No, I don't think so," said Brigitta.

Zhay fell forward onto his hands and knees and began to shake. His body radiated a heat so intense it warmed them all. They watched, stunned, as bright silver symbols appeared on the ends of his wings. Large round shapes within squares within circles, like miniature Purviews.

When Zhay stopped trembling, Brigitta helped him to his feet and turned his head so that he could see his new markings. "I think those spirits just gave you your entire Change all at once."

"Next time," said Zhay, still shaken up, "perhaps they'll warn me first,"

Brigitta hugged Ferris, trying not to cry. Devin and Zhay kissed her on each cheek. Abdira and Uwain stepped forward, lowered their heads, and touched Brigitta gently on the forehead with their lip horns.

"You know where to find us if you change your mind," said Brigitta.

She stepped closer to the Purview and looked down at the ring around her finger. She was about to step through, then stopped and removed her pack. She took out the jar of sorcery sands and handed them to Zhay.

"You should take these. Study them and maybe you'll learn some new tricks to defend against Dugald. You are part Ancient, after all."

She turned and gazed into the Purview. She concentrated on her home, on the White Forest, on the faces of her momma and poppa and Himmy. She pictured the Great

Hourglass and the High Council seated in front of it. She pictured Auntie Ferna and Gola and Minq and Glennis. She pictured Ondelle and stepped through.

Chapter Twenty

Brigitta's body was ripped forward through the air. Images and colors collided, and she saw both worlds simultaneously. There was nothing to hold onto, yet she felt held in place as she traveled, faster and faster, unable to breathe. She let go, knowing breath would come again.

Everything stopped moving. She collapsed to the ground and lay there in the dark, waiting for her vision to clear. The tops of the trees came into focus and the Great Blue Moon beyond. A loud hum filled her head, blocking out any other sounds.

The hum faded, and hushed faerie voices drifted in the air. Flashes of light bombarded the leaves above.

Someone touched her, and wetness landed on her cheeks. Where was she?

A face came into focus, Thistle's, grinning through her tears.

Brigitta sat up on her elbows and looked around. She was sprawled in the festival arena before the Great Hourglass of Protection. Elder Dervia headed her way, wringing her hands as she jetted through the air. Behind her, Earth Elder Adaire was tending to Jarlath's battle wounds. Roane hid in the folds of Granae's tunic as she spoke with Elders Hammus and Fozk.

"What's wrong?" Brigitta managed a hoarse whisper.

"Why are you crying?"

"Oh, Brigitta!" Thistle wrapped her arms around Brigitta's neck, almost choking her. "Wait," she said and looked around, "where are the rest?"

"They stayed behind to—" Brigitta started, then grabbed Thistle's arm, "Ondelle!"

"That's what I've come to tell you," said Dervia, landing next to them. She helped Brigitta up and hugged her forcefully. Brigitta's surprised eyes nearly bulged out of their sockets.

"The Perimeter Guards took her to Gola's." Dervia pulled back, looked her square in the eyes. "Her wings . . ." She shook her head. "Well, there's nothing that can be done about that. But Gola is a master healer and I'm sure—"

Brigitta tried to speak the dreadful truth to Dervia, but she couldn't get her mouth to make the words.

Dervia's own mouth dropped open as she sensed the elemental change in Brigitta, and she let go of her. "By the Dragon's breath . . ."

It was obvious by her knitted brow and murmured bewilderment that Elder Dervia had never heard of a faerie transferring one of her elements to another faerie. But then again, deodytes were rare, so few faeries would have ever had a second element to transfer to anyone.

"Who would have taught Ondelle such a thing?" asked Brigitta after she had related her story about receiving the element of air in Mabbe's burl.

Globelights in hand, she and Dervia flew southeast through the forest on the main throughway, skirting the northeastern tip of Bobbercurxy. A few young faerie couples sat on the edge of the village-nest in its popular tree park, which was strung with breathlanterns and candlewebs. They looked up as Dervia and Brigitta flew past.

"One isn't always taught," said Dervia. "Sometimes one just learns, intuitively, if she is inquisitive at heart."

Brigitta nodded. This was something she definitely understood.

When Brigitta and Dervia landed at Gola's tree, Minq was sitting among the chatterbuds at her door waiting for them. The chatterbuds didn't greet Brigitta with their usual joyful chorus, but instead drooped against each other sadly.

"She inside," said Minq softly, touching Brigitta's arm with his ear. Brigitta squeezed it back with her hand.

Minq stayed outside while Brigitta and Dervia ventured through the door. It was dark, and as Brigitta's eye's adjusted, she saw Ondelle lying in Gola's bed under layers of blankets. Gola was puttering about her kitchen, Eyes perched on her shoulder. The Eyes hopped around as Gola continued mixing whatever concoction she was making.

"There is nothing I can do for her," came Gola's gravelly voice, "other than keep her comfortable until the end."

"No!" Brigitta rushed to Ondelle's side. "There must be something. Please, Gola!"

Ondelle looked many season cycles older than when they had left the White Forest. Wrinkles Brigitta had never noticed before lined the High Priestess' mouth and forehead. Her black hair was woven with gray. And without her air energy, she appeared more ordinary.

Still, Brigitta thought, she was stunning. It seemed impossible that such beauty could die.

"Why?" asked Gola as she shuffled back to the bed. "Her life is complete." Gola placed an herbal compress on

Ondelle's forehead. "More complete than most."

Elder Dervia squeezed Brigitta's shoulder as they gazed upon their dying priestess. The Eyes hopped from Gola's shoulder to the headboard and blinked.

"Ondelle . . . I'm so sorry . . ." sobbed Brigitta.

Ondelle's eyes fluttered open and she managed a smile. "Why are you sorry, my child?"

"I don't know if I made the right choices."

"There are no right or wrong choices, only the choices themselves . . . We must make them, that is the important thing, and go on."

"I choose for you not to go!" Brigitta cried. "I choose to give you back all your air so you can heal yourself."

"I do not think you could." She nodded to Gola and closed her eyes again. "Goodbye, Brigitta of the White Forest."

"No!"

Gola was suddenly in front of Ondelle, an unfamiliar object in her twig-like fingers. It was round and opaque, about the size of Brigitta's fist, and made of something similar to Gola's moonstones.

"You must take her outside," Gola instructed Dervia as she leaned over Ondelle.

Bewildered, Brigitta allowed herself to be led from the cottage. As she stepped through the door, she heard Ondelle shriek out in pain.

Brigitta looked back at the bed. Gola stooped over Ondelle's body as it relaxed, and she expelled a long, final breath.

As they emerged from the tree Brigitta was enveloped

in a tearful group hug. Someone had retrieved Pippet, Mousha, Himalette, and Auntie Ferna when Brigitta had arrived. Even Roucho, her poppa's featherless delivery bird, was there solemnly perched in Gola's tree with a pack of broodnuts on his back.

"Ondelle of Grioth has completed her Life's Task in this world," said Dervia. "I will inform the Center Realm."

Her parents and sister wailed in disbelief as Dervia flitted into the trees. Pippet rocked Brigitta back and forth in her arms. She suddenly stopped and let go.

"You . . . you're . . . " she stammered.

"Yeah, I know."

"But how?" Mousha examined Brigitta all over, as if being a deodyte would include some outward physical change. When he saw the sliverleaf scar on her wing he reached out and touched it. Brigitta braced herself for the shock of poison pain, but there was none.

Mind and body spent, she dropped to the ground. "I guess we'll never know," she said softly as everyone gathered around her.

"Oh, lola," said Pippet, enveloping Brigitta in her plump arms once again.

What should have been a welcome home celebration turned into a strangely melancholy gathering as, one by one, each village-nest's residents drifted into the Center Realm the following morning. Even when faeries dispersed, there was generally celebration. But the appearance of the Watchers, the unexpected death of their High Priestess, and Brigitta's unprecedented change into a deodyte disquieted everyone.

Fear or no fear, the White Forest faeries deserved to hear the truth. At least as much as Brigitta knew of it. Some of it, she had a feeling, was lost forever.

As everyone gathered beneath the Great Hourglass, a realization struck Brigitta, and she wondered how she could have forgotten. She pulled Jarlath aside as the Elders took their seats.

"Jarlath," whispered Brigitta, "has there been any sign of Croilus?"

"No," he replied, "I'd almost forgotten about him in all of this."

"Me, too." She looked around. "And no one mentioned anyone emerging from Noe before you got here with Ondelle."

"Maybe he couldn't do it? Maybe Zhay was wrong."

"Either he never left or he landed somewhere else."

Both options troubled her. There was no way to go back to warn the others. "We got here by knowing the White Forest. If Croilus couldn't know it, maybe he couldn't appear here."

"So, where is he, then?"

"Lost in some between world, I hope."

"Wherever he is, he has Mabbe's staff," Jarlath reminded her.

Brigitta nodded and thought about Zhay, Ferris, and Devin. She suddenly wished she had convinced them to come.

They made their choice, she thought. We must go on.

Brigitta climbed the stairs to the dais. When she got to the top, she bowed to Ondelle, who lay in a glass box in a fiery red gown that would have matched her wings. This was the final time she and Ondelle would share this platform together. She felt older and younger at the same time. A child who knew too much. A child who wanted to crawl into her momma's lap and listen to an old faerie tale. One with a happy ending.

Ondelle's scepter stood in the center of the platform, just as she had left it. Brigitta stepped up to it and cleared her throat.

"My dear kin."

The White Forest faeries looked at her warily, definitely wondering how she had acquired a second element. For Brigitta, the two elements had interwoven and moved like long-lost parts of each other, so familiar that she marveled how she had lived with only one element before.

Was that what Ondelle had meant when she said, *I do not think you could*?

"We are here to celebrate the life of our dear High Priestess," spoke Brigitta. "It's because of her protection and wisdom that I stand here now. I'm afraid I can't offer you what she could have, but I think the gift of her air element was so that a part of her would remain."

The crowd murmured and the Elders stared up at her strangely. For them, she realized, everything about this was unfamiliar territory. The transference of an element, a Second Apprentice speaking for a dead High Priestess, losing touch with the Ancients. She almost felt sorry for them.

Welcome to my world, she thought grimly.

"The best I can do is offer the truth, because at this point, not knowing it might do more harm." Brigitta took a deep breath and gestured to the Noe Watchers gathered behind the Elders' chairs. "We traveled to Noe, where we met all these faeries, the Watchers. Their kin had somehow been tricked into staying behind after the Great World Cry. The Ancient who tricked them is now gone, but there are others, dangerous faeries who have caused a lot of misery in Noe.

"We will have to learn to defend ourselves, because—" a frantic buzz went up from the crowd, and she waited for them to quiet down again. "Because the truth is . . ." Brigitta peered down at the Elders, who now looked particularly panic-stricken. Adaire stood up from her chair, but Fozk took her arm and shook his head. She sat back down, and he nodded for Brigitta to continue.

"The truth is that the White Forest is falling into imbalance, because we have lost touch with the Ancients."

The crowd gasped and once again broke into excited chatter. Brigitta once again raised her hands to silence everyone.

"That's why Ondelle and I traveled to Noe. We had hoped the sacred artifact would help reconnect us with the Ancients, and in some ways it did. It reconnected us with our past and these Ancient descendants, so at least our elemental faerie line will continue. But sacrifices were also made and there will be more to come." She took a breath and gazed upon Ondelle's remarkable face.

"No faeries will be given destinies at birth. When these new children grow up, they will have to decide their Life's Task on their own. We will have to decide for ourselves who our next leaders will be."

"Brigitta of Tiragarrow!" someone shouted from the crowd, and a few faeries cheered. Brigitta blushed.

Dervia made her way to the stage, and the rest of the Elders Followed.

"I'm afraid she's not ready," Dervia said, placing her arm around Brigitta's shoulders.

Brigitta tightened her fists and felt anger rising up from her stomach. None of the Elders had ever faced a warwump or even so much as glimpsed the River That Runs Backwards. She glared at Dervia but then caught sight of Ondelle in her glass box and quickly calmed her energy.

She looked back at her mentor, but instead of the disdain she expected, she saw only concern. In her own way, Dervia was trying to protect Brigitta, too. She felt ashamed. If she could not control her emotions, then they were right. She wasn't ready.

Besides, she thought, looking out over the crowd, she was tired. She needed to rest for a while and show her new friends around their adopted home.

Her eyes locked with Glennis's, who stood next to Himalette beside the Water Faerie stands. New markings graced her wings: four yellow-orange lines in four directions. Glennis had gone through her Change while Brigitta was away. She had the markings of a Wising.

Poor Glennis, Brigitta thought, destined to serve. Then she recalled Uwain and Abdira's steadfast pledge: *service is our highest endeavor.* No, not poor Glennis. She was exactly what she was meant to be.

Once the Elders had said a few words, the ceremony ended, and all the faeries began to feast. The festival grounds were still more solemn than usual, but filling their bellies helped to relieve some of the anxiety.

Brigitta sat with her family and the Watchers, who were to disperse Ondelle's spirit later that evening in a private ceremony. Roane sat next to Brigitta on the grass and leaned into her. She poked his nose and he smiled.

Jarlath sat down opposite them with a plate piled ridiculously high with faerie specialties. He had a pink frommafin mustache. "Here," she laughed and wiped his lip with a napkin. Their eyes locked and he smiled.

"Thanks," he murmured, and she knew he meant for everything.

Suddenly shy, she changed the subject. "How come Roane's voice hasn't come back? Didn't all the voices get released during the battle?"

Jarlath playfully messed with Roane's hair. "Mabbe didn't take his voice," he said. "It was just easier to tell everyone that she did. I didn't want the Watchers to think there was something wrong with him and lock him up."

He looked down at his little brother. Roane nodded that it was okay to go on. "He stopped speaking when our parents were killed. They managed one of the sky farms. He was messing around, hiding from them, and it grew dark. The birds got them." He swallowed hard.

"Mabbe was going to sentence him to chiseling for his behavior, so I became one of her guards in exchange for a lighter sentence." He indicated the burn marks on Roane's wing. "I was already involved with the rebels, so we thought it might help the cause, you know, to be on the inside."

Brigitta didn't know which impressed her more, that Roane had kept himself quiet all these moons, or that Jarlath had taken so many risks.

"Thistle mentioned that you started the rebels because

of the voices," said Brigitta. "What did they say to you?"

"To lead the faeries to a new land," he said, drifting off at the memory. "But I was afraid to listen. I didn't want to become like Croilus, mad and vain."

Brigitta shot him a wicked grin. "Well, at least you're not mad."

"Ha ha," Jarlath poked her arm and leapt up, grabbing Roane by the hands. He spun him around until they were both off the ground. Roane kicked his feet playfully and began to laugh, at first raspy and quiet, and then heartier as his body remembered how.

Brigitta started laughing, too. She watched as Jarlath twirled, taller and stronger than he had seemed to her in Noe. His skin would grow redder in the White Forest sun, she decided. And as it darkened, his eyes would shine more brightly than ever before.

Brigitta dashed toward the Apprentices' chambers to prepare for Ondelle's dispersement. All the First Apprentices— Flanna, Thane, Na Tam, and Mora— were waiting for her at the end of the hall beside her door. Thane cleared his throat and held out his hand, palm up. Brigitta hesitated before brushing it with her own. This was a gesture reserved for the senior Apprentices.

"I—" began Flanna. The others nodded for her to go on, which was obviously difficult for her. "I have been unfair to you."

Brigitta didn't respond for fear she would be less than gracious.

"After tonight, you may be one of us," added Mora, a sinewy Air Faerie with deep aqua wings and a pale, angular face. "Well, if Dervia is revealed as the new High Priestess."

Brigitta hadn't even thought of this. If Dervia became High Priestess, then Flanna would become an Elder and Brigitta would move to First Apprentice. Flanna didn't look particularly happy about the idea.

"It won't be Dervia," said Brigitta to Flanna.

"How do you know?" asked Flanna, forgetting her dislike for Brigitta and grabbing her arm. "Are you sure?"

"Pretty sure," said Brigitta, then she smiled. "She's not ready."

The rest of them laughed.

"Thanks," said Brigitta, not quite to Flanna. "I need to prepare." She turned to open her door.

"Apprentice Brigitta," asked Mora, "what is it like being a deodyte?"

"It feels," Brigitta thought for a moment, "like having someone else with you. Someone you know really well."

When Brigitta was finally alone in her room, she climbed onto her bed, curled up into the tightest ball she could, and began to sob.

How could any of this be her destiny? How could Ondelle leave her with such a mess? She caught a wisp of a shadow close to her bed. She sniffed and lifted her head up.

"Ondelle?" she called.

The shadow shifted in the air, and then it was beside Brigitta. It gave off no elemental energy. She looked into it, held her hourglass, and relaxed her mind. Nothing happened. She could not get through.

Granae had been chosen to disperse Ondelle's spirit, since she essentially had the most experience. The Elders also agreed that using the eldest member of the Watchers would be more respectful.

They first supervised Jarlath in dispersing Jorris's spirit in the Elders' ceremony chambers, and then Granae stepped forward to receive Ondelle's. Jorris's body was given to the earth outside of Rioscrea, and Ondelle's was taken to her childhood home, Grioth, the smallest village-nest in the Fire Faerie realm.

Before dawn, Air Elder Fozk of Fhorsa's markings had already turned gold.

That's that, thought Brigitta, staring into her Thought Mirror the next day. Destiny was still alive in the White Forest. For now.

Maybe there's an Apprentice already with gold High Priestess markings under her Elder symbols, waiting to be revealed, the image in her mirror said.

She turned away from her mirror. She didn't want to think about that.

❦

Brigitta didn't attend Ondelle's burial. She had already said her goodbyes. But she did watch from afar, perched in a tree, as the faeries Ondelle had grown up with lowered her body into the ground. Her Auntie Ferna was there. Brigitta had almost forgotten that she and Ondelle had served on the Council of Elders together for a short time. That they had even been friends.

Only a moonbeat from Gola's place and Brigitta had never been to Grioth before. Some day she would ask the Grioth faeries to tell her about the Ondelle they had known.

After the ceremony she snuck away and headed west until she found the Lola Spring River. She flew above its tranquil surface until it sunk into the warm ponds, where several Fire Faeries were floating, contemplating the sky.

She meandered for most of the morning, following whatever path opened for her, skirting the village-nest of Rioscrea, as she did not want to make conversation. Midday she found herself at Precipice Falls. She dropped to the soft ground and stared at the glistening streams, so tame compared to the River That Runs Backwards. The Mad River, she corrected herself.

She lay on her stomach, staring into the water as it splashed over the rocks into the caverns below. She didn't try to empath the water or rocks or trees or anything. After awhile, she rolled over onto her back to stare in the other direction.

She put her hands in her tunic pockets. There was something soft at the bottom of one. She pulled out a pink fire flower, the one she had stolen from the garden on her way to visit Gola before she left for the Ruins of Noe. She straightened the petals and marveled at the flower's tenacity.

There was a rustle from the trees. Brigitta sat up. Jarlath stood a few feet away with a sheepish grin. Minq fluttered around him a few times before landing next to Brigitta.

"I show him waterfall," he said, proudly stretching out his ears. "Favorite place to be alone."

"Yeah, exactly," Brigitta scolded, then laughed as she

caught Jarlath's sparkling crystal blue eyes.

Minq sniggered and pulled his special move, twirling up and then diving down over the edge into the falls. Brigitta scooted over and sat with her legs dangling off the embankment. Jarlath sat down next to her.

"Everyone seems to be settling in," he said.

"I hear Momma and Poppa will look after Roane?" Brigitta twirled the flower.

"Yes, and Granae and Thistle decided to live in Grobjahar, near the marsh farms."

"It's strange . . . all these destinyless faeries . . . "

"They all managed to find something to do," teased Jarlath.

"Our destiny markings really only reveal what we already know," said Brigitta.

He looked up at her wings and squinted. "You know, that sliverleaf scar looks like it's supposed to be there."

She twisted around to look at her right wing. The silver scar did look like it was melting into the eye glyph, and the edges of the scar were taking on some of her mark's deep green coloring.

"Everything is as it's supposed to be," she murmured.

The White Forest is good for him, she thought, studying his own wings. They were actually quite brilliant in the right light. She caught herself staring and quickly looked away again.

"What about you?" she asked, watching Minq fluttering about the falls.

"Minq took me to meet Gola," he said. "She's amazing."

"Mmmm, she is." Brigitta traced her lips with the flower.

"I might apprentice with her," he added.

"Wheeeeeeee!" Minq called as he flew up and sprayed them with an earful of water.

Jarlath leaned hard into Brigitta's right shoulder. A strange sensation shot up her arm, but this time, it didn't sting.

Brigitta blushed as he pulled away, and she handed him the fire flower. He took it without thinking, and before their eyes, as he held it, the flower grew a deeper shade of red.

White Forest Lexicon

blossom bells
Hanging chimes, shaped like flower buds, used during many faerie festivals and a favorite of the Twilight Festival, which takes place at the end of the **Green Months**.

broodnut
Its "shell" is soft and thin, so that when carved into, the red meat of it is exposed. Named "broodnut" because love-sick faeries often use it to carve messages to their heartthrobs (and the evidence can be eaten). Also sometimes used in faerie games because it is light and soft so it doesn't hurt to catch one. The meat of it is plain, but when cooked and spiced makes a great party snack. Broodnut trees grow best in the forest between the Earth and Water Realms near Green Lake (see White Forest map).

ceunias leaf
It takes a Master Gardener to grow ceunias. It must be frequently trimmed, and meditation is essential while it sprouts. There is no blossom, the leaves are shiny and waxy, and when placed on the tongue the "wax" melts and gives a calming effect. The more peaceful the meditations while caring for the plant, the better the calming effect, as it essentially carries this meditation within. The leaves are slightly fragrant, but not used for cooking.

chygpallas
Found primarily in southeastern Foraglenn (see Foraglenn map), they are a bit like big, fat mice but without ears or tails. They are completely deaf and have large round eyes and tiny mouths with

long tongues for catching tiny beasts inside hollow branches. Noe Valley children like them as pets because they are docile, although a bit skittish, and have soft fur. If you keep a steady supply of buggy beasts, they'll stick around.

Croilus

Croilus refers to both the male Watcher who rebelled against Mabbe and the palace lands. Croilus named the area after himself when he retreated there with his rebel force. The land was originally home to the Ancients and lesser faeries and the palace was the seat of the World Sages. At that time the area was called Noe, part of the larger Noe Valley. (See Foraglenn map)

Dragon's breath / by the Dragon

Whenever faeries use the term Dragon in reverence, they are referring to the Eternal Dragon, Tzajeek, a sea serpent with the ability to absorb elements. Tzajeek is **Faweh's** true Keeper of the Elements and the only one of its kind. Its origin is unknown. When exclaiming something in great awe and wonder, faeries often say, "by the Dragon" or "by the Dragon's breath."

When a new High Priest or Priestess takes their position, he or she must journey, alone, to the Sea of Tzajeek to seek audience with the Eternal Dragon. The serpent imparts private wisdom, often things that must never be shared with another being. In addition, Tzajeek infuses the White Forest scepter (a gift from the Ancients) with the fifth element, essentially giving the High Priest or Priestess the ability to conjure Blue Spell and therefore reset the hourglass each season cycle.

durma

The only somber instrument in the White Forest. Used in Elder ceremonies, in particular ceremonies celebrating the life of a deceased faerie. A thick **silverwood** branch is used, but it must have fallen naturally, symbolizing the branch having fulfilled its first destiny. It is hollowed out and one end encased in sunbleached strips from the Reed Forest (see White Forest map) of the Air Faerie Realm. It resembles a drum, but the durma is rubbed with the palm of the hand, rather than beaten. Each instrument has a unique sound somewhat like a low wind.

dustmist

A diverse and useful tool (created most often by a talented Air Faerie) used to spread spells, aromas, sounds, or any other light item through the air or to make it stick or stay in one place. Can also be used to conceal things. With a great deal of practice, one can learn to send messages using dustmist. Mothers can leave lullabies in the air above their babies. Festival grounds can be sprinkled with dustmist to keep sparkles or musical notes in the air.

empathing

A skill developed during Elder Apprenticeships. Water Faeries are particularly adept in this area, so the task of teaching it generally lies with the Water Faerie Elder. It is the ability to enter the "mind" or "body" of other things with one's own mind. Inanimate objects are easier because of the lack of messy thoughts and resistance getting in the way. One can "be" a cloud because the cloud doesn't care one way or the other.

Eternal Dragon (Tzajeek)
(see **Dragon's breath**)

Faweh

What the faeries call the world outside the White Forest and the world in general. There are five continents on Faweh, and the White Forest is on Foraglenn. The remaining continents are Pariglenn, Araglenn, Carraiglenn, and Storlglenn. The Nhords are from Araglenn.

Featherkind, Orl and Edl

Most faeries go by their first name and the name of their birth village-nest (Brigitta of Tiragarrow, Ondelle of Grioth, Mousha of Grobjahar). There is no need for any further naming, but some couples take on a joint name of their choosing, particularly if they do not have children. There is, of course, a name-revealing party to go along with the choosing. Edl and Orl, both of Tiragarrow, chose Featherkind as a second name because they thought it sounded friendly.

Firepepper

A Fire Faerie specialty, of course. Fine spell-treated granules used to make something hot to touch. It can really burn, so it's not often used full-strength. More generally it is diluted and used in anything you'd want warm, like a compress, blanket, or water to bathe in. Some Master Gardeners use it to keep beasties from getting into their gardens.

Folgia tree

A tall, thin tree found throughout Foraglenn and Pariglenn, with fibrous bark that can be pulled apart and used to bind or weave. If you soak the fibers, they can be woven into cloth.

Font

A metal bowl on a pedestal used by the Ancients for both ceremonial and practical purposes. Every element, and combinations thereof, can be called into a font if one knows how to do so. For instance, if one were thirsty or wanted to wash one's hands, water could be filled in the font. If warmth were needed, then fire could be called.

frore dagger

An ice-cold dagger that immediately heals the cut it makes. Originally used by the Ancients on anything that needed to be trimmed. For instance, if a tree had a sick limb, it could be cut off with a frore dagger and not leave a wound. Mabbe has a few frore daggers, but she uses them for nasty business, like slicing off wings without killing the faerie.

gargan

A big ugly spider. The only thing the birds of Noe are afraid of. Luckily for Noe faeries, they primarily stick to the mountains away from the mist, because the moisture makes their hairs heavy. Every once in a while, one will venture down and build a web in the forest around the valley. You do not want to get caught in a gargan web.

green zynthia

Before the Great World Cry, the zynthia crystals found inside the caves beneath Dead Mountain, and in parts of Araglenn, were harmless. They were never harvested but were sometimes meditated upon. They were mesmerizing even before the Great World Cry. After the Great World Cry, and the subsequent elemental chaos, they became strongly hypnotic and dangerous. Few have had a chance to study them and fewer still have developed a way to resist their effects.

Grow, Green, and Gray Months

These are the three seasons in the White Forest that make up a **season cycle**. Each season, all birth celebrations take place at the same time in each village-nest (otherwise there would be nothing but celebrations). For instance, everyone in Tiragarrow who was born in the Green Months (like Brigitta) is honored all at once. The Festival of Elements takes place as Grow transitions to Green, the Twilight Festival takes place as Green gives way to Gray, and the Festival of Moons (also called The Masquerade) takes place as Gray moves into Green.

hennabane

A plant grown in the shadow of Moonsrise Ridge east of the Earth Realm (see White Forest map) used for dying items different colors, mostly shades of red (from light pinks to dark browns and everything in between). With the right combination of ingredients, one could color almost anything, even grass or clouds.

Hive, the

The Hive was created by the Ancients to house the Apprentices, Elders, High Priest or Priestess and give them privacy for their magical practices. No one knows when faeries started calling it the Hive, as this was not its original name. It is a curiosity in that it is mostly underground, which seems counter to faeries' attraction to light and air. The Elders know it was meant as a protective fortress in case of a forest invasion, though none think this likely. One can get to any village-nest through the underground tunnels that start beneath the Hive, but almost everyone prefers to fly above ground.

Hollows, the

Contrary to what many of **Croilus's** and Mabbe's faeries think, the Hollows were not where the "lesser" faeries lived during Ancient times, although they did spend plenty of time there and some of the younger ones might have wanted to live there had their parents allowed it. The trees were not bound mercilessly by poles, but rather grew in natural circular formations, which were perfect for parties, camping, games, dances, concerts, and theatrical presentations. The Hollows that Mabbe bound together were an attempt to recreate this environment for the faeries that she convinced to stay behind.

hoopflute
Just like it sounds, a flute in the shape of a hoop. Different sizes can be made from different types of tree branches, but the branches must be harvested while still green, then formed, hardened, and lacquered with uul tree sap. Very talented musicians can fly or dance while using multiple hoopflutes.

hopplebugs
Tiny annoying sand beasts that get under the Nhords' armor-like skin and make them itch. Not fun.

hrooshka
Like gundlebeans are to White Forest faeries, hrooshka are to **Nhords**. They are meaty sand mushrooms, grown in the oases of the Araglenn deserts. When they are picked, they shrivel, but when cooked, they take in moisture and plump back up. Really quite satisfying.

mind-misting
Mind-misting is a way of "reaching out" to things around you without physically touching them. Elders use it as a meditative practice and encourage Apprentices to use it as well. The faerie closes her eyes, relaxes into her breath, and sends her mind out to feel the energy of objects or sentient beings. Very talented mind-misters can identify other faeries and species of plants and beasts. One can mind-mist without **empathing**, but one cannot empath if she has no talent for mind-misting.

moons / moonbeats / moonsbreath

Faeries use the term "moons" and "suns" interchangeably, depending upon the occasion and their own personal preference. When being more specific they typically use suns, as in, "The festival is in three suns' time!" When being vague, they use the term "moons" to represent the passing of time, as in, "it's been many moons since your unveiling." A "moonbeat" is specific, however. It equals just under 15 minutes. They use it when measuring time or distance. For instance, Brigitta's village-nest is about half a moonbeat long, meaning it takes an average faerie about 7.5 minutes to fly across. If you are a less than average flyer, take that into consideration. An unspecified short moment in time is a moonsbreath.

Nhords

Araglenn is the second smallest continent on Faweh. After the Great World Cry, it was overridden by the element of air, which produced a harsh, arid climate. Its ancient civilization consists of the Nhords, who have developed rhino-like skin, multiple-eyelids, and flat, aerodynamic limbs and heads. They can navigate through sand and have buried their homes in the earth.

The Nhords are a very proud, very communal culture. They believe in doing things democratically, so there is much discussion before anything changes. They were the last civilization to join the World Council at Noe but were considered the most loyal.

sand cycles

Since the **Nhords** live in the desert, there is very little to indicate seasons. They tell time by sand cycles. The winds move the sand like clockwork across the desert. Four sand cycles (North, South, East, West) are equivalent to a season cycle in the White Forest.

seasons / season cycle
(See Grow, Green, and Gray months)

silverwood

Don't confuse silverwood and **sliverleaf** (although it would be hard to do so for any competent faerie). Silverwood is the most common type of tree in the White Forest. Its bark is sturdy, its branches and leaves numerous, and it looks like someone's dusted it with a silver powder. Even though the White Forest looks white from a great height or distance, up close, it is actually silver hued. The myth around the forest is that there used to be three moons in the sky and one of them fell to Faweh, littering the trees with moondust.

sliverleaves

Only found in the mountains around the Valley of Noe, razor sharp sliverleaves travel in flocks at night. When they drop from the sliverleaf tree they are immediately drawn to the River that Runs Backwards like metal to magnets. The only warning a faerie gets is the rustle as they drop and the humming sound as they fly through the air. They can slice through a faerie's wings and leave gashes on the skin. The wounds heal extremely fast, trapping poison inside, which can sting for many suns afterward. The more sliverleaf scars, the more poison, and the more pain.

stranglewood vine

Stranglewood grows throughout Foraglenn (except in the White Forest). The ivy loves to wrap around things and squeeze. Hrathgar spellcast some, adding her special thorny touch, and captured Brigitta and Himalette in her spell chamber. Mabbe used stranglewood as shackles. Stranglewood vine is quite willing to cooperate if one has knowledge of how to use it.

thought mirror

Thought mirrors have been used by Apprentices and Elders alike since the elemental faeries came to the White Forest. They were actually invented by the Saarin of Pariglenn and brought to the Ancients of Noe as gifts. They allow gazers to meditate on one's thoughts, basically having a conversation with oneself, but they only work when no one else is around. Extremely helpful when working a problem out. No other faeries in the White Forest use them as there are only enough for the residents of **the Hive**.

transformation

A practice of the Ancient High Sage in which he or she reshapes things with his or her thoughts. Every Ancient could perform some level of transformation. The White Forest Elders aren't as knowledgeable, but they can perform some basic transformations (i.e. water to ice or mist) as well as change the state of their own mind by transforming their thoughts. Elder Adaire is the best "transformationist" on the Elder Council. She's so talented that, if she chose to do so, she could change the state of another faerie's mind by transforming *their* thoughts with her own.

triple lyllium suclaide

A specialty of several Feast Masters, though many would agree Brigitta's mother Pippet holds the best recipe, which has won much recognition. Suclaide is a sweet that melts in the mouth. It's sort of fudgy, but not as rich, and usually has a hint of mint or fruit. Triple lyllium suclaide is known to bring happy and healing dreams from the use of lyllium roots, leaves, and petals in the mix.

wingmitts

An item of clothing that no faerie would ever wear on her wings unless she didn't want her destiny markings to be seen before her unveiling ceremony. Faeries can't fly very well in them unless the mitts are especially thin and tailored exactly to that faerie's wing measurements, which no Clothier wants to do since they are only worn once by any faerie. The material is fairly light and dyed with **hennabane** to hide the wing markings from curious eyes.

Wising

There are always one High Priest or Priestess, four Elders, and a combination of eight Apprentices and Wisings in the Center Realm. Elder Apprentices are mentored far longer than any other faerie in the White Forest and have greater and greater responsibility as they proceed. Some magical skills take many season cycles to master. First Apprentices generally assume Eldership later in life, but not all Apprentices become Elders. These servants of the Center Realm are called "Wisings" and live to be of service to the Elders, the other Apprentices, and the community. Their markings are different—they have the four direction symbols, but no center eye glyph. This is not a shameful position. It is a sacred calling, just like any other destiny.

About the Author

Danika Dinsmore is a writer, performance artist, and educator. *Faerie Tales from the White Forest* is her first novel series. She lives in Vancouver, British Columbia, with her husband and their ferocious feline Freddy. She likes to put maple syrup and goat milk in her coffee. She also talks with trees.

You can find more about Brigitta on Facebook or at:

http://thewhiteforest.com

Coming Fall 2013
Book Three in the *Faerie Tales from the White Forest* series

Ondelle of Grioth

Ever since the High Priestess gifted Brigitta with the element of air, Brigitta has felt more powerful. But she has also been disturbed by visions of Ondelle's life. When she reveals this phenomenon to the Council of Elders they are more worried than supportive. When she tries to gain understanding from the Air Faeries, she is met with suspicion. And when the memories that plague her convince her that the new High Priest must seek an audience with the Eternal Dragon, he refuses to make the journey.

Driven by what she knows she must do, Brigitta steals the High Priest's scepter and, along with her friends Jarlath and Minq, makes her way to Eternal Beach. The problem: someone else has gotten there first, and the Ancients are now under his command.

CPSIA information can be obtained at www.ICGtesting.com
Printed in the USA
BVOW032353150712

295186BV00001B/2/P